THE COST OF LIVING
AND OTHER MYSTERIES

THE COST OF LIVING
AND OTHER MYSTERIES

SAUL GOLUBCOW

WILDSIDE PRESS

CONTENTS

THE COST OF LIVING

Thursday, May 11, 1972.

I took the three flights up to my grandfather's office two steps at a time. That morning, I had completed my first year law school exams. I was jaunty, sure that I had done well, the day was warm and clear, and I wanted no intellectual burdens for a while. I thought an afternoon out watching a ball game with my grandfather was just what I needed. I planned to pick him up, have a quick lunch, and out to Shea Stadium to see the Mets take on the hated Dodgers.

I burst into his office. The sign on the door's smoked glass read: **FRANK WOLF DETECTIVE AGENCY**. Grandfather was sitting in his swivel chair with feet propped on his desk cluttered with newspapers, magazines, and books. He was reading a Ross Macdonald novel. Bookcases covered every wall. It was warm in the office, but a single window that looked out to the next building's red brick facade was fully open, and an incoming breeze made it bearable.

"Hello Zaida," I said using the Yiddish word for grandfather. "Tell Lew Archer you've got to go because I've got plans for us!"

Grandfather didn't answer. He didn't move his eyes from his reading. I should have known that he wouldn't. When he read, he wished his family to understand that he was not to be disturbed with anything unimportant until he came to a natural point of interruption. When reading a novel, it was at the end of a chapter when he would look up to see if anyone had anything to say to him.

I just couldn't wait for his natural pause. If he had just started a chapter, I might have needed to delay speaking up to a half hour. By that time it would be too late for the game. I chose to risk his annoyance and announced my plans for the afternoon.

"Nuh," he said with a pinched smile. He spoke English with a cultured European accent. "I know for you to talk into my reading means to go to the Shea must be important. But how can I help you?

You see," he said with a sweeping gesture, "I am at my occupation. Can I leave the office on a business day?"

My first impulse was to tell the truth. It may have been weeks since anyone besides me or my mother had walked into his office unannounced. He was lucky to get a call a week from a prospective client. I grandly thought myself not stupid. I had studied some psychology and had done well in a recent moot court competition. If the truth would hurt Grandfather's feelings and make him at the same time resistant, why shouldn't I speak around the truth?

Accordingly, I said: "Zaida, you deserve a half day off once in a while. If a client calls or comes to the office, I'm sure they'll leave a message or try again tomorrow."

Grandfather nodded as if what I said made sense. I had him convinced. As he slowly got up, straightening his fedora and suit jacket, I readied the cardboard out-of-office advisor and could already taste the hot corned beef sandwich I was going to have for lunch. I hoped the game would go into extra innings. I was in the mood for a triple header.

"We will go," he said giving his baggy pants one final hitch. "A half day off will be good for the health."

I shook my head vigorously and moved toward the door. Grandfather was right behind me. I opened the door and came face to shoulder with a man about to enter the office. He was well over six feet and wore a grey, three-piece pin stripe suit. His dark brown hair with some silver at the temples was short and razor cut.

"Mr. Wolf?" the man asked glancing from me to Grandfather who shot me a look that said: *"Do you see what I almost missed?"*

"I am Mr. Wolf," Grandfather said bowing slightly.

"Wesley Post, New York Mutual Insurance." Post plucked a card from his vest pocket and handed it to Grandfather who looked at it and then pointed to me.

"Mr. Post, my associate, Mr. Gordon." The man also handed me a card. I gave Grandfather a surprised look. He beamed at Post who in turn beamed at me. We all moved back into the office. Grandfather sat down behind his desk, and Post seated himself in the guest chair. Since there were no other chairs in the office, I stood.

"I'll get right to the point," Post began. "A Joseph Stein was shot to death last Monday morning in his butcher shop. Did you happen to hear about it?"

Grandfather's brows furrowed for a moment. "In Boro Park, on the 13th Avenue?"

"Right," Post said leaning back in his chair and crossing his legs. "The case seems open and shut. A bunch of young toughs tried to hold up his store. They got nothing but killed Stein while they were at it. Stein's partner, a Mr. Kacew, saw it just as the gang members were fleeing. The thing is that Stein just three months ago took out a $100,000 life insurance policy with us. He was 60 years old, but since he passed the physical and was quite willing to pay the high premium, he was given the policy.

"Now please don't misunderstand me. Nothing seems to be out of order in Stein's death. It's just a matter of routine for us. But when a man takes out a large policy and dies three months later, we investigate. Normally, our own people handle it. But in this case, we feel inadequate and would like to call you in. You see, Mr. Stein was an orthodox Jew and didn't speak English well. His widow also speaks English poorly. We note from your ad in the Yellow Pages that you speak their language. If you would agree to take on the investigation, we are willing to pay a $1000 retainer plus another $4000 if you should discover something favorable to our company. Are you willing to help us out?"

Grandfather did not hesitate. "Mr. Post, to solve anything, one needs the will and the effort. You will be glad to hear that we can give you both."

"Great, I'll have a contract and a check out to you by courier tomorrow morning. When will you begin?"

"Ah, that shall depend. Could you please tell me when Mr. Stein, may he rest in peace, was buried?"

Post appeared puzzled. "On that very Monday afternoon, just as soon as the coroner released the body. I understand it's the Jewish way to have the burial before sunset. We would have liked to have had a full autopsy as the law requires, but we tried to be sensitive to your people's religion on that matter. The coroner who is also of your persuasion quickly ruled, in what was presented as autopsy results, that ballistics indicated that Stein died from a non self-inflicted, single gunshot wound. We also have the testimony of his partner. As things stand now, we have no grounds to deny payment."

Grandfather eased himself back in his chair. "Today is Thursday. We can begin our investigation early on Monday morning."

Post seemed annoyed, shooting me a quick look that begged for intervention. But before he could say anything, Grandfather continued: "You are wondering why we don't start immediately. The family will be sitting *shiva*, observing the seven days of mourning, through Sunday. I am sure the store will be closed all week. It will be plenty of time to begin Monday. The investigation should take a few days, and I promise you an expertly typed report no later than 15 days from Monday."

Post's face relaxed. "I would have liked you to start right away, but if you're sure you can produce results that quickly, your time-frame is fine with us." He rose, shook hands with Grandfather, nodded to me, and left the office.

I had said nothing while Post was in the office. Now I blurted out: "Zaida, why did you introduce me as your associate, and are you sure you can handle a murder investigation?" My second question betrayed more incredulity than I had intended.

"Joel, Joel," Grandfather said swirling to face me. "Is it possible that your lack of confidence comes from never having worked with me?"

I reddened and said nothing. Grandfather continued. "As for your first question, at first I introduced you as my associate to give my firm what we might term as gravitas. When dealing with a major insurance company, it is of benefit to have a young man in the business. But after accepting Mr. Post's proposal, I truly want you as my associate. You are finished with your law studies until September and you have no summer employment yet. Will you not work with me as an equal partner on this case? Half of the $1000 is yours, and if we earn $4000 more, half of that will go to you also. Is this not a satisfactory arrangement?"

"Sure it's satisfactory," I mumbled, "but how can I help you?"

"Ah," he poked at his temples a few times, "my powers of critical analysis are still working well, but for me to utilize my mind completely, I need all the information placed before me. I promised Mr. Post an expertly typed report within 15 days. I need your young feet to run around gathering some of the information. I also am in need of your beautifully spoken English to ask questions in places where an old man with a funny accent might not be welcome. Nuh, again, do you agree to work with me?"

I shook my head yes.

"Good," Grandfather said, "now let us rush to lunch and then to the Shea Stadium where during the enfolding of the game, we will discuss both Mr. Hodges' managerial acumen, and I will inform you of what I want you to accomplish before Monday in the preliminary phase of our investigation."

* * * *

In what now seems to have been an almost different type of world, the Stein killing in the spring of 1972 was the first case I worked together with my grandfather. There were others to come. As it happens to many of us at my current age, each passing year swells nostalgia and accentuates the sense of loss. Memory often becomes imagination, and over time has a way of rearranging the past, sometimes embellishing, and sometimes minimizing events. I may be fooling myself, but I think I have a clear recollection of what occurred.

And oh yes, if my cadence is clipped, even snappy, as if I were chronicling scenes from a Philip Marlowe or Sam Spade investigation, know that I do so purposely to pay homage to the profession in which my grandfather felt himself to be a full-fledged member.

Obviously, Grandfather was not your usual private eye. That's why before continuing on to tell you about the Stein case, I'd like you both to understand my grandfather and how it was that this elderly man, broken by the Holocaust, took on with confidence and enthusiasm being a private eye committed to the pursuit of justice.

Raised an orthodox Jew in Vienna, he was born Velvel Franck, but in a transposition of his first and last name and play on the translation of the Yiddish "Velvel," he used Frank Wolf as his professional name. Although he completed rabbinical training, he did not employ his ordination but instead accepted a professorship at the Vienna university where he had completed his doctorate in philosophy at the age of 23. He was the university's youngest professor at that time. He married the first woman the matchmaker proposed, fell in love with her after they married, and my mother was born in 1925. She was their only child.

From pictures I've seen from before the War, he was broad faced and powerful looking, probably 5'10" and around 170 pounds with a shock of wavy brown hair and a sculpted brown mustache. His cheeks were rounded, and he displayed a strong, square chin. His dark eyes, exuding a sharp confidence, were always lifted as if he were self-possessed and comfortable in his surroundings.

But by the time I knew him, he appeared much shorter, a hunched spinal stoop distorting and reducing his height. At 145 pounds, he trailed a frailness, with his face angular except for the same rounded cheeks as in the pictures, albeit greatly caved in. His hair was silvery and wispy, with a hairline that receded each year I spent with him. He still sported a mustache which he tended with daily care, but it also was silvery and pencil thin. His eyes were still sparkly, but he wore glasses daily.

I can remember my father often telling my mother out of Grandfather's earshot, "The dear man isn't much of an eater. He takes in just enough to sustain himself."

And my mother always replied, "It was the War."

Each day when he sat down to breakfast with *The New York Times*, he was already dressed in one of two brown suits he owned at any given time, each always worse for wear, a white shirt, and somewhat matching brown tie. A brown fedora hat lay nearby, at the ready, since he always wore a hat if he left the house. When he stood, he looked rumpled, pants baggy, jacket hanging, and shirt sleeves too long. When a garment became much too threadbare even for him, he would take the train to the Lower East Side and return with a replacement that just somewhat improved on what he was discarding.

"Do you see how Orchard Street has a plethora of very fine haberdashery stores?" he would exclaim proudly showing off his purchases.

During my adolescence, I too often was embarrassed to be seen on the street with him. After failing to sway him directly, I sometimes pestered my mother to buy him some "decent" clothes.

"Leave it alone," she would answer me sharply. "He is comfortable in his clothes, and they do you no harm. Leave it alone."

I would relapse, but for the most part, I left it alone.

In 1938, when the Nazis began the attacks upon and round ups of the Austrian Jews, Grandfather wrote to dozens of universities in England, the United States, and Canada asking for sponsorship as a visiting professor. None was forthcoming. In 1939, days before deportation was certain, he, his wife, and daughter were saved by a non-Jewish university colleague who snuck them out of Vienna and hid them in the cellar of his isolated country home. For the next six years, my grandfather and mother left the cellar only once to bury my grandmother who caught a chill and fever in the damp, cold winter of 1942 and died within a few days. In nearby woods during the night, my grandfather and mother, using a spade and their hands, hacked and dug through the frozen ground to hollow out a shallow grave.

My grandmother died on February 2, 1942, on Tu Bishvat in the Jewish calendar, a holiday marking the New Year of the Trees in anticipation of the coming spring. As a young child, I was confused about the day. At my Jewish day school, we would celebrate with songs and a Tu Bishvat Seder featuring a fruit medley of olives, grapes, figs, pomegranates, and dates.

When I would come home from school, my mother and Grandfather were usually together at the kitchen table. Often they would be filling out forms for the purchase of trees in the newly restored State of Israel. As my mother wrote with her jaw clenched and eyes moist, my grandfather would beckon me to him and holding me would say gently, "We are planting trees in memory of your grandmother Rivkah, may she rest in peace."

Once on a Tu Bishvat evening, as my parents sat close together in the living room, my father holding my mother's hand which he rarely did in front of me, I asked my grandfather: "Should I not be happy during Tu Bishvat? At school, we sing and laugh, and dance. Am I doing something wrong?"

"Yoeli," he answered using my Hebrew name in diminutive form, "it is my thought that it is perfectly correct that you be happy today. Yes, your grandmother, may her memory be for a blessing, died on this day in a horrible manner before my and the eyes of your mother, and we had to bury her somehow. But Tu Bishvat is a holiday of the rebirth of what is meant to grow, and your grandmother once told me she believes that we all exist on a tree of life where we are the leaves of certain seasons on that tree, and when the leaves drop and branches have become longer and stronger, we are replaced by new leaves such as yourself from which new boughs will sprout. So be happy on Tu Bishvat as she would have wanted you to be, as do I and your parents."

Then, motioning me to approach him, he added: "I would be greatly pleased if you could teach me a Tu Bishvat song you learned today so that we may sing it together."

Professor Lindemann, my grandfather's university colleague or his wife brought provisions to the cellar, mostly canned foods which had to last until the next visit. Since the Lindemanns could not predict the timing of their return, the food was rationed to allow for at least a two month period.

Besides the rats which increased markedly over the six years, the cellar contained a flush toilet, a spigot with running water, cots and blankets for sleeping and some warmth, and dozens of books on a variety of subjects. The Lindemanns had recently purchased the home from the heirs of the previous owner, and when the heirs indicated they had no use for their parents' extensive book collection, the Lindemanns asked to keep the books. Receiving permission, they stored box upon box in the basement until they could comb through the contents.

My mother received her education from these books. Literature, history, mathematics, sciences, she alternated subjects and had Grandfather explain what she didn't understand. Every book that was taken out to be read was carefully restored to the same box with name and author carefully written on the side as if the boxes constituted an organized library collection.

Grandfather would have had not much new to read had it not been for three large boxes piled to the top with books. Several were paperbacks, a publishing media with which my grandfather had little familiarity. As he once whimsically confided in me, "paperbacks were then connected with readerships and subjects assumed to be less erudite than with which I was acquainted."

There were around 100 detective and mystery novels including all the great works of Wilkie Collins, Conan Doyle, Dorothy Sayers and Agatha Christie translated in the mid-1930s into German. He had never read a detective mystery before and was fascinated by what he had discovered. As an example, Grandfather told my mother that in reading Christie's Hercule Poirot mysteries, he had come across a mind employed in the practical application of critical analysis skills my grandfather had learned through the study of Talmud and philosophy. When he finished all the books, he re-read them. My mother claimed that by the time the liberation came, Grandfather had completed at least 10 turns through the collection.

Liberation, of sorts, came on April 14, 1945 when Professor Lindemann appeared. For two weeks my mother and grandfather had heard the sounds of explosions and the movement of military vehicles all around them, but their hideout remained secure and unscathed. Grandfather said that Lindemann previously had always been impeccably groomed and neatly attired with tie and jacket, his shoes always shined. This time Lindemann looked gaunt. His eyes that had expressed sadness for the past six years were flashing fright, his clothes disheveled and grimy, and shoes covered with dust and mud.

While Vienna had fallen to the Soviets, and the war was over in their region, fires burned throughout the city with widespread pillaging and violence against civilians. Lindemann advised that my mother and grandfather stay hidden a while longer as their safety, especially of my mother who would be vulnerable to rape assaults by the victorious troops, was precarious. Lindemann promised to return as soon as order was imposed. My grandfather and mother agreed.

They waited for a month. Their food supply was nearly at an end when Lindemann, along with his wife, returned. They came by car and brought fresh clothes and toiletries. The war in Europe had officially ended the previous week, and the Soviets had instituted martial law in Vienna and its surroundings. The building where my grandfather and mother had lived in Vienna was now rubble. The Lindemanns drove them straight to a Jewish relief agency that had just begun operations.

Thanks to a cousin who sponsored them after the War, my grandfather and mother came to the United States and settled in a small apartment in the Flatbush section of Brooklyn. Mother spent one year getting her high school equivalency degree and then entered Brooklyn College finishing in three years. When she graduated, she married my father who had just completed law school a year earlier and worked as a real estate attorney in downtown Brooklyn. Grandfather moved with them into one unit of a duplex dwelling on East 7th Street off of Avenue P, also in Flatbush. I was born a year later. My father, a habitual back porch smoker, nagged constantly to stop by my mother and grandfather, died of lung cancer when I was 14. My mother never remarried.

Since Grandfather's professional credentials were worthless in this country, upon arrival he went to work as a security guard at the 42nd Street Library where he sat at the exit checking if books were being properly taken out. During those moments when patrons weren't passing before him, he read. He loved this country, and anything that pertained to America interested him including a Superman or Batman comic book. Oh yes, he continued reading detective stories, paperback Raymond Chandlers, Dashiell Hammetts, Ross Macdonalds, and Mickey Spillanes. Every morning he read the *New York Times* along with his breakfast. When he wasn't reading, he listened to the radio and later watched television "to acculturate myself to the essence of America," as he put it. He painstakingly learned the rules of baseball since my father and then I loved the game so much.

After I was born, Mother went to work at the midtown jewelry store that she managed until she was 77, and Grandfather quit his job at the library to take care of me. When I was five and started school, he was 55. That's when he became a private detective.

Grandfather came home one evening and announced that he was now in the "investigative business." My parents, who at first thought he was joking, believed him when he showed them his license, the rent receipt for an office in downtown Brooklyn, and an ad in *Der Tog-Morgen Zhurnal*, a Yiddish newspaper advertising his services. He then added:

"My children, you must understand that this detective profession is perfect for me. If you know America, you know I will not be without business. I have with thought selected my office. It is just two blocks from the Boro Hall and courthouses where people in need of my services are always to be found. When I am in my office, I can hear from the street below the sound of thousands of feet walking by every hour. If just two of those feet came to me as a client each day, I would have a most successful business."

My parents were appalled. They had visions of Grandfather engaged in night long stakeouts and shootouts with gangsters. But they said nothing in opposition. They simply hoped no one would hire as a private detective an elderly man who spoke a quaint English.

For the most part they were right. Up to the time of the Stein case, in the 17 years Grandfather was a detective, he had no more than 50 paying clients. Since both my parents were financially successful, they didn't mind meeting the rent for his office. While my father was alive, Grandfather would gently badger him for "investigative" jobs stemming from his law connections. Even after my father died, my mother continued the financial support.

The few cases he did get came as a result of the ad that he regularly ran in the Yiddish newspaper and the Yellow Pages. A few were investigations of the character and financial condition of a future marriage partner. A few others were at the request of a spouse who suspected infidelity.

"It would seem," I heard him tell my parents after completing one of these cases, "that when people are apprehensive or suspicious, they have every reason to be so. My cases are very sad with little difference between who may be a victim and who a victimizer."

My grandfather was not in the least a bitter, cynical, or hardboiled character like his fictional heroes. Quite the opposite, he was always gentle, old world courtly, soft spoken with European inflections that transformed any statement into a form of inquiry.

When I was nine or so, I asked him a question that had been troubling me for a while. "Zaida, if you're a detective, why don't you carry a gun?"

He stroked my head and answered: "I am your grandfather. What do I know from guns?

Monday, May 15, 1972.

Dawn was just intruding through my bedroom's curtains when Grandfather with orange juice in one hand and a coffee mug in the other awakened me, urging me to rise quickly.

"Your research last Friday discovered for us that the butcher store opens at 8:30. Mr. Kacew arrives even earlier. It is important we be there not much later after he arrives."

As I washed and dressed, Grandfather said his morning prayers. My mother scrambled some eggs for us. My poor mother! She was concerned that we were involved in a murder case. Years later, not long before she passed away, just as her memory began to fade, for the first time in my hearing she started talking about the six years she and my grandfather hid in the cellar. In slightly accented English, she told me about the daily hunger that had to be, to use her term, "managed" so that the rations lasted until the next Lindemanns visit.

She told me about the days her mother lay dying and she feeling helpless to do anything but wipe her mother's burning forehead with a cold cloth. She told me about the night she and Grandfather buried my grandmother, the frozen numbness of body and mind in hacking out the grave, dragging the body of her beloved mother to it, and spadeful and handful, one after another, piling sufficient earth over the body so that animals would not burrow in. She told me that as much as she knew Grandfather was taking care of her, she was determined that she would also take care of him.

"The first day when we went down into the cellar, I was 14. "That day your grandfather called me 'Malkeh' and not 'Malkehleh, ' or 'little Malkeh,' as he always called me before. He never called me 'Malkehleh' again."

Unasked, unprompted, she said one more thing to me. "I didn't want to make you afraid, I never wanted to show you my insides, even though I was always afraid. You were my only child, but really even if I had a dozen children, I would have been equally afraid for all of them, a terror that I would lose each one, and it would have been my fault."

"Your fault?" my voice faltered. "Why your fault?"

"Because," my mother answered fiercely grabbing my arm, "I couldn't do anything when my mother lay dying, I couldn't stop your father from smoking, and I couldn't do anything about the cancer that took him from us just after his 40th birthday. You'll now try to argue with me, I know, but please don't. No one was better than your grandfather in making logical arguments to me about how I have felt, but it has never been a matter of logic."

My mother said she was worried that the Stein killers might find out that Grandfather and I "are snooping around." I assured her that it was a routine matter and that we were to make an easy $1000 for just a few days of work. And with half a bagel still to be eaten, I walked with Grandfather down Ocean Parkway to the B9 bus which we caught at 7:15 and headed to Boro Park and the butcher shop.

Having fulfilled Grandfather's earlier instructions, I was convinced Mr. Post was correct – the Stein murder was an open and shut case. The insurance company supplied me with a copy of Stein's medical examination. It showed nothing wrong with the man, not even a minor ailment.

I also obtained a copy of the police report. At around 7:45 on Monday morning May 8, Stein's partner Kacew, who was working in the back of the shop, heard noises and then a gunshot from the front. He rushed out and saw five or six youths fleeing the shop. Down near the cash register lay Stein's body with a meat cleaver next to it. The apparent motive for the murder was robbery. Stein was shot with a gun the butchers kept in their store for protection. Based on the information provided by Kacew, the report speculated that the killers took the gun away from Stein and then shot him when he tried to defend himself with the meat cleaver. The gun was found later in the day in a garbage can a few blocks away, prints wiped clean.

"Talk with the Stein and Kacew neighbors on Sunday," Grandfather had directed me. "Friday is not a good day as many will be busy preparing for *Shabbos.* Find out what you can."

"They'll talk to me?" I asked having never done this before.

Grandfather just winked at me.

Folks certainly like to tell strangers about their neighbors. Without even showing identification, I introduced myself as a private detective investigating the Stein murder. I read the information straight out of my notebook to Grandfather. While I had a lot written down, I didn't see that what I reported was helpful.

The butcher shop was on 13th Avenue between 52nd and 53rd Streets. Both families lived within walking distance of the shop, the Steins on 46th Street and the Kacews on 63rd. Stein was a pious man who prayed at a small Orthodox congregation nearby. He had a wife Gittel who was a homemaker, a son Jack and a daughter Rachel. The neighbors claimed Joe and Gittel were wonderful people, but afflicted with bad children. Jack was some sort of a political radical living in the Bronx, and Rachel, who a few years ago married what one neighbor woman called "a lazy Italian boy," lived in Bensonhurst and was no longer welcome in her parents' house.

The Kacews, according to neighbors, were the perfect family. They were prominent members of a large, Conservative synagogue and donated generously to various charities. David Kacew was somewhat of a neighborhood celebrity. He fought with the Jewish Partisans in Poland during World War II and just a few years ago foiled a mugging in Manhattan. Mimi, his wife, was American born, very attractive, and came from a wealthy family. They had one son, Arthur, who had been an honor student at Columbia.

"Excellent bit of sleuthing," Grandfather remarked enthusiastically after I had completed my report.

"Really, what have we learned from all of it?"

"Time will tell us that over the next few days," Grandfather answered. "Let us allow time to do its work."

* * * *

The B9 dropped us at 60ᵗʰ and 13ᵗʰ Avenue. We walked down 13ᵗʰ to the butcher shop. The door was ajar, so Grandfather and I walked in. My thumping a bell on the meat case brought a man out from the back who stopped at the side of the case where a manually operated National Cash Register sat on the counter. Tall, broad shouldered, and dressed in a white apron, he had a large, wide-boned face over which he wore a painter's cap that set off by a series of Jewish stars that read "*Kacew & Stein, Fine Kosher Meats.*"

"Good morning," he said with a slight accent. "I am not yet open."

Grandfather stepped forward and handed the man a card. "Good morning, you are Mr. Kacew?"

When the man nodded yes, Grandfather continued. "My name is Frank Wolf, and this is my associate, Mr. Joel Gordon. I am afraid we are here on distasteful business. Mr. Stein's insurance company asked us to do a private investigation of his death before they pay his beneficiary. You know that he had such a life insurance policy?"

Kacew moved forward and shook hands with us. "May Joe rest in peace. Such a terrible thing." Kacew dropped his voice and his head at the same time. "No, I did not know he had taken out a policy. I will be glad to do whatever I can to help."

Grandfather gingerly moved behind the glass case, and I followed. Kacew remained on the other side. "This is where the unfortunate man was slain?" Grandfather asked pointing down at a figure of a person outlined in yellow chalk in the sawdust that covered the floor. Back then butcher shops commonly laid down sawdust to absorb the meat drippings. Next to it was the outline of a meat cleaver. I was shocked that cleanup hadn't taken place with the shop reopening in just another 30 minutes.

"Yes," Kacew replied visually shaken. "I was about to sweep out this horrible sight, wash down the floor, and put down new sawdust. As early as Wednesday after they had taken pictures, the police said I could clean up the store. I just couldn't bring myself to do it during Joe's *shiva* period. I'll need every bit of my strength to do so now before the first customers arrive in just a while."

"We will not keep you too long," Grandfather said sympathetically. Then, stooped over even more than usual, he slowly paced the whole area behind the counter, carefully avoiding the outlines. While still pacing, he looked at Kacew and said: "Just a few questions, and we will let you recommence your business. First please, on that morning, did you both arrive at the same time?"

Kacew shook his head. "No, we never arrived at the same time. Joe always went to the synagogue for morning prayers before coming to work. I am satisfied to pray at home. I believe it says in the Talmud that if the prayer comes from the heart, it makes no difference if it is said alone or with a congregation. So it was our habit for me to arrive first and begin preparations. Joe would stay a little later and close up."

"And that morning, what time exactly did he arrive?"

Kacew thought a moment. "Exactly I cannot say because I was in the back until I heard the shot, and I had not seen him until then. I imagine he came when he usually does from synagogue, around 7:40."

"Mr. Stein was a man of constant habits?"

"Yes, a simple man, a religious man who was a wonderful partner. Very dependable. In every morning after synagogue, home for lunch at 1:00, back at 2:00, and everything put away and the floor swept when he closed up."

"It is wonderful for business partners to work so well together, Grandfather noted. "About the gun, please. Where was it kept?"

"Here," Kacew answered pointing under the cash register.

"Why did you have such a weapon in the store?"

"A few months ago Joe came in with it. He said we needed it for protection."

"You have had some robberies?"

Kacew shook his head. "No, but in Brooklyn these days it is always possible. It was for just in case."

"Yes," Grandfather agreed, "much happens in Brooklyn. Tell me, were you and Mr. Stein trained in the use of this weapon?"

"I was during the war when I was with the Jewish partisans in the Polish woods. "I'm not sure about Joe."

"Just a few more questions, Mr. Kacew, and we will be out of your way. What did the boys who shot Mr. Stein look like?"

Kacew shrugged. "Like boys in a gang. You know it says in the Torah that because of Cain's sin, we will have a world full of many nations and many tongues. So it was with the gang, a few white, a few black, and a few Spanish."

"Ah, that is good," Grandfather said. "Such a gang the police will catch easily."

"No," Kacew answered fiercely, "I don't think I could identify them. I only saw them from behind."

"Don't worry," I spoke up with first year law school confidence. "You'll be surprised how much you remember when the time comes to pick them out of a police lineup."

Kacew looked down and shook his head no.

Grandfather walked over to a chair near a wall on the other side of the counter near the shop's door. He picked up a *Daily News* lying on the chair and thumbed through the pages. "This is from the last Monday. May I surmise that it belonged to Mr. Stein? Such a man of habit probably bought a newspaper every day?"

"No," Kacew answered wearily, "it belonged to Rachel, Joe's daughter. She left it here after she came upon the tragedy."

Grandfather's eyes grew animated, but his voice remained neutral. "Rachel, she was here that morning? What time? And would you also know why she came?"

"I can't tell you why. I hadn't seen her for quite a while. She burst in around 8:00 just after the police arrived. She screamed and collapsed to the ground when she understood what happened and dropped the newspaper. Terrible, it was terrible."

Grandfather shook hands with Kacew. "Thank you for your help. We will let you get on with your work."

Grandfather started for the door, and I shook hands with Kacew. Grandfather had just opened the door when he turned back to Kacew: "And yes, just a last question. Was anyone else here between the time you came to the shop and when Mr. Stein was killed?"

"No one," Kacew answered quickly. "The store was not yet open for business."

After we left, Grandfather asked: "What is your opinion of this man?"

I answered without hesitation. "I liked him. Doesn't come across much like a butcher. He could pass for an old time Hollywood actor, the Gary Cooper type. He's a religious man, very grieved about his partner's murder."

"Yes, he is very handsome. Why do you think he is religious?"

"Don't you agree," I answered petulantly. "His quoting from the Torah and Talmud suggests it."

Grandfather halted, caught my eye, and held it. "It seems my young associate is impatient with my questions. I am still formulating my thoughts about Mr. Kacew. To help me, please find the newspaper report of the time Kacew was a hero in Manhattan. We will meet back home and then visit Mrs. Stein tonight."

"Ok," I said still a bit peeved. "What will you do today?"

Grandfather started walking again. "I will wander about the 13th Avenue. I see that many of the stores are offering bargains. We will discuss the case further during dinner before we go to see Mrs. Stein."

* * * *

I left my grandfather on 13th Avenue and took the D train to the *New York Times* building in Manhattan, then at W. 43rd Street between 7th and 8th Avenues. An old-fashioned card file in the paper's massive library told me the exact date of David Kacew's Manhattan story. Since newspapers including the *Times* had recently placed its historical copies on microfiche, I found the story quickly and took notes as I spun the text.

From the *Times Building*, since I was close by, I walked over to my mother's jewelry store on 47th Street between 5th and 6th Avenues to see if she could have lunch with me. But prior to departing, I called her from a pay phone to let her know I was coming. I had learned at a very early age that she did not like surprises. Had I not called, as soon as she saw me, for the minute it took for her to buzz me into the store, a terror would have enveloped her fearing that something bad had happened to Grandfather.

After a hug and ascertaining why I had come, she called over to a clerk and gave him a sandwiches order to bring in. Following some light chit-chat, my mother's face turned serious.

"How is your first day working with Zaida? I still should not worry?"

"There's nothing to worry about," I said firmly. Then my voice turned irritable. "I honestly don't know how I'm doing so far. Zaida just tells me what to do while he acts sphinxlike. I'm not even sure I'm allowed to tell you anything more."

My mother drew me close to her and hugged me again. "That's all right, I received five years of education through what you've called the "sphinxlike" method of pedagogy that Zaida always assured me would sharpen my "critical analysis" skills. Eventually, he would be direct and share his insights, but only after I did some processing on my own. But again, please, please be careful."

I assured my mother that we would, and after a quick lunch and putting up with Mother's clerks coming over to tell me how grown up I looked and asking me about my career plans, I headed back to Brooklyn on the F train.

* * * *

By the time I arrived home, it was nearly 4:00, and Grandfather had not yet returned. My frustration was boiling over and tiring me more than the running around. It still seemed an open and shut case to me. Why did Grandfather care what I thought about Kacew? If Grandfather did not agree with my thinking Kacew was a nice guy and a religious man, why didn't he just say so? Why did what happened with the Kacews 10 years ago in Manhattan have anything to do with this murder? The whole thing shouldn't have been complicated, but Zaida seemed to be making it so.

Shutting my eyes and mind to the case, I dozed off until I heard Grandfather return around 5:00. The jewelry store my mother managed was open until 9:00 in the evening on weekdays, so when I was home for dinner, it was just the two of us. Grandfather and I would eat what my mother had prepared in advance. My mother always drove home, arriving around 10:00. She was frightened to take the subway, especially at night.

I helped Grandfather warm dinner, but I was still childishly sullen when we sat down. While eating Grandfather said nothing about the case. Instead, he brought up mundane domestic matters and bragged about the food and clothing "bargains" he had purchased on 13th Avenue. I was annoyed with him. Here I had spent most of the day running around the City and traveling subways, and all he could talk about was his petty purchases.

Right after dinner we went to see Mrs. Stein. We took the train to Boro Park in silence. I wasn't going to offer any information until asked. As we began the short walk from the train at 50th Street and New Utrecht to the Stein house, Grandfather stopped to light a pipe he sometimes smoked, but only outside of the house. Before resuming the walk, he said: "Nuh, I have been waiting to hear what you uncovered this afternoon. Are you a stranger that you need a personal invitation to address me?"

I felt stupid, the way I usually do when caught in a pout. I still do, whether I am discovered by my wife or two grown children. To smooth over my embarrassment, I quickly told Grandfather what I had learned.

"It goes back 10 years," I answered opening my note pad and reading from it. "Kacew and his wife had just gotten out of a Broadway show and were walking to the subway. A guy with a knife came up and forced them into an alley. He made Kacew give over his wallet and then told Mrs. Kacew to hand him her purse. She was frightened and dropped it, which may have angered the mugger. He pushed her away and reached for the purse. As he did so, Kacew lunged at him, took away the knife, and stabbed him to death."

Grandfather winced. "He took away the knife and stabbed him? Tell me, the mugger was a young boy?"

"No, he was 26 and weighed over 200 pounds. The paper made a point of his size to play up what Kacew had done."

"Quite an elucidating event," Grandfather noted while pushing up his glasses and closing his eyes for a moment's thought. And then looking at me with pride, he added, "Excellent leg work, Joel. Well done."

While the child in me swelled from the approval, I didn't have a clue what was so "elucidating" about what I had reported.

* * * *

We turned up 47th Street from 13th Avenue and looked for the Stein home which turned out to be a modest two story duplex. We walked up the stoop and rang the bell. A very overweight woman with brown speckles over her neck and hands answered the door. She had a round face with small, trusting brown eyes, and age lines from both sides of her mouth down to her jaw. In the manner of the Orthodox, she wore a dark brown *sheitel,* a wig, short and even in its contours that covered her head to her ears. The wig lay slightly off center with a tilt to the left as she faced us.

Speaking Yiddish, Grandfather introduced us and, after determining that he was speaking to Mrs. Stein, extended his card and explained why we had come. I knew Mrs. Stein couldn't be more than 60, but she looked at least 20 years older.

"Kum arein, kum arein," she happily motioned us to come in. Following Grandfather's lead, we swept our right hands over the mezuzah on the door frame and entered the house. Mrs. Stein led us into a dark, small front parlor that was overstuffed with a large velour textured light brown sofa and matching arm chairs. The material showed scenes of *shtetl* life, women holding happy babies, men in *yarmulkehs* and *payess*, and Klezmer-like musicians. A large brown coffee table placed much too close to the sofa and arm chairs took up the middle of the room. A few pictures of what I guessed to be family members scattered across the walls.

Mrs. Stein seated herself on the sofa, and Grandfather and I took the armchairs to the sides of her.

"Please excuse the intrusion," Grandfather said. He continued to speak in Yiddish.

"It is nothing to excuse," she responded also in Yiddish opening her hands to us. "Your coming is welcome."

And then looking at me, she asked in English: "You too can understand the Yiddish?"

When I nodded, she continued in Yiddish. "I never had so many people around as during the seven days of mourning. Day and night someone was with me. Then after this morning there was nobody."

Grandfather nodded. "It is very hard to suffer such a loss. But you have two children. They are a help at a time like this?"

"Yes, they were both here. You know children. They grow up and have their own lives. So now I sit alone."

Grandfather sighed. "Tell me, you heard the news from your daughter? I believe she came upon the tragedy, no?"

"Yes, Rachel came running. In our shock, we sat and cried together. Rachel called Jack, and David, bless his soul, came over as soon as the police were finished with him. He made the funeral arrangements."

"David, that would be Mr. Kacew, yes?" Grandfather asked.

"Yes, he has always been very good to us."

Grandfather paused for a moment. "Tell us please, your daughter often visited her father at work?"

Mrs. Stein's sorrow seemed to deepen. "No, I am ashamed to say that she hadn't spoken to him in the last two years." Mrs. Stein lowered her voice. "She married out of our faith and to a bum, and Joe said she was lost to us. I wonder why she was at the store. All week I didn't want to ask her."

"Then your son, he was a comfort to your husband?"

Mrs. Stein put her hands to her face and shook her head. "When he was very young, Jackie could do no wrong in Joe's eyes. Then in high school Jackie took up with politics. He said people were suffering from the capitalists, and he had to save them, to make a revolution. For the last five years, he works for an organization, the Workers United Party. They pay him nothing so he would come to Joe for money. 'Give your money to the people,' Jackie would hound him. Joe said 'no, not a penny for your organization, but take $50 a week for yourself. I can't let my son starve.'"

"I am sorry," Grandfather said. "This aggravation must have hurt your husband's health?"

"No, thank God, he was a healthy man. I thought for sure his blood pressure would be bad, but it was normal. For the last few months he had some headaches, but that was all."

"Then you were surprised when he took out the large insurance policy?"

Mrs. Stein appeared to be thinking back for a moment. "One day he came home and said, 'Gittel, I want you to know about this policy.' I asked him why we needed it since we already had a $10,000 policy and the mortgage paid off on the house. He said, '$10,000 is not enough so you should not have to go to a nursing home.' I am an old-fashioned wife. I accepted what my husband told me and forgot about it."

"And this was about three months ago?" Mrs. Stein nodded yes. "And the children," Grandfather quickly followed, "the children, did you tell them about the policy?"

Mrs. Stein answered with some intensity. "You know how it is. A mama talks with her children. She tells them what's new, both the important and not important things."

She looked to me as though I certainly would understand her point. I gave her a half smile in return.

Grandfather drew her attention away from me. "Yes, Mrs. Stein, a mama is a mama and a wife is a wife. Mr. Kacew told us that your husband went home for lunch every day?"

Mrs. Stein, who had looked as if she would cry, now smiled. "Yes, for the 19 years that he owned the shop, the man came home the same time every day for lunch. You can imagine how strange it was for the last three of four months not having him home for lunch on Fridays."

I almost leapt to ask the question, but Grandfather calmly did it for me. "And did he explain why he didn't come home on Fridays?"

"Of course, why shouldn't he tell me? He said that we should feel fortunate that the business at the shop had become very heavy before the Sabbath, and he couldn't leave David by himself during those times."

"Truly," Grandfather said leaning in toward Mrs. Stein, "the man was a good husband and a good partner. I imagine you are quite close with the Kacew family?"

Her voice was firm as she responded, "Never a quarrel, never a bad word did Joe bring home about David." And then softly, "But our families were never close. We were the greenhorns, and they like established Americans. Mimi, Mrs. Kacew, was born in this country. She grew up in a luxury apartment in Manhattan."

"They just have one child?"

"Yes, Arthur." She used a hard *t* for *th* when she pronounced the name. "He is a very nice boy. They sent him to a private school in Riverdale for high school, but not a Jewish one. I have not seen him for a while, but Joe told me some things. Arthur did very well in college. A very practical boy, not a spender like some today. Everything he buys is quality. Now he is a stockbroker, and with his ambition and good sense, he will own all of New York. It is funny how life takes its turns. For about a year, he had been pestering Joe to sell out his half of the shop. Now he will have no trouble doing what he wants. I will gladly sell my portion."

"Why did he want your husband to sell?" I asked in English. While I comprehended what was said in Yiddish, I spoke it poorly. Grandfather translated to make sure she understood.

"Arthur wanted to expand, to take over the store next door, break the walls, and make a large market and delicatessen. He didn't want a partner besides his own father. Arthur would ask Joe to sell in such a nice way that Joe said it was hard to say no. But what would Joe do without his business? What a relief it was when Arthur stopped asking."

"When, please, did he stop?" Grandfather asked.

"Exactly, I cannot say, but a few weeks ago I asked Joe if the boy was still nudging him. Joe said 'no, not in a while.'"

We sat for a few minutes with no one speaking. Grandfather was content to think, and Mrs. Stein seemed just glad to have company.

I was edgy and ready to go. Finally Grandfather stood up, thanked Mrs. Stein, and as we left, Grandfather offered Mrs. Stein the traditional words of consolation, *"Hamakom yenachem etchem bitoch shar aveli Zion V'Yerushalaim."* (*May you be comforted among the mourners of Zion and Jerusalem*)

"Nuh," Grandfather asked as we waited for the train to return to Flatbush, "do you understand more now?"

I just shook my head no. Nothing had shaken my stubborn belief that there was nothing in this case to think about. But I did have a question.

"You didn't ask Mrs. Stein if she knew about the gun her husband bought for the shop recently. Why didn't you?"

"Ah," Grandfather said looking pleased. "That is an excellent observation. Mr. Stein would not have mentioned the gun to his wife. It would have only served to frighten her. And I did not wish to anguish her further during her time of grief. I think my hypothesis will be validated after questioning of the Stein children."

I had not been looking at Grandfather directly as he spoke, but when I turned to face him, he suddenly looked tired to me. "Today," he said as the train pulled in, "I understand a few things and don't understand many more. Tomorrow we will investigate further, and the end will be that we will both understand better."

Tuesday, May 16, 1972.

The next morning we took a bus and the N train to the 18th Avenue stop to see Rachel Scotto, the Stein daughter. She lived on 70th Street between 16th and 17th Avenues, a quiet street in Bensonhurst. It was about a half mile walk from the train, and Grandfather seemed fatigued when we had climbed the stoop of the light colored duplex. I opened the grilled screen door to the right of a bay window with a crack in the glass and rang the doorbell.

A young woman about my age with streaked blonde hair and wearing a bathrobe opened the door. A cigarette dangled from chapped lips. She appeared nervous as if it might be the landlord coming for rent that could not be produced. She had an angular face and large green eyes that begged sleep and easing of tension. All made up, I thought, she probably would be attractive.

Following Grandfather's earlier instructions, I did the introductions including handing her Grandfather's card and explained why we had come. As we entered the darkened apartment with a living room to the immediate right, she put a finger to her lips and pointed to a man asleep on a red sofa. Bare feet stuck out of a sheet that covered him to his waist. The room was cluttered with odd pieces of furniture, not one matching another. Newspapers and magazines were all over the floor. Rachel closed the door to the living room, and we followed her to a small kitchen deeper into the house. She motioned us to chairs at a table with dirty dishes.

"Please excuse us," she said removing the soiled dishes to an already full sink. She then sat down and looked at me. "We were out late last night. You know how it is."

I wasn't sure if Grandfather wanted me to begin. I shot him a questioning look. He spoke immediately. "Mrs. Scotto, thank you for seeing us. We have only a few questions."

"Your answers will help speed payment on your father's policy," I added peeking at Grandfather who seemed pleased with my statement.

"O.K.," she said yawning and again looking at me. "Ask away."

Grandfather's tone was conversationally steady. "Please, what time did you arrive at your father's shop the day of the tragedy?"

Rachel lit another cigarette. "I dunno, I don't wear a watch, but it was plenty early. Around 8:00 I guess, a little before, a little after. There was a crowd already there."

"And please, why did you go see your father that morning?"

"Can't a daughter just drop in and say hello to her father?" Rachel snapped in my direction cinching the sash of her robe. "Did I need a reason to go see him?"

"Mrs. Scotto, I beg your pardon," Grandfather said neutrally, "but we were led to understand that he had refused to speak to you for the last few years. Now I ask you very kindly, what did you want of him that morning?"

"You know about that?" she said meekly looking like a little child caught in a lie. I nodded my head.

"I went because we really needed some money. Tony's been out of work for months, and we're flat broke. I would have asked Mom, but Dad controlled all the money and gave her what she needed each week for shopping. I was ready to beg him. I came early because I thought it would be better if I got there before customers started coming in. If I came to the house, he'd run into the bedroom and not talk to me. I thought I could corner him at the shop."

"A sad thing for a father and daughter not to speak. But good that you could still talk to your mother, no?"

"Yes," Rachel said cheering some, this time turning to Grandfather. "Mom and I spoke two or three times a week."

"Then she mentioned that your father purchased a gun for the store?"

Rachel looked confused. "No, that was a real surprise when David told us. Daddy's buying a gun would have been big news, and Mom would have told me."

"The same like when she told you about the insurance policy?"

Rachel's eyes narrowed into a glare and she turned back toward me. "Yeah, like she told me about the damned policy. I know what you're getting at. You think I'm glad Daddy's dead so I can hit up Mom for some of the insurance money. Well listen, I won't say I won't take some if Mom offers, but I didn't want him dead to get it. I don't care what you think." She sobbed and wiped her eyes with her sleeve.

I felt sorry for Rachel and felt helpless as to what to say or do. So I was glad when Grandfather leaned toward her and said with a voice choked with his own emotion:

"We know you are sad that he is dead, and under such terrible circumstances. It is never easy to lose a loved one."

* * * *

"I must spend more hours on the 13th Avenue," Grandfather advised me after leaving Rachel's apartment. "Would you please go to the Bronx address of this Workers United Party and speak to the Stein boy."

More time on 13th Avenue! Whatever for, I wondered but said nothing. But going to the Bronx to the Workers United Party office to speak to Jack Stein! That was another matter. I became very nervous and stopped our walk. "But what shall I ask him, Zaida?"

"We have now done together three interviews so you are acquainted with the interviewing procedures. I trust you to find your way. But before you go, employ your legs to do a little work." Grandfather flashed his shy but self-satisfied look whenever he came up with an English language play on words. "And see what the newspapers have written about the Workers United Party."

Still nervous, I took the train to the 42nd Street Library. There were two small *New York Times* articles about the committee. The first in July, 1965, described an announcement by Ervin Green that he along with three other Columbia University students had broken off from SDS, Students for a Democratic Society, to found the Workers United Party, as the article quoted, "to fight for economic justice, racial equality, and brotherhood among America's working class." Claiming that SDS leaders such as Tom Hayden had become "coopted" by the establishment, Green vowed that "WUP will never accommodate compromise with the rapacious, capitalist oppressors."

A second article, from February, 1968, reported that Ervin Green had filed to run as a candidate for the United States Senate from New York under the Workers United Party. I couldn't resist. I looked up how he wound up doing in the election. Green received 328 votes.

The 42nd Street Library did not house *Daily News* archived articles, so with my legs still strong and a "what did I have to lose attitude," I hustled over to their nearby building. Rolling through their microfiche, I found a story that took my breath away. An article from March of 1971, blared a headline of "COMMIE PARTY JACKS UP VIOLENCE IN BROOKLYN," with a picture of shopkeepers standing before a candy store with a shattered glass front on 4th Avenue in Brooklyn's Sunset Park section. The story quoted merchants as saying that about six months ago, the Workers United Party had started a campaign to radicalize Brooklyn street gangs, particularly in the Boro Park and Sunset Park neighborhoods. They accused WUP of inciting the gangs to steal to fund the group's activities.

But here's what made my eyes open wide. The article contained an interview with a Jack Stein who was identified as the Workers United Party's "Youth Officer." Stein said he started WUP's youth arm in these Brooklyn areas because he grew up in Boro Park and was very familiar with "the exploitation that takes place in these neighborhoods." He rejected the merchants' "deliberate distortions" of his work. "What you are getting from these capitalist exploiters is the usual smear accusations. They don't want us to raise the consciousness of the young who fall prey to accepting the degrading work practices that store owners here and throughout America are employing to grow their wealth at the expense of their workers."

I paid a quarter to have the story printed. I felt excited and energized, filled with a newfound bravado that made me even willing to skip lunch as I headed to the subway to take the #4 train to a W. Burnside Avenue address in the Morris Heights section of the Bronx where the Workers United Party was headquartered.

My mind was racing with a suspicion that perhaps this case wasn't as simple as I had thought. I had not met him, but I disliked Jack Stein. Perhaps he was behind his own father's murder. After all, he was well acquainted with the butcher shop's hours, set up, and who would be there before the morning opening for a gang to swoop in and steal a few, easy dollars. I wondered if he even might have known about the gun and had tipped off the gang to watch for it. I knew I had to constrain my animosity, but my adrenaline was pumping, and I looked forward to a confrontation.

WUP headquarters turned out to be a small storefront between a Firestone tire center and Dunn-Rite Dry Cleaners. The harsh whirring of air compressor drills attacking lug nuts dominated the neighborhood sounds. As I approached the WUP entrance, I was perspiring. Late May, the days were becoming hot and humid. The smell of rubber competed with the acetic odor of the dry cleaning chemicals, and rubber was winning. I stopped before an open streaked, glass door with paint flaking all around its dirty, white frame. The door was held open by two triangular wooden door stoppers. Crudely stenciled large block letters proclaimed WORKERS UNITED PARTY.

I walked in and saw two men behind desks speaking on phones. Both desks were grey steel industrial models. Dozens of tag board placards with wooden handles were propped against the walls. One, I could clearly see, read **GREEN FOR SENATE**. He must be keeping it for another run, I scornfully told myself. Two bulbs screwed into ceiling sockets gave the room some additional light. The air was warm and fetid. I spotted a small brown door ajar toward the back wall with TOILET painted on it in white.

The man sitting at the desk closer to the door was Ervin Green. I recognized him from his picture in the *New York Times* that accompanied his Senate filing story. He was a red head, from his short cropped, wiry hair down through long sideburns and stubbly beard. Wire rim glasses gave prominence to bushy red eyebrows. He was wearing a powdery blue short sleeve shirt which allowed me to see the forest of freckles that made its way from his hands to wrists, and up arms. He kept his fingers to his mouth spreading them when he spoke rapid fire and closing tightly when listening.

Much of Green's desk was covered by a ragged, stained brown desk blotter with frayed, lifted edges on which were a black rotary dial phone, empty and half empty bottles of soda, various papers, and multiple copies of what I could read as *Workers Voice*.

After a few moments of looking at me with narrowed eyes, he spread his fingers over the phone and barked, "wait a second."

And then directly to me, "You a reporter?"

"No." I shook my head trying to keep my expression neutral and hiding my antagonism. "I'm here to see Jack Stein. It's personal family business."

"About his Dad's death, I'm guessing." And before I could respond, Green rocked one shoulder and a tilt of the head toward the other desk and then spoke again into phone, "Yeah, I'm back."

I moved forward and positioned myself near Jack Stein's desk. He too was on the phone, and I tried not to act impatient as I waited around 10 minutes listening to his discussion with someone at what seemed to me to be the bureau that gave out permits for political rallies. Actually, the delay gave me a chance to look Jack over, and I was surprised.

I guess my mind had raced with its stereotype of a political radical. I thought Jack would have dark, wooly hair, several days of face stubble, and be bespectacled like Green. I was sure his arms up to his knuckles would be furry, and chest hair would be tufting through the top of an unbuttoned worker's shirt.

Well, I was right about the work shirt. It was sunwashed blue canvas which might have come even back then from the L.L. Bean factory. But it was neatly buttoned to the neck. He was wearing the blue jeans I imagined, but they were clean and not frayed.

Jack sat forward while he spoke into the phone, obviously frustrated, but his voice was firm and modulated, not at all harsh. His desk was clean with neatly stacked papers and copies of the *Workers Voice*.

He was thin, no more than 125 pounds, and later when he stood up, I saw that he was around 5' 6". His sandy colored hair was slightly wavy and grown out down to the nape. He did not wear glasses, and his hazel eyes looked tired to me, especially as brown circles sat underneath. Probably insomnia, I suspected. His small, angular face was clean shaven.

"Yes," Jack intoned several times into the phone.

"Yes, we are sure we want to have it in Cadman Plaza in Brooklyn."

"Yes, we know about last time. This time we will easily have over a 1000 people."

"Yes, again, the rally is called 'Delivery Workers United Against Greed.'"

"Yes, I know there is a permit fee. I'll drop it off tomorrow at your office."

Finally he hung up, gently dropping the phone receiver into the cradle. By this time, both my antagonism and adrenaline had for some reason receded. "Mr. Stein?" I asked wanting to be formal and polite.

Even though I had thought that he must have known I was waiting for him, he looked up surprised and nodded yes to me. I moved forward, introduced myself, and offered condolences.

After I had told him why I had come and had a few questions, he stood up but did not extend his hand. He looked at me, and with the tone of someone deeply disappointed with the person in front of him and perhaps with all of humanity, softly said: "Well, insurance companies are always true to form. I suppose if I don't answer your questions, you'll just use it as an excuse not to settle with Mom, so ask your questions." He sat back down.

I felt myself disarmed. I would have done better with a frontal, verbal assault, but the mildness of his response oddly unnerved me. I was going to get right to the point, no niceties, and do my interview machine gun fashion. Now I felt myself faltering as I proceeded to ask my questions in the order I had prepared in my mind.

"Mr. Stein, did you know your father kept a gun at the shop?"

"No," he retorted blandly.

"Did you know about the $100,000 policy before your father's murder?"

"Yes."

"Do you expect to get some of that money?"

To this question, he hesitated for a moment. "I don't know. That's up to Mom."

I worried that Jack might take my next question badly. "Since you work with the kids in Boro Park, any ideas which gang it may have been?"

But he took the question well. For that matter, he lost himself in a moment's thought. Then, looking as if he were battling confusion, he answered: "No idea. The description Mr. Kacew gave the police doesn't fit any of what you call the gangs I work with. The ones I know are not racially mixed."

Did I have to ask the next question? I'm not sure even to this day. But I remember I had to pluck up my nerve to do it.

"Is there any truth to the accusation that you get your gangs to steal for your organization?"

But while Jack's eyes flashed anger, he remained steady. "Mr. Gordon," he said forcefully, his voice rising somewhat. "I'll bet you did some homework before coming all the way up the Bronx and saw the article in *The Daily News* where you've probably seen my refutation of these absurd charges. If you haven't, look it up, it's the March 4 of last year edition."

Before I could say anything, Jack picked up the phone and said, "So if that's it, I have important work to do. You'll probably find a way to screw my mother out of her money. That's just the way it is, until we make some real changes in this country. Good bye Mr. Gordon."

I wasn't going to get into an argument with Jack, so I turned, walked by Ervin Green, and out the door. The heat was even more stifling, tires were going on or coming off cars, clothes were being martinized in one hour, and I was pretty much satisfied with my day's work.

* * * *

I returned home around 4:00 famished from not having eaten since breakfast. Grandfather was asleep in our living room's easy chair, the Yiddish weekly unfolded in his lap. Although I was excited to report on my day, I didn't disturb Grandfather. Instead, I grabbed a snack and read the *Times'* sport section. I heard Grandfather stirring a half hour later.

When I walked back into the living room, Grandfather was still in the easy chair. He greeted with me a wide smile. "I didn't hear you come home. Nuh, how are you and what discoveries did you make today?"

I was bursting with self-satisfaction about how well my day had gone. I pulled up a chair in front of Grandfather and sat down, leaning toward him. Rapidly, I told Grandfather what I had learned from reading the *Times* and my initiative in running to the *Daily News* Building and finding the article that mentioned Jack Stein working with the young gangs. After giving Grandfather a description of the Bronx neighborhood where WUP was located, I repeated almost verbatim my conversation with Jack. Shrugging off any import, I also shared how wrong I was in my expectation of him.

When I finished, I leaned back and expected a compliment or two, but instead Grandfather said: "Two things, please Joel. Do you not find it most interesting, as I have for a good portion of my life, how we are dominated by preconceptions and formulas that are useful for our getting through each day, but are the stumbling blocks to critical analysis. Certainly we would never cross a street if we didn't have in our heads that cars will stop at a red light. But for excellence in detective work, we must always challenge our own minds' entrenched stories."

Thinking back, I must have appeared flustered, the way I looked when I wanted validation and approval from Grandfather but instead received a pedantic teaching moment. I think Grandfather always understood my reaction but thought our bond was strong enough to withstand momentary exasperation for longer term development. He was right, and I'm still working on it.

His expression benign, Grandfather continued. "Thank you for your dedicated work today. But I must ask that you perform one more task tonight. I know you may be fatigued, but please go back to Manhattan and see if you can interview Arthur Kacew. I called his father at the butcher shop, and though he was hesitant, he gave me his son's address and phone number after I told him that to complete our thorough investigation, we needed to talk to Arthur briefly. Let us take the approach of not calling first. The master detectives of fiction believed that approaching those we interview unawares will provide us with a more honest assessment of behavior and information."

I would rather have put on a ball game and relaxed at home, but I made no objection to Grandfather's request. After all, I was making at least $500 for a few day's work.

* * * *

I took the F train up to Lexington and 63rd Street. Even with an early supper, by the time I arrived, it was 8:15, and the heat was just beginning to subside. Arthur's address checked out to be on 63rd off of 1st Avenue, one of the newly emerging fashionable Upper East Side apartment buildings. Walking up to the building, I spotted the mural of Sherlock Holmes with smoke wafting out of his pipe above a sign for the Baker Street Pub at the corner of 63rd and 1st. I took it as an indication that history's greatest detective was smiling down at my work.

I never got past the doorman who was dressed out of a movies set in a heavy coat, cap, and white gloves. A large, metallic whistle hung from his neck. How in the world, I thought feeling sorry for him, does he bear the heat? But exhibiting not a drop of perspiration, he told me that Arthur was out-of-town. He didn't know when Arthur would be back.

I dropped a dime into a pay phone and called Grandfather. "Do you have two $5 bills with you?" he asked.

Puzzled, I checked my wallet. I did have two $5 bills.

"Go back to the doorman," Grandfather directed, "and give him one of the bills. Tell him if he answers some questions, you will give him the other. Ask him: When did Arthur leave? Why did he leave? Does he remember anything special about a week ago Monday?"

I went back wondering that Grandfather knew about such tactics. The $10 "gratuity" worked. Somewhere from within his voluminous coat, the doorman, who suddenly became chatty and told me his name was John Regan, took out a ledger book and thumbed through it. The day Arthur went out of town, he came down around 6:00 in the morning "looking dapper" and headed for the garage. The door-man remembered quite well because he was tired toward the end of his 8:00 at night to 8:00 in the morning shift, and Arthur's good cheer irritated him so early in the morning.

"Just wanted to check my memory, sir," Regan said indicating the ledger book to me. "Yep, it was a week ago Monday morning this happened."

Just before 8:00, Arthur returned in his Continental, pale as a ghost, hair ruffled, tie askew, and a shirt that didn't match his suit jacket. Arthur ordered the doorman to watch his car while he went upstairs.

"I can tell you sir," Regan said with a voice seeking sympathy. "That wasn't right sir, no sir, not right to make me delay my knock off time. But these days I'm glad to have work, and our building's motto is 'the tenant is always right'"

Just 15 minutes later, Arthur rushed down with a small suitcase and wearing a change of clothes.

"More casual like," Regan recalled. "Mr. Kacew was mumbling something to the effect that he was suddenly called away on business. Jumped into that beautiful Continental of his and roared away turning north on 1st Avenue."

I gave Regan the second $5 bill and thanked him profusely. He tipped his cap to me as I said goodbye and turned to head back to Lexington.

I knew Grandfather liked to be in bed by 9:00, so I dropped another dime into the pay phone and within my three minute time limit before I needed another coin, I filled in Grandfather on what I had learned.

"Thank you Joel, again good work. I find myself a bit weary this evening, so let us reconvene in the morning."

On the train riding home, I stopped thinking of Jack Stein as my prime suspect. I was now sure that Arthur Kacew was implicated in Joe Stein's death. So much had occurred in the last two days. I thought about the murder scene, the Stein children, and Arthur Kacew's seemingly strange behavior as described by the doorman. But a lesson acknowledged late is better than a lesson not acknowledged at all. "Arthur Kacew is one more puzzle piece," I lectured myself thinking about what Grandfather had said earlier in the day. "The puzzle pieces have to all come together. Be patient."

Wednesday, May 17, 1972.

By the time I rolled out of bed, it was around 9:00. My mother had already left for work, and I found a note from Grandfather on the kitchen table asking me to meet at the office. I badly needed a shower and shave, and so it was around 11:00 when I made it to downtown Brooklyn.

"You are well rested, I presume," Grandfather greeted me from behind his desk. Not waiting for a response, he added: "I called Lerman Equities, Arthur's place of employment. They told me he has been ill for over a week and to call him at home. There was, of course given what you reported to me last night, no answer when I called his home number."

"There's something strange somewhere," I said seating myself in the guest chair.

"Ah Joel, that is a much too simple conclusion. I trust you have more complex thoughts?"

My mind's engine quickly kicked into revving mode, and I blurted out: "Well Zaida, I don't know what to think given that David Kacew saw the gang fleeing the shop. Following your guidance on my need to engage what you call critical analysis, that fact really makes any of my thoughts just conjectures."

Grandfather said nothing for a while but made sure that his eyes caught mine. I relaxed a bit. He then replied: "It is appropriate for a moment to be hypothetical, to operate in what you have called the area of 'conjectures.' Let us see how they survive when placed against our critical thinking. So I am most interested in your confusions. They often pave the way to clarity."

I thought briefly before answering. "Like any good detective, I look for motive and access to the victim. Who could gain by Stein's death? There's Arthur. Stein stood in the way of his market. Arthur probably knew about the gun in the shop, something happened to him at the very time the murder occurred, and that he suddenly disappeared right after.

"There are the Stein children. They both knew about the insurance policy and might have known about the gun, but probably not. And Jack could have engineered the whole thing behind the scenes. He might not have wanted his father killed, just the shop robbed for the cause. But Zaida, my feeling is to discount the possibility of the Stein children being involved. I can't believe that one of his own kids could have had a part in it."

"Tcha, tcha," Grandfather cautioned. "When I was a young man in the 1920's, the most gripping news of that decade for many of us was not the stock market crash or Lindbergh's flight, but the Leopold and Loeb murder case. We could not comprehend how two wealthy boys, so refined and well-educated, could commit such a crime.

What many concluded, in America and abroad, was that America may be called for good reasons the Golden Land, but where there is gold, life always exists at a cost, and not just of the monetary. We should automatically not rule out that one of the Stein children, or even in collaboration, could have engineered their father's murder. But neither Jack nor Rachel did such a heinous act, and we arrive at that determination using our analytic skills and not our emotions."

"How so?" I wondered.

"Because obviously David Kacew made up a street gang that could not possibly match any the police or Jack Stein know. Also, would a gang make a holdup so early in the morning when the shop would only have a few dollars for the change making?"

"So that leaves one prime suspect, Arthur Kacew," I said bounding up. "That's where he went when he left his apartment early that Monday morning. He wanted one more try at convincing Stein to sell. When Stein again refused, Arthur lost his head and shot him with the gun he knew was there. I'm now sure Arthur killed Stein, and his father is covering for him."

Grandfather smiled. "Do you remember what time Stein was killed? According to the police, it was around 7:45. Do you remember what time the doorman said Arthur returned to his apartment? It was a few minutes before 8:00. Could Arthur have travelled from Brooklyn to Upper East Side Manhattan in such a short time?"

I was deflated and again confused. I liked certainty, and this detective work was constantly eroding feeling sure about things. "That would put him in the middle of rush hour, and he couldn't have made it. That leaves out Arthur, doesn't it Zaida?"

"No Joel, it does not," Grandfather said looking directly at me. "You see, Stein was murdered earlier than 7:45."

I was even more lost. "What makes you believe that?"

"Because Stein did not go to synagogue that morning. He could not have gone."

I was totally lost. "What makes you believe that?"

Grandfather eyed me affectionately. "It is impossible the man did so. You see it was a Monday morning and also *Rosh Chodesh*, the monthly Jewish celebration of the new moon. Do you remember when you were younger in the summers when you weren't in school and up in the early morning, and I sometimes asked if you wished to accompany me to synagogue? This was before you became a teenager and slept long into the day. Before agreeing, you would inquire, especially if it was a Monday or a Thursday, if it was also *Rosh Chodesh*. Do you remember why you would ask me such a question?"

"Sure, the services were already long on Mondays and Thursdays because portions from the Torah are read on those days, and if it's *Rosh Chodesh* too, the service with the additional prayers is even longer. So usually I wouldn't want to go on those days."

"And how long would such a service take, Yoeli?"

"At least an hour and 15 minutes."

"So do you see why it was impossible for Stein to have been at the shop at 7:45. He would not have left services in the middle. During my walks on the 13th Avenue, I learned that at the synagogue that Joe Stein frequented, services started at 6:45 that day. Even so, Stein would not have arrived until after 8:00."

"Wait a minute, Zaida. What you say might be true, but wouldn't a religious man like Kacew know all this? He would have taken this into account in formulating his story."

I saw the smile on Grandfather's face. "You believe he is a religious man because he quotes the Talmud and Torah? When we spoke to Kacew Monday morning, neither of his seemingly learned references was correct. On the 13th Avenue, those who know Kacew said he gives his money generously to charity but comes to synagogue only three times a year on the High Holy Days. Kacew would have neglected to take *Rosh Chodesh* into account in creating the murder story."

Frustrated and feeling a bit stupid, I spit out: "So my conclusion was correct. Arthur Kacew killed Stein."

Grandfather drummed his fingers on his desk. "No Joel, the evidence may point in that direction, but I do not think Arthur killed Stein. I believe David Kacew did the shooting."

When I looked incredulous, Grandfather went on. "I cannot rely on my analytic skills to convince you as much as on intuition, the second most valuable asset for a detective. Look at the history of the Kacew father and son. The son grew up in a comfortable, protected environment. The father was a hero during the Holocaust fighting Nazis for five years. In America, he engaged a mugger and killed him with his own knife. What I am suggesting is the ability to kill, and certainly the father possesses it more than the son.

"But what would his motive have been?" I asked hardly convinced.

"Good," Grandfather beamed. "You pose a most important question. I cannot satisfy you at this moment. I would also like to know why Joe Stein did not go to synagogue that morning. And we have neglected other puzzling aspects of this case. Prior to the day of the murder, does any one time period stand out?"

I very much wanted to come up with the answer, but just shook my head.

"Listen, it is quite evident," Grandfather said swinging around to face me. "Three months ago, Stein bought the gun and the insurance policy. In the last few months, he stopped coming home for lunch on Fridays, and a few months ago he started getting headaches. Also, in the last few months, Arthur stopped asking him to sell the shop."

"There's a connection among all these facts?" I asked trying to put the pieces together.

"I am quite sure, but what it is I do not fully know yet. But I will tell you this. Just yesterday I discovered that Joe Stein at the time of his murder had a terminal illness."

I didn't even try to betray my wonder. My look begged an explanation.

"Where did Joe Stein go on Fridays?" Grandfather asked without really expecting an answer. "Yesterday I walked down the 13th Avenue in the direction of his home away from the shop and spoke to shopkeepers. Most knew Stein by sight. They told me that for years he had passed by around 1:00 and back again around 2:00, but lately not on Fridays. I then started in the other direction from the shop. Only a few of the merchants knew him, but those who did said for a few months before his death, Stein passed by on Fridays also around 1:00 and 2:00. Yet past the 52nd Street, not one person ever saw him go by. So I turned up the 52nd Street toward the 14th Avenue. Where would he be going? I asked myself. When I thought of his headaches, the answer was obvious.

"I stopped at the first doctor sign and was very lucky. I explained my representation of the insurance company, and he admitted Stein was his patient. But he would not tell me why Stein went to see him. I pointed out that he would be subpoenaed for depositions and possibly a court appearance where he eventually would have to disclose the information and that he could save himself the time and expense by telling me now and signing a deposition later at his convenience.

"The doctor was reluctantly convinced and informed me that Stein had a brain cancer, gioblastoma multiforme, with no reasonable intervention. Every Friday Stein would come and ask the doctor if he knew any better how much longer he had to live. The doctor felt sorry for Stein and didn't want to dissuade him from his repeated visits to which the answer to his question at first was six months and decreasing thereafter. At the time of Mr. Stein's death, he maybe had another three months to live."

"OK, Zaida," I said trying to get all the pieces to fall in place. "Then how did Stein pass his physical for the insurance policy?"

"Ah, a good question which I asked the doctor. He didn't know anything about the policy but indicated that the physician for the insurance company would not have known about the condition if Stein hadn't mentioned the headaches."

All of a sudden Grandfather ranked with Poirot and Holmes in my mind. "Zaida, that was fantastic work you did."

"Well boychic, it is nice to hear that the young are sometimes capable of appreciating the work of the old, but do not forget we still have unanswered questions. What is the connection of the murder with Stein's illness and all the other events of the last few months?"

"Excuse the unintended play on words, but I guess we are at a dead end, Zaida. I don't see where we can go for those answers. Can you?"

"Yes Joel, I can. We will ask David Kacew, and he will tell us."

"David Kacew!" I was quizzically amused. "He's going to tell us? Really?"

Grandfather remained serious. "The venerable Hercule Poirot mused that 'if you confront anyone who has lied with the truth, he will usually admit it – often out of sheer surprise. It is only necessary to guess right to produce your effect.'

"So we will simply present him with your original theory that Arthur shot Stein. If he is the man I believe him to be, he will not allow his son to be implicated falsely."

I jumped up and headed for the door. "I'm ready," I said. "Let's go to the butcher shop."

Grandfather waved me back with a "sha, sha, the man is working and making a living. Why should we interfere with that. He is not a common criminal who might run from the city. Let him work, let him eat supper. Around 8:00 tonight will be soon enough."

* * * *

While most of the homes on 63rd Street off of 13th Avenue were two or three level duplexes with stoops leading up to the entrances, the Kacew residence was a large house with a street level one-car garage, white balconies across the second and third floor fronts, and a few manicured concrete steps up to the entrance. When we rang the bell, the door was opened by a strikingly attractive middle-aged woman wearing a good deal of make-up, well-dressed in a red linen suit, matching pearl earrings and necklace, and silver hair puffed and teased.

After greeting us and ascertaining who we were, she welcomed us into the foyer and called behind her, "David, there are two gentlemen to see you." And then to us as she headed to the door, "Please excuse me, I have a meeting tonight."

When Kacew saw us, he smiled broadly and waved us into the living room which was neat and meticulously clean. The long wall was covered with Jewish art, a Chagall that was easy to recognize, and other works depicting biblical scenes. Family pictures were stacked on chests and end tables. The short wall caught my eye with its large reproduction of Bierstadt's Rocky Mountain Landscape.

A highly polished wood mantel was built into the wall beneath the Bierstadt, which, along with end tables, held family pictures, some recent and in color, many in black and white including what appeared to be a 19th century tintype of a large family gathered around a bride and groom. A richly colored Persian rug adorned the wooden floor, and Kacew directed us to a wine colored sofa. He faced us from a matching easy chair.

Grandfather spoke gently, but got right to the point, immediately stating our suspicions of Arthur and presenting the supporting evidence for the contention just as we had reviewed it at Grandfather's office.

Kacew stopped smiling. "All you say cannot be proven," he said sharply looking hard at Grandfather.

Grandfather answered in a neutral tone. "You might be correct, but please be sure of the following. When we go to the police and give them Arthur's motive, when we tell them about Arthur's car parked in front of the shop around the time of the murder which we are sure it was and a witness will certainly be found, when we tell them you lied about Arthur's being there, your son will be arrested for murder and you for covering up. A good lawyer could get both of you off, but the arrests will take place."

Grandfather took out a handkerchief and, as he wiped his glasses, looked directly at Kacew and said firmly. "Know this completely, we will go to the police with these facts even though I don't believe Arthur murdered your partner. It was you who fired the gun, am I not right?"

Kacew, who had gone from belligerently self-assured to agitated as Grandfather spoke, slumped back and gave a grudging, painful smile. "It seems very hard, Mr. Wolf, for one greenhorn to fool another. And I find myself relieved to say it, Mr. Wolf, yes, you are correct, I shot Joe. I made up this gang so that no boys could fit my description. I did not want any innocent people hurt because of what I did."

"We believe you are not a bad person," Grandfather said quietly. "Please, why did you shoot your partner?"

Kacew's gaze looked beyond us. "To explain why, I must go back about three months to the morning Joe came into the shop with the gun. He told me he was dying from cancer. He made me swear I would tell no one else, including Gittel. Before I could get over the shock, he gave me an even bigger kick in the stomach. He told me about the insurance policy and very calmly asked me to shoot him because if he died of the cancer, the company would not pay out. They would have realized that he lied on the application. He had it all figured out. I would shoot him and make it appear that he was killed in a robbery. I told him, no, absolutely not. 'I could never shoot you,' I said. 'You are like a brother.' Joe kept begging me, wept to me, screamed at me, but of course I would not give in. That was the end until the morning of his death."

"And around then, around three months ago, Arthur stopped bothering Stein to sell because you told him Joe was dying?" I asked.

Kacew jerked his head toward me as if he had forgotten that I was present. "No, I did not tell Arthur. I only insisted without explanation that Arthur stop pestering him. Arthur listened until that morning. When I came to work, Arthur was already there. He had just pulled his car up in front of the shop. It was around 7:00. I let him in with me. He was very excited. He talked about the economic upturn and predicted a boom period ahead. He wanted one more chance to convince Joe to sell.

"I again said not to bother the man, but before I could get him out of the shop, Joe walked in. On the way to the synagogue, he must have seen Arthur's car parked outside, and he waited for me to arrive. His face had a happy look I had not seen since he told me about his sickness. Arthur and I were behind the counter. 'You say that you cannot kill me, we will see,' Joe hollered in Yiddish without even giving us a hello. He ran over and got the gun out from under the register. 'What are you doing? What are you doing?' I kept pleading over and over.

"He rushed over and after jamming the gun into my hand, shoved me back a few steps in the direction of the door. I don't know why I didn't put the gun down. I kept holding it. In another quick motion, he pulled a cleaver off the wall and ran toward my son. He grabbed Arthur by his shirt and looked right into my eyes for a second before lifting the cleaver as if to strike at Arthur.

"The look was like in the paintings of Abraham holding a knife to Isaac's throat, and Joe, using similar words from the bible, roared at me, 'Is this not Arthur, your son, your only son? Aren't you his angel that will save him from his slaughter?'

"Arthur is my son, my only son, so I shot, just once. I learned well when I was with the Partisans. And God forgive me, I aimed at Joe's head. Even as I pulled the trigger, even as Joe fell, I knew through my twisted insides that he would never have struck Arthur. But it was too late. For that split second, I could do nothing but shoot him.

"The rest you can probably guess. In the few seconds it took for Arthur to rush over to where I was standing, gun still in hand, he had become hysterical. I calmed him down and made him wash up. He didn't have his suit jacket on, but his shirt and tie had blood splatter. I had him remove his shirt and tie and put on an old dress shirt I kept in the back. I kept hoping that at that time of day before the other shops open, no one heard the shot.

"My son is a good boy, never in trouble, a boy with a wonderful future. I worried that his present job would be lost and his future ruined. I also considered what you yourself realized that the police might not believe the truth and would suspect us because we would gain by Joe's death. Then Joe's suggestion came to me. I would tell the police about the gang robbing the store. I made Arthur leave immediately, told him he was in shock, not to go to work, and instead to leave for our bungalow in the mountains. He was to stay there until he calmed down enough to function without betraying what occurred.

"With Arthur gone, I wiped the gun of fingerprints and hid it in the freezer with the shirt and tie. I knew that if I called the police then, people would ask why Joe hadn't gone to the synagogue that morning. Also I needed to give Arthur time to return to his apartment in case he needed an alibi. So I waited a half hour before calling. I figured a half hour difference in death is hard to discover. Of course, I wasn't aware about *Rosh Chodesh*. Later, I threw the gun away in the trash and burned the shirt and tie. Had the insurance company not contacted you, no one would have ever known."

We sat in silence with Grandfather gently rocking back and forth and Kacew holding his head in his hands. "I am sorry," Grandfather finally said. "But of course, you would have known all of your lives, and both of you would have carried a heavy weight."

"Thank you, Mr. Wolf, I am sorry too. Do you know what I did waiting for the half hour to pass? I stood over Joe's body, watched his dear blood seep into the dust, and spoke to him the whole time? 'Yossi,' I said speaking of course in Yiddish, 'is this why you suffered through the Holocaust? Is this why I lived like an animal for five years fighting the Nazis? Did we both do these things so that you should be lying at my feet dead from my own hands?' Over and over I repeated this."

"If this is consolation," Grandfather said, "it is possible you will not be prosecuted if you suggest the shock caused your lapse in judgment."

Kacew continued speaking in Yiddish, his head up. "Yes, perhaps, as it is the truth. I am usually quite calm and with good judgment in difficult situations. But it was my son after all, and I panicked when the truth would have been the best option. I will take the consequences, and hopefully not Arthur."

Kacew then looked imploringly at Grandfather. "You will do me one favor? Do not go to the police. I will call Arthur and tell him to come back. I will talk to Mimi. She knows nothing of it. Then we will all go to the police together, as a family."

Grandfather also answered in Yiddish: "Of course, tonight, tomorrow, go when you are ready."

Kacew remained sitting as we let ourselves out. On a beautiful twilight night, children were still playing in the street. People sat on the stoops and porches of their homes talking, and television pictures flickered in the windows. I was very pleased and babbled about our success in cracking this case.

When Grandfather had not said anything for a few minutes, I turned and saw my beloved grandfather looking tired and trying to keep up with me. I stopped and faced him.

"Zaida, is something wrong? Aren't you glad that we've solved the case?"

He sighed and shook his head. "I am satisfied, but happy is another emotion. Consider the great Sherlock Holmes who fought battles with real hardened villains, murderers, spies, and blackmailers. A victory over a Moriarity was a victory for good over evil. Such work truly merits satisfaction, but still, a sadness would envelope Holmes who would fall into depression and opioid addiction.

"In my career as a detective, I have accepted money from one sad person to reveal the unwanted truth about another sad person. Now we discover that one fine man shot to death another fine man. Why did such a thing happen? Such sorrowful reasons for this tragedy."

"And Mrs. Stein won't even get her $100,000, will she Zaida?"

"It is probable she will not. When the insurance company receives our report, they will reject the claim because Joe Stein lied on his application and, in effect, committed suicide. Bah, what is the difference? I have a feeling her children would wind up with most of the money anyway."

My high flying balloon came down to earth. "I feel bad for you." I said stopping and putting my hand on Grandfather's shoulder.

"Ach," he answered grabbing me gently by the neck. "You are new to the business. Let's go home. If the Mets are playing tonight, we can watch the last few innings."

Friday, May 19, 1972.

A short item in the *Times* reported that David Kacew had confessed to the involuntary homicide of his partner, Joseph Stein. Arthur Kacew was charged with obstruction of justice. They were freed on bond. A few months later, he and Arthur were let off with a $5,000 fine, the cost to the city in dealing with Joe Stein's death.

A LITTLE BOY IS MISSING

Wednesday, May 23, 1973.

Success isn't all it's cracked up to be, I thought as I stopped before the smoked glass door to my grandfather's office that read: **FRANK WOLF DETECTIVE AGENCY**. It was 9:55 AM. A year before, Zaida, using the Yiddish word for grandfather, had with a bit of my assistance solved the murder of Joseph Stein, a butcher in the Boro Park section of Brooklyn, and so saved New York Mutual a $100,000 life insurance payout to Stein's family. If you want some details, you can find them in the May 19, 1972 issue of the *New York Times*.

I was sure that when word got around the orthodox Jewish communities in Brooklyn and perhaps beyond, business would really pick up for Grandfather.

"That's all he needs," my mother had lamented when I shared my enthusiasm. "I don't know if it was the Stein case itself or something more, but your grandfather seems tired to me. He says he's fine, but I'm worried."

My mother could have saved herself the worry. Business hadn't picked up and may have even dropped. Although he went daily to his office near Brooklyn's Boro Hall to wait for the phone to ring or a client to walk through the door, he had only a case or two a month come his way: a check on a future business associate, background on a proposed partner in an arranged marriage, or an investigation of suspected infidelity.

Grandfather wasn't surprised when I brought it up. He rubbed his eyes under his glasses, and in his elegantly accented English commented: "I expected this result. I have angered many in our community who believe I violated a certain code by helping the insurance company 'against one of our own.' I stand indicted for depriving Joseph Stein's widow of the money that would have bolstered her after her husband's death, regardless of the claim's illegitimacy."

"Are you sorry we took the case?"

"Not at all, Yoeli." That was Grandfather's pet name for me. "When I took on this honorable profession, I committed to seeking justice with no favor nor disfavor to the rich or poor, the weak or the powerful. I am greatly sorry the outcome negatively impacted Mrs. Stein, but New York Mutual also deserves justice. I ask of you, what would have occurred if the original police report had remained indicating that Stein was killed by a youth gang that included various minorities? Suspicion, hatred, revenge all arise when justice fails."

Just a few hours earlier, I had been fast asleep after completing my second year law school exams the day before. I wanted to sleep late and spend time with my new girlfriend, Aliya, for the next two weeks before I started my summer clerkship at the Brooklyn DA's office. Although I dreamily heard the phone ringing in our Flatbush apartment where I lived with my mother and grandfather, I was jolted fully awake when Mother knocked on my door.

"Joel," she said tensely. "That was Zaida calling. He wants you at his office by 10:00."

"By 10:00!" I sputtered. "But why, and what time is it now?"

"It's now a few minutes past 8:00, and I don't know why. But Zaida said it is 'critical' that you come by 10:00, and when he uses the 'critical' word, it's something very important. So you'll get up and rush over?"

"I guess," I answered half-heartedly, sitting up at the edge of the bed. "Is there any coffee?"

"Yes." My mother came over and stroked my hair. "I also must run to open the store on time." She meant the jewelry store that she managed in Manhattan. "There are some hard-boiled eggs in the refrigerator that you can eat quickly with the coffee."

She kissed me on the cheek, and as she was about to leave, turned toward me, looking worried. "I hope your Zaida hasn't gotten himself into anything dangerous."

I felt sorry for my mother. I knew that the six years she spent as a young girl in hiding with my grandfather in the Austrian countryside during the Holocaust, her mother dying during that time, and my father's early death when I was 14 had left her constantly fearful.

"I'm sure there's no danger," I said in a soft voice and got up from bed. "I'll get dressed, eat quickly, and hurry over there."

When I entered my grandfather's office, I saw the back of a heavyset man seated facing my grandfather. A large black velvet skullcap sat over the man's short, cropped hair. He glanced my way when I entered.

"Joel," my grandfather called out. "This is Avi Raskin from the Williamsburg Shomrim Society. A little boy is missing in Williamsburg. He is here to ask our assistance in finding him. Mr. Raskin, this is my grandson and at times associate, Joel Gordon."

Mr. Raskin stood up and shook my hand. He was stocky, about 50, with glasses, had a few days of stubble, and wore a white shirt that showed stains around the neck. The shirt was badly tucked into dark trousers, and knotted ritual fringes or *tzitzit* dangled on both sides of his pants pockets in the manner of some orthodox Jews.

I indicated to Raskin to resume his seat. I moved to the side of grandfather's desk. "Shomrim Society?" I asked.

"Yes," Raskin said eagerly. His accent was half Yiddish and half Brooklynese. "We are a Jewish civilian patrol in Williamsburg. We are unarmed and patrol mainly at night to prevent muggings, burglaries, vandalism, and domestic violence. We also help to locate missing people."

My two years of law school provoked a sense of law and order being circumvented. "But shouldn't these matters be left to the police?" I asked sharply.

Raskin answered calmly. "We are not vigilantes. We don't make arrests, and we immediately call the police if we come across criminal behavior. Many Jewish families in Williamsburg were victimized and murdered by fascist or communist police and military units in Europe. It's not just they have no trust in the police; they also fear the police. So we serve as intermediaries between the community and the police."

My grandfather rarely was impatient, but he became clearly so, "And a little boy is missing now two days. The Shomrim are assisting the police, and we must also try to assist."

Grandfather handed me a few pages of stapled papers. "Mr. Raskin brought us the police report. Joel, please make a quick perusal."

I thumbed through the reports quickly. Eight-year-old Yosele Rosenstock disappeared around 4:00 in the afternoon the previous Monday. Raskin had also brought a photo that showed a wispy looking boy, slight for his age, with wiry dark hair cut short, ear locks, and piercing eyes. He was last seen leaving his yeshiva, a religious school, at 95 Boerum Street and never arrived home. His older brothers at the school, Shimon 12 and Levi 10, explained that Yosele was not permitted to walk alone, but when they came to meet him at the school's entrance, they learned that he had already left, heading west down Boerum toward Leonard in the direction of the family's apartment.

They ran to catch up with him so as to avoid their mother's anger if Yosele showed up by himself. Looking in all directions, they hurried two blocks down Boerum to Union Avenue and a long block up Union, turning a short left to 468 S. 5th Street, where they lived in a second floor walkup. They asked boys playing punch ball on the street if they had seen Yosele, but the boys said no. Hoping that Yosele had eluded notice and was in the apartment, they ran upstairs, but no Yosele.

Their mother Leah said she immediately ordered the boys along with their older brother, Reuven, 17, to join her out on the street to look for Yosele. Sister Dinah, 15, was left at home in case Yosele appeared.

They searched to no avail. When the father, Yaacov Rosenstock, came home at 6:00, first unleashing his verbal fury on Shimon and Levi and then the other family members for not finding Yosele, he contacted the Shomrim, who also took up the street search after notifying the nearby 90th Police Precinct. The Williamsburg Jewish Community Relations Officer, Sgt. Max Fink, along with a canine search unit, came within minutes. But it had turned dark, the stores along the route were closed, and the search dog picked up no scent.

The next day, Tuesday, Fink's team worked with the Shomrim to question every merchant and resident along Boerum and Union. No one remembered seeing Yosele. Boys at the school confirmed what his brothers had reported. Was he carrying anything? Yes, he had his usual ragged, plastic backpack. The K-9 once again sniffed out the route. Nothing.

After finishing my reading of the report, I addressed Raskin: "But what can we bring to the search that the police or you can't?"

"A good, important question," Raskin acknowledged. "Your grandfather is an experienced investigator in the Orthodox Jewish community, and we hope his knowledge and analytic skills will lead us to the boy, as we are totally baffled. Your solving the Stein case may have caused resentment in some of the community, but we in the Shomrim, when we learned of your work and understood how you unraveled the intricacies of the death, we were struck by the brilliance of the detective work.

"And," here Raskin stopped and looked at my grandfather who signaled permission to go on, "we looked into your grandfather's background and learned that he knows the Rebbe, the spiritual leader of the missing boy's family, Rabbi Moshe Koenig. We've arranged for Mr. Wolf to meet the *Rebbe* and ask him to direct his community to cooperate with the investigation. Right now, there's very little they're telling us, including the boy's own family.

"So around 5:00 yesterday, I decided to contact your grandfather. The first 24-48 hours are critical with missing children. I called the number here, but there was no answer. I took a chance, and at 7:30 this morning, I was at your door. Mr. Wolf thankfully arrived 15 minutes later."

After a few more minutes of conversation, Raskin left. I then asked Grandfather: "How do you know Rabbi Koenig?"

Instead of answering, Grandfather stood up with more energy that I had seen over the last year and pointed to papers on his desk that were maps of Williamsburg.

"A little boy is missing, and there is much to do quickly. I will explain more about my relationship with Rabbi Koenig later, but now let us gain an understanding of the boy's neighborhood and the facts behind the case, yes?"

I had plans to go into the City with Aliya, but I had rarely seen Grandfather this agitated. I didn't know Aliya very well yet, but I would call her and hope she understood.

"What do you want me to do, Zaida?"

"Thank you, Joel, for your support. It will be of immense help in our endeavor." He then opened a desk drawer and took out a Polaroid Land camera and two rolls of film. I had no idea that he owned a Polaroid.

Sensing my surprise, Grandfather handed me the camera and film: "A modern detective must obtain information quickly and also document environments. A modern detective cannot wait for the film to be developed. The Polaroid is a great advance in the technology that supports my work."

"And I'm to take pictures of what, exactly?"

"Ah," Zaida responded with a twinkle in his eye that always charmed me as a child, "have you ever been to this particular Williamsburg neighborhood?"

"No. What would have ever brought me to that neighborhood?"

I immediately realized how childish I sounded, as if I were casting a neighborhood of Brooklyn no more than five miles away from where I lived as some forsaken habitat into which I never would have tread.

I'm sure my grandfather noticed my conceit, but he let it go. "Good then, since the area will be new to you, why do you not let your curiosity guide you? Certainly, we need pictures of Yosele's school, his home on S. 5th Street and the immediate neighborhood, and the route he was expected to have taken between the school and his home. In addition, if you find something of interest, take a picture. Good?"

I nodded. Hopefully Grandfather's trust in my sense of curiosity would be well founded. "And you want me to go right now?"

"Yes, yes, quickly, a little boy is missing. No time should be lost. Use up both packs of film, which will give us 24 photos. It is now half after 10:00. I will meet you at Epstein's delicatessen where Broadway and Union Avenue come together at 2:00 for a quick lunch, and you will show me the pictures you have taken. Then we will walk over to Rabbi Koenig's dwelling on Harrison Avenue. Mr. Raskin has established a 3:00 appointment for us. It will be of a short duration. No more than 20 minutes."

Grandfather reached into his suit pocket for a skullcap. "You will wear this *kippah* when we are eating and during our visit to Rabbi Koenig, yes?"

"Yes, of course," I answered quickly. I was amazed how well my grandfather knew Williamsburg.

I was about to head out when Grandfather added, pointing to a location on a map: "And Joel, there are additional activities on our schedule. At 4:00, you are to meet with Sgt. Fink, the Williamsburg Community Relations Officer at the 90th Precinct just here at Division and Lee. He will have materials for you to review. While you are at the precinct, I will do my own perambulation of Yosele's neighborhood."

"Wow, is that all we're doing today?" I asked. "After my time at the precinct, we meet up and head home together?"

"No," Grandfather smiled, suddenly hurrying me toward the door. "At 5:30, every member of Yosele's family is to be present at the Precinct for interviews. I will speak to each individually and expeditiously. Mr. Raskin is also making this arrangement with the family. Immediately after the interviews, we will determine our next actions."

* * * *

I walked out of the underground Union Avenue exit of the Broadway Station into bright sunlight. The temperature in the window of the Williamsburg Savings Bank read 90 degrees, unusually hot for late May. Dozens of posters littered the street or were attached to lampposts, mailboxes, garbage cans, storefront windows, and entrances to apartment buildings. I picked one up and saw the same picture that Raskin had given us in Grandfather's office, a little boy's face smudged with a city's grit along with "missing" and the Shomrim's's contact information. The poster promised a $500 reward for his safe return.

I stuffed a poster into my shirt pocket and walked a short distance south to Boerum Street intending to make my way to Yosele's school and then retrace the path to where he lived. While I noted a mixed ethnicity, particularly of Hispanics, Blacks, and Asians with a mélange of languages, my eyes and camera that I carried at my ready were on the ultra orthodox Jews that heavily populated Williamsburg. Pictures I later reviewed with Grandfather showed a man walking determinedly alone, head and back bent forward, looking neither to the left or right, as if he were shielding out distractions to his mission. Another caught two men facing each other in heated discussion. I got close enough to hear their conversations in Yiddish, which I understood much better than I spoke. They were discussing the price per pound of used clothing shipped out of the country. Two other men nearby were in passionate Talmudic debate which I could not follow at all. Neither pair took notice of me.

Most of the men wore large black fedoras over curled ear locks, some to the chin, and full beards. Despite the day's heat, black frock coats over fully buttoned white shirts came down to their knees over baggy black pants and black shoes, quite a contrast to my floral shirt and stovepipe pants that were tight to my knees and slightly flared at my ankles.

Married women appeared in groups of at least three and wore coiffed wigs under kerchiefs or dark berets. Each, for the sake of modesty, was outfitted in a long-sleeved blouse and ankle-length skirt that barely exposed stockinged legs.

Some rocked baby carriages or dealt with the tugs of young children as they discussed food prices, children's ailments, or the plight of certain still-unmarried friends. There were no school-aged children with them. After all, it was late morning on a school day.

The women also took no note of my picture taking.

But at Boerum and Lorimer, my eyes and camera lingered on a group of five girls in what I pegged as their late teens or very early twenties. Each wore white, long-sleeved blouses buttoned to the neck and black or navy skirts falling below the knee to stockinged mid-calf. Each had pinned long hair of different hues, not wigs as Grandfather later explained, which was required only after marriage. When I eased close enough, I heard them speaking giddily in a combination of English and Yiddish about marriage prospects of various acquaintances.

I found each attractive. I never shared this thought with Grandfather, but I arrogantly romanticized their falling for my alluring modern look and escaping from arranged marriages to the pale, old world-looking young men who passed by.

When I pointed my camera and took the picture, one of the girls with shiny red hair noticed and pointed me out to her friends. Immediately they linked arms and walked in the other direction from me. As they did so, the red head turned and glared contemptuously at me.

Embarrassed, I increased my pace and headed east the few blocks on Boerum to Yosele's school, taking photos of a mixture of structures along the way: high-stooped brownstones that were probably grand decades before, a hardware store, a grocery, a fruit market, a three-story building claiming to be the **Breslau Pickles Building**, and a four-story apartment building. As I crossed Leonard Street, on the north side of Boerum, a decaying large structure with a large sign hanging over a façade of broken windows exclaimed **Williamsburg Can Co.**

But what stopped me right before Yosele's school was music pulsating out of a double-spired brownstone church with a high, brightly colored sign indicating **Life of the World Church—Pentecostal Puerto Rican** and right below, faded but still visible, the etching of **First Methodist Church of Williamsburg**. Probably as part of a mid-week service, the blend of guitars, maracas, and piano filled the street, and with my high school knowledge of Spanish, I made out the repeated lyrics of "Dios abre nuestros ojos"—God open our eyes.

As I moved just a bit further east on Boerum to the edge of the building that housed Yosele's school, the church music and the hum of a few hundred voices in Talmud study played against each other, neither vying for center stage. The school's three-story light brown brick building looked well maintained. Concrete steps with a rail in the middle rose to a first-floor entrance framed by thin Doric columns. A half-moon window sat over two closed oak doors. and over that lay a white sign giving the name of the school.

I glanced at my watch and saw it was noon. Then the doors burst open, and a swarm of boys ran down the steps. Some stopped to eat their lunch along a railing that fronted the school almost to Manhattan Avenue, while others took over the street to play punch ball.

Dodging cars and sometimes causing them to come to sudden halts, they ran to bases designated by certain parked cars. I was an avid baseball fan, and having often played punch ball in my Flatbush neighborhood, I smiled hearing the slap of a ball followed by a call in Yiddish of "Leif, Moti, leif,"—"Run, Moti, run." I wanted to join in their play, and as I snapped a picture, I became distracted from why I was there.

But that distraction didn't last long. I felt a large hand on my right shoulder from behind. I spun around to look at a bear of a man, well over six feet and probably around 300 pounds. with a black, bristly beard, ear locks, and black fedora.

"What are you doing here on this block, and why are you taking pictures?" he asked in unaccented English. His voice was not at all threatening, but it didn't have to be given his size compared to my 5'8" and 135 pounds.

"I'm part of a criminal investigation," I answered looking up and trying to exude coolness. Extending my hand, I added, "My name is Joel Gordon."

Later at the deli when I recounted what happened, my grandfather complimented me on my quick thinking.

I was afraid that he would ask me for identification, but instead, after shaking my hand, he nodded, turned, and walked away. Grandfather was sure that the man thought I was a police officer looking for the little boy and did not want to appear obstructionist nor overtly helpful.

"It is their way," Grandfather explained. "You will come to understand more fully as our work progresses."

* * * *

I headed back toward Broadway and Union, passing by Lindsay Park on the right. The park took up a whole block between Leonard and Lorimer Streets. I entered the park and took two pictures of older boys playing handball and basketball, mothers gathered in clusters around children and strollers, men on a grassy area kicking a soccer ball, and young couples sitting closely together on park benches. Later, at the deli, I pointed out to Grandfather that there appeared to be no ultra orthodox Jews in the park.

"Yes, that's a good observation, Joel. The park is *issur*, out of bounds for the ultra orthodox. They especially do not want their children exposed to, let us call it, the more liberal behavior of others."

"So they reject all the advances that modern life has brought us?"

Grandfather did not hesitate, and his voice rose. "What advances, they would counter, pointing to the slaughter of millions just 30 years ago in the Holocaust?"

At Boerum and Broadway, I took note of Epstein's Deli, where I would meet Grandfather. I replaced the first roll of Polaroid film and turned right for a hundred yards and then north on Union. Since I had only 12 shots on my second roll, I decided to conserve my picture-taking to Jewish establishments, a total of eight.

Each Jewish establishment announced itself in English and Yiddish: a combination kosher butcher and market with a neon sign blinking "GLATT KOSHER; " a women's wig store; a women's dress shop with hats prominently displayed; a large men's clothing emporium with double-breasted suits in the window and advertising "100% wool"; a caftan store with its wares presented in black or gray gabardine or worsted; a men's hat store that featured mostly fedoras but also *shtreimels*, rounded fur hats worn by some ultra orthodox

Jews on the Sabbath and holidays; a religious bookstore with large tomes in the window along with ritual items; a linens mart emphasizing tablecloths and lace embroideries.

Thinking Grandfather would want a full inventory that also included non-Jewish establishments, I took from my knapsack a notebook and Bic pen and wrote down: A Russian Orthodox Church with three onion spires that took up a quarter of the street's west side near S. 5th; a candy store, a bodega, multiple fruit and flower markets, an insurance agency, two law firms, one specializing in visa cases and the other personal injury, a liquor store, a Chinese take out, and a small Bohack Super Market.

S. 5th hit Union at a 60 degree angle, so I turned left and made my way to 468 on the right side. It was a three-story edifice with four rectangular windows facing the street on both the second and third floors. Rusted steel fire-escape ladders hung down from the far right windows. Both sides of the street, up to the Hewes intersection, had similar looking apartment buildings of three or five stories. The street and sidewalks were fairly clean for Brooklyn at that time, with a smattering of graffiti on the bottom floor of some of the buildings on the left side of the street.

Things were very quiet, unlike the bustle described by Yosele's brothers when they arrived home on the day he went missing. Here, S. 5th was a one-way street, with few cars passing from Hewes to Union. I noted two elderly women pushing wheeled shopping carts and several more mothers with young children. I took photos and found myself relaxing, but Grandfather's crackling words of "a young child is missing" brought me back to my task and to my watch dial.

It was 1:40, time to head back to meet Grandfather for lunch. I had hoped to discover something that had been missed. But nothing. It was as if Yosele Rosenstock had disappeared into thin air.

* * * *

I arrived ten minutes early, but Grandfather was already at Epstein's, seated in a two-person vinyl booth. He saw me in the doorway and motioned me to put on my skullcap. At the height of lunch hour, all of the tables were taken, mostly with Jewish diners, but I also spotted a few Black and Hispanic workmen. The retail counter had salamis, bolognas, pastramis, corned beefs, and stuffed dermas hanging from ceiling hooks, and its glass case held an assortment of prepared foods. There was a long line of customers holding paper numbers.

I slid into the booth opposite my grandfather. The pickles and sour tomatoes piled into a steel bowl in the middle of our table took my appetite from hungry to ravenous. While we talked, I devoured a corned beef on rye with two Dr. Brown's cream sodas, but Grandfather ate his turkey breast on wheat with lemoned water much more slowly.

I handed Grandfather the 24 Polaroids which he sorted into three piles. Shuffling through the first pile, Grandfather pronounced: "In these photos, you are showing me pictures of the few blocks Yosele would have traversed between his school and where Boerum meets Broadway. I take note that all of the pictures are of the Boerum's north side. Is it possible you may share with me what went into your judgment not to show the south side? That aside, what do you remember of the south side?"

Even though Grandfather had spoken gently, I was stung and answered rapidly and testily. "Well, Raskin's report said that children at the school saw Yosele bolt down Boerum on the north side, and I was thinking he had no reason to cross the street, which would have delayed his getting home. Besides, the south side between his school and Leonard didn't have anything to draw him over. Just a few apartment buildings, an auto repair garage, and a large, empty lot. Make sense?"

Grandfather maintained his gentle tone. "At this time, very little makes sense to me. But is that not the way good detective work progresses? Do we not at first gather the information upon which our critical analysis skills are employed? Our immediate problem is that we have so little time. A little boy is missing. And as we assess, can we be sure that Yosele's intent was to go directly home?

"Also, Yoeli, there are no pictures of Broadway past the Union Avenue. Did you happen to walk further in that direction in case Yosele missed the turn to Union and found himself lost shortly after?"

I hadn't, and I was now caught twice with my thinking-pants down.

Picking up the second pile of the Union to S. 5th pictures along with the written list of non-Jewish establishments, Grandfather nodded approvingly. He explained that the men's clothing store advertised "100% wool" to assure compliance with the Orthodox injunction against mixing fibers, which I knew by myself, but I didn't resent his explanation.

"Good, Yoeli, good." Grandfather smiled, setting down the Polaroids and note paper. "But I doubt Yosele disappeared along Union Avenue. According to Raskin's report, every establishment and resident was interviewed. Of course, I may be wrong, but unless something is being hidden, someone would have seen the boy running at a time when so many shopkeepers were at their storefront encouraging customers to enter."

I nodded. "That makes sense."

Grandfather picked up the third pile of photos. "Let us move on to Yosele's neighborhood, yes."

I had taken three pictures of the Rosenstock building from first floor to roof line and one picture of the three-story 469 S. 5th building across the street to show how similar both sides of the street looked.

"Do you think so?" asked Grandfather. "Look carefully." He spread the four S. 5th Street pictures before me. "Is there not one remarkable difference between the building at 469 and all the buildings on the right side of the street?"

Of course, now plainly staring me in the face, I saw it. "The 469 building has a TV antennae on it," I said enthusiastically, "and as I remember, so did the other buildings on that side of the street, but the buildings along the right side of the block where the Rosenstock house is situated, none has an antennae."

"Yes." Grandfather beamed. I felt like kicking myself for not picking up something so obvious on my own.

"Everyone who lives on the right side of the block doesn't watch television? Could that be right?" It seemed incredible.

"Yes, you are correct," Grandfather replied giving me back some of my dignity. "Where the little boy lives is a mixed block, with one side ultra orthodox and the other side not so. If you go around the surrounding neighborhood, you'll see some other streets mixed just like this one, some all ultra orthodox residents, and some without any ultra orthodox. And if one did not wish to spend much time observing this phenomenon, then the presence of TV antennae provides an indication."

"And why no TV watching," I asked even though I mostly knew the answer.

"Ah, because it is the firm belief of the ultra orthodox leaders that television provides unwanted secular distractions that tempt one away from the prescribed religious path. Like the Amish, they believe to survive in a vastly secular world, they must maintain their differences or succumb to assimilation."

Grandfather's explanation washed over me, making sense and not making sense. But before I could react, he looked at his watch and said: "Shortly, we must leave to see Rabbi Koenig. But let us take five minutes for you to share your thoughts with me. Then, on the way, I will tell you how I am acquainted with Rabbi Koenig."

"My thoughts?" I came back plaintively and a bit uneasy. "But I haven't put anything together yet."

"Ah Joel, I did not ask for conclusions, which your instincts correctly are declaring as premature. Tell me what paths might we pursue to find the boy."

"Ok, here goes," I began marshaling my focus. "On his way home, he was somehow stopped and abducted?"

"Yes, possibly, and for what purpose?"

"Well, for one, ransom, but I guess no ransom demands have been made. So no." Here I stopped, perhaps because I felt uncomfortable or that I might make Grandfather uncomfortable about my next conjecture.

"Something else?" Grandfather prompted.

"Yes, there are perverts in the world. Maybe he was lured away for that purpose."

"You are referring to pedophilia," Grandfather said calmly. "That possibility did enter my mind, yet without coming to a conclusion, how do you assess the probability?"

"Low," I responded quickly. "If Yosele was motoring his way home with his brothers on his heels, he wouldn't be an easy target to stop. Just a few minutes' delay would have allowed his brothers to spot him. As we said, the streets were full of people at that time in the afternoon. Even a pervert wouldn't take such a chance."

Grandfather reflected for a moment. "Yes, I agree, but let us not at this point rule out any possibilities. Those you term as "perverts" are known to take risks. What else is on your mind?

I still felt sheepish for my failure to take Polaroids of Boerum's south side and Broadway past Union, so I threw out: "He was observed running down Boerum on its north side, so as I said, I don't think he crossed over because there's nothing there that would have tempted him. But maybe he never turned up Union from Broadway and instead kept going, got lost, and fell into bad hands." The thought of pedophilia reentered my mind, and I shuddered inside.

"It is possible as you now suggest that Yosele continued on Broadway, but why? Raskin's report indicates the addresses of all Rosenstock relatives, and none is located to the west of Union. Why would he deviate from the route he had taken hundreds of times since he began school? I have a notion why he left on his own, and I will verify it when we speak to the family tonight. But just in case, let us call Mr. Raskin from a pay phone on our way to Harrison Avenue and ask him to send men to ask questions on Broadway west of Union. Again, what else?"

"One more hypothesis, Zaida. I saw statistics that the case of a missing child is usually solved close to home. Maybe Yosele did make it home and encountered a violent reaction from his mother or father. A smack to the head that unintentionally killed him? I know the police went through the Rosenstock apartment and basement and found nothing, but in the few hours the family say they were looking for Yosele, maybe they found a way to dispose of the body."

"Certainly a possibility," Grandfather acknowledged, looking sad. "But any other thoughts, Yoeli?"

I shook my head, even though I felt that Grandfather had dismissed my last conjecture too quickly.

Grandfather rose, removed his skullcap, and put on his fedora. "Then let us proceed to Rabbi Koenig's residence. We have just enough time to arrive without being late."

Linking his arm through mine as we walked, Grandfather recounted. "I grew up with Rabbi Koenig in Leopoldstadt, a very Jewish section of Vienna, then home to many of the ultra orthodox. Moshe was the third son of Rabbi Herschel Koenig, the fourth generation leader of a Hasidic movement with adherents not only in Vienna but also throughout Hungary and northwest Rumania.

"Since he was the third son, there was no thought that he would inherit the leadership position upon his father's death. Therefore, after much imploring by Moshe, his father permitted him to attend university under three conditions: he would focus his studies on mathematics and the sciences; he would spend a minimum of four hours a day studying Jewish texts assigned by his father; he would be quizzed regularly and accept rabbinical ordination if worthy. To this Moshe readily agreed and kept his word. That is where I became friends with him, during both of our studies at the university.

"He earned a degree in electrical engineering and soon became the head of the Vienna Electrical Power Commission. He was credited with bringing reliable lighting to every neighborhood and electrical energy to every store and factory. By 1930, widely recognized for his achievements, he left Vienna's employ to become an electrical consultant to cities throughout Europe including Berlin, Frankfurt, Paris, and importantly for what I am telling you, Geneva, where he, his wife, and two children found themselves on March, 12, 1938, that terrible day, when the Nazis marched into Vienna.

"During the short period of time in 1938 and 1939 when the Nazis permitted Austrian Jews to emigrate, Moshe brought out his two younger sisters, but his father, believing the events to be just another episode in the millennial history of hatred directed at Jews, would not leave, saying he must stay with his adherents until this latest phase of Anti-Semitism receded. His two older brothers refused to abandon their father and mother.

"Of course, no receding occurred, and soon World War II and the full Holocaust ensued. Moshe's family in Vienna was sent to Dachau and Buchenwald, where they were murdered."

I reflexively squeezed Grandfather's arm guessing that the Rabbi Koenig narrative must have brought back awful memories of Grandfather's own tragic experience during the War. But Grandfather went on in a steady voice.

"After the War, Moshe started hearing from remnants of his father's adherents around the world, especially a few hundred in Williamsburg. Some asked, some begged, some demanded that as the remaining son of their *rebbe*, he assume the mantle of leadership. Whether he agreed willingly or reluctantly, I have no knowledge. He arrived in the United States in 1949 and settled in Williamsburg. Today, his adherents are projected to number around twenty thousand."

We reached 62 Harrison Avenue, Rabbi Koenig's residence, and Grandfather stopped speaking. I had not said a word during the seven-minute walk, as I usually didn't when in those few instances Grandfather or my mother spoke of the Holocaust. As much as I wanted to say something, ask questions, I didn't know how.

* * * *

Two ailanthus trees, one in the front and one to the right, set off Rabbi Koenig's building. The trees' light grey bark, reddish twigs, and bronze leaves complemented the immaculately maintained purplish-gray masonry of the three-story brownstone. The windows of the basement and first floor and the front glass double doors displayed decorative bars that muted the reason for their installation and a sense of danger. As Grandfather and I climbed the stone steps to the front door, Grandfather stumbled slightly, but he waived me off when I extended my hand.

I rang the bell, and a stooped, elderly man opened the door and asked of my grandfather in Yiddish: "You are Velvel Franck?" my grandfather's name in Europe before he came to the United States and changed it to Frank Wolf. Grandfather nodded, and the man opened the door wider to let us in. Later, Grandfather explained that the man was Rabbi Koenig's 'beadle," an old fashioned term even back in 1973 for being the rabbi's administrative assistant, especially in regulating the flow of visitors constantly seeking an audience with the *Rebbe.*

His adherents would come for various reasons: blessings for an upcoming marriage; prayers for the birth of a child after a few years of what was called back then, "barrenness"; problems with children; mediation of business disputes; answers to complex religious questions; blessings for medical recovery; depression; challenges of faith.

We entered a long, dimly lit vestibule. Spindle-back wooden benches lined both sides of the hallway with an oak door straight ahead.

"Come with me," the beadle directed.

A young couple, about my age, dressed in the ultra orthodox fashion and wearing wedding rings, sat on a bench to the left near the oak door. They looked up with anticipation. Without stopping, the beadle said, "You will be next."

At the door, he knocked and stuck his head in. "Velvel Franck and his grandson have arrived." Seconds later, he opened the door wider and motioned us through. The door closed behind us.

Rabbi Koenig sat in a large green armchair. He was a big man with a long, flowing white beard and curled ear locks that came down almost as long as his beard. But what I remember most was that he wore no glasses, and his grey eyes exuded a pleasantness that drew me to him.

Although it was mid-afternoon, the large window at his back was enclosed in heavy drapes and several lamps provided ample light. The large desk behind him was heaped with books. Packed bookcases lined each wall from floor to ceiling. Everywhere my eye passed, I took in religious works—biblical texts, various publications of the Talmud, and countless tomes of commentary.

One smaller bookcase in the far right corner of the room held multiple volumes of the *Encyclopedia of Science, 1972,* texts with German titles, and (because I owned my own similar looking copy), John F. Kennedy's *Profiles in Courage.*

Rabbi Koenig did not rise when we entered. Instead, he threw his hands open wide in greeting and pointed for us to sit on two smaller chairs that flanked him.

"Velvel, we have not seen each other since before the War." The Rabbi spoke softly to Grandfather in Yiddish. "You suffered greatly and lost Rivkah. I heard and I am sorry." He then smiled at me and in barely accented English said. "This is your grandson, your daughter Malkeh's son, I assume? He looks just like her."

"Yes, Moshe, this is my beloved grandson, Joel. And he does look like Malkeh."

"Then Joel, I hope you also have your mother's soul, which I had the honor of watching flourish when she was a child."

He then turned from me, looked at Grandfather, and reverted back to Yiddish. "Nuh Velvel, from a professor of philosophy in Vienna to a private detective in Brooklyn, how does it happen? And if I may add, an excellent one. I heard of your success in finding the truth about the death of the butcher in Boro Park. A tragic occurrence."

Sadness spread out from my grandfather's eyes. "The Nazis, may their deeds be blotted out forever, destroyed the records of every Jewish faculty member at the university. So when I came to this golden land, I could not demonstrate the required credentials to teach. I at first worked as a guard at the 42nd Street Library and then found a profession that best matched my love of *Yiddishkeit*, philosophy, the exploration of the human mind and soul, along with the use of critical analysis skills. And that profession for me is being a private detective."

Grandfather's sadness carried to Rabbi Koenig's eyes. "And here you are after all these years to see me in your official capacity as a private detective assisting in trying to find Yosele Rosenstock. I am certainly glad to see you, but how can I help?"

Grandfather got right to the point. "First, Moshe, if you know anything about what happened to Yosele, you will tell me? A precious little boy is missing. I feel he is still alive, but time to save him may be running out. Second, please put out the word to your community that they are to cooperate in the investigation. The Shomrim went store to store and house to house, and your followers hide, are silent, or are angry that there is possibly an insinuation that he has been harmed by someone in the community. Third, I will be interviewing Yosele's family at 5:30. Please tell them to be fully open."

I couldn't believe Grandfather had spoken so bluntly, and I watched Rabbi Koenig intently. I expected a burst of anger in response, but instead Rabbi Koenig's eyes expressed acceptance.

"I give you my word, Velvel, that I have no knowledge of what happened to the boy. And that my community also does not know. They believe he fell prey to an outsider. But I had lived in the greater world beyond these few Williamsburg streets and know that any individual or group can perpetrate an evil act, including my own. I promise, I will immediately request full cooperation be given, and I will personally call the Rosenstock family."

Rabbi Koenig halted and put his hand out for Grandfather to shake. "It was nice seeing you again, Velvel, even under these circumstances."

Rabbi Koenig then looked toward me and said in English: "I wish you luck, happiness, and prosperity."

The Rabbi remained seated and once again threw his hands open, this time to indicate our need to leave. "If you will excuse, there is a young couple waiting to see me who have been married three years without the joy of a child joining them. I must speak to them."

* * * *

Once outside, Grandfather and I separated. I headed to Division and Lee, and Grandfather walked back towards Union and Broadway. Stopping to take in the red, three-story terracotta 90th Precinct building, I guessed it was built in the late 19th century with eye catching artistic features of ironworks, stained glass windows, and gargoyles both catching rain at the roof edge and sending signals to miscreants. With what must have been an attempt at historical preservation, the driveway to the left of the building through which police cruisers were steadily moving contained an archway that read "To the Stables."

As I walked up the six concrete steps to the weathered wooden doors, I was buffeted by streams of people going in and out. Inside, a din of plaintive voices filled a long hallway with men, women, and children sitting along benches oddly like those in Rabbi Koenig's home. Victorian wall sconces, peeling, yellow paint, and two chandeliers lit the way toward a high reception desk with two officers dealing with a long line of people.

I stopped at the end of the queue. It was already 3:50. How long would it take to ask for Sgt. Fink? I need not have worried as seconds after I began my wait, I heard, "You, back there, Mr. Stovepipe Pants, are you Gordon?"

When I shouted, "Yes," a rotund officer behind the desk beckoned me forward.

"Sgt. Fink is waiting for you!" he barked at me, already looking at the next person in line. "His office! Room 29! Second floor!" He gestured toward a curved, ornate staircase.

A short man, around 40 and built like a weight lifter, opened the door to my knock. The name plate on Room 29's door indicated that this was the office of Sgt. Max Fink, Community Relations Officer.

"Joel, right?" Fink greeted me and handed me a manila folder. "C'mon in and have a seat. That's the Rosenstock family file I prepared for you."

He had a wide, clean shaven face, was crisply dressed in a police uniform, and exuded cologne popular in those days. I liked him instantly.

I liked him even more when he said: "The way you and your granddad figured out the Stein killing last year, that was brilliant. My friend Marty Kramer over in the 66th in Boro Park told me that it saved them a good deal of money and energy chasing down bad info and irritating the hell out different ethnics. Well done, and I'll tell your granddad myself when he comes by a little later to do the Rosenstock interviews."

I was emboldened to ask, "Before I start reviewing the file, what does a community relations officer do?"

"Well, it's something new the department introduced a few years ago, basically to help us understand the people in our precinct and to help them understand us. There's a couple of us in the 90th, and my focus is on the Jewish community, which now is basically the ultra orthodox, what most officers call 'the bearded ones'."

"'The bearded ones.' Huh. Hard job?"

Fink chuckled. "Yes and no."

"Can we start with the 'no'?"

Fink sat down behind a small desk and motioned me to sit across from him. "Sure. You see, there's no real crime coming out of the communities I deal with, and I say communities because there's probably ten ultra orthodox groups, each loyal to its *rebbe*. There are no gangs, juvenile delinquencies, robberies, surface violence, prostitution, or numbers running. They hardly bother us with any conflicts which they take to their *rebbes*. We'll get involved when they suffer assaults or break ins by those they're sure are outsiders."

And here Fink smiled broadly. "And some times we get involved when we come across a fistfight on the street between men or even groups of kids—different factions all worked up about some interpretation of Jewish law or perceived insult to a *rebbe*. But nothing will come of it because no one ever presses charges or blames the other for starting the row."

"And the 'yes'?"

"Well, when something like this happens, they retreat into themselves. It's as if they don't know whether to be more afraid of us or criminals. When we make inquiries, apartments go dark and knocks on doors aren't answered. If they do answer, we get one-word responses. And I often think because I'm also Jewish and not as observant as them, they hold me in disdain and clam up even more."

I nodded. "I see."

"One other thing. You notice I said 'surface violence'?"

I hadn't but covered myself with, "I think so, please go on."

Fink pointed to the file I was holding. "Stuff always goes on behind closed doors, and we know domestic violence against women and children occurs within the ultra orthodox—as in any society. But with them, it's never reported or acknowledged even when it clearly happened. Take a quick look through the Rosenstock file and tell me what jumps out at you."

The folder contained copies of a few documents: a 1955 Brooklyn marriage certificate in the names of Yaakov Rosenstock (born in Hungary in 1930) and Leah Lavonsky (born in Rumania in 1935). There were two traffic citations for Yaacov, a slew of unpaid parking tickets, and a summons for Yaacov to appear in traffic court to pay outstanding tickets and court costs.

But what stopped me cold were records of visits to the Kings County Hospital emergency room by Yosele Rosenstock in 1970 and 1972 and an attempt by Miriam Bender, MSW, to visit the Rosenstock home following Yosele's second emergency room visit. In the first, Yosele was treated for a broken arm that the mother—with Yosele's confirmation—said occurred "when he slipped in the tub." The second, also claimed by mother and child, was for a concussion incurred by "jumping from a couch while playing and hitting his head." The report also indicated that a Dr. Pasquale referred the injury to Children's Protective Services for possible child abuse.

On Children's Protective Services letterhead, Miriam Bender wrote in long hand: "Tried to visit on: 3/20, 3/22, 3/24, 1972. No answer to buzzer request for entry. Spoke to neighbors who said they did not know the Rosenstocks."

"I looked up. "So you think Yosele was hit each of these times, probably by his father?"

Fink looked angry. "Yeah, I think. But like I said, they never come forward and let us help them. Really frustrating."

I thought for a moment. "Obviously, the father has a car."

"Yep, a '69 Buick station wagon. That's in the traffic documents."

Coming back to the theory I had earlier shared with Grandfather, I said: "So the father may have lost his temper when he found out Yosele scampered home by himself, hit him too hard causing his death, and then hid his body in his car and dumped it in, say, Red Hook."

Fink snorted out a laugh. "You've been reading too much *Daily News*. I don't know about Red Hook, but yeah, what you say is possible."

"So Yaacov Rosenstock is your main suspect?"

Fink looked resigned. "I guess, since I don't have another one. Let's see what your grandfather can get out of them."

* * * *

I heard a knock on the door and looked up. It was Grandfather with Avi Raskin.

"If it is acceptable to you, Sgt. Fink," Grandfather said, "I've asked Mr. Raskin to both watch the interviews, which will proceed at a rapid pace, and then deliberate with us after as to next steps. An idea is crystallizing in my mind that will require immediate action if what I suspect is confirmed in the interviews."

"Of course," Fink said springing up to lead the way to the interview room. "Avi is certainly welcome."

The interview room was also on the second floor away from Fink's office. As we approached, we could see the Rosenstock family in the hallway, the father Yaacov pacing angrily, his wife Leah and daughter Dinah close together on one bench, Dinah clutching her mother's hand, and the brothers Reuven, Shimon, and Levi sitting on an opposite bench.

Reuven, tall with long legs tucked awkwardly under the bench, was wispy thin, his face pale with down fuzz. His eyes were riveted on a tiny, leatherbound book, to which his lips moved and his body rocked back and forth. He did not look up as we neared.

Shimon and Levi, both dark haired and solidly built, were spitting images of each other except for Shimon being two-years bigger and already showing some face fuzz. They were poking and elbowing each other until they spotted us and quickly became still.

Yaacov Rosenstock met us head on. In broken English, he sputtered looking at Grandfather. "We have received the call from our rebbe, and we will answer your questions."

And looking between Raskin and Fink, Rosenstock spat out: "But why are you standing here and not catching who took our Yosele. You must know it is an outsider, so I do not understand what you want with us. We already answered your questions many times."

Also in English, Grandfather responded. "Thank you for your coming and bringing your family. I think within a half hour, I shall be done speaking to all of you. Mr. Rosenstock, if you will, you first."

And looking at the rest of the family, Grandfather added: "When Mr. Rosenstock comes out, separately Mrs. Rosenstock, then Reuven, and after Shimon and Levi together, and last Dinah."

Grandfather pointed to a door to an interview room and motioned Rosenstock to follow him in. Fink nudged me and said, "this way," so I followed him and Raskin to an adjoining observation room with a two-way mirror. Before entering, I looked back at the family and noticed a petrified expression on Dinah's face. She clutched her mother more tightly. Reuven kept to his book, but the younger boys glared at Dinah as if she were a traitor in their midst.

After Grandfather and Rosenstock were seated across a metallic, rectangular table from each other, Grandfather addressed Rosenstock in Yiddish, but more the street variety than the high Yiddish Grandfather had conversed in with Rabbi Koenig.

"Please tell me, Mr. Rosenstock, who are the outsiders you believe took your child?"

Rosenstock was immediately angry and flustered. "Who, who, you need to ask me who?"

Grandfather paused for a moment. "Yes, I must hear the answer in your own words. Is it possible you mean non-Jews in the neighborhood? Might you also mean other Jews not in your community?"

Rosenstock's eyes spewed venom. "You are the famous detective that took away a poor woman's money. Everything is possible, no?"

"Yes, I agree with you. Everything is possible. Good then, to help me. Better, Mr. Rosenstock, if you will tell me about Yosele."

Rosenstock looked perplexed. "What is there to tell? He is a little boy, a wild little boy who doesn't listen to his parents and teachers. I wouldn't be surprised if he is at least partly the cause of what we're going through."

Grandfather took a minute to thumb through the file Fink had put together. I smiled to myself. It must be for the sense of drama; Grandfather had looked at the file quickly when he had arrived.

Grandfather returned the file to the table. "So, there are times you had to discipline the child, yes, even with *paches*, hitting him on different parts of his body?"

"*Paches* never hurt a child; they only make him better," Rosenstock snapped.

"And did Yosele become better after you sent him to hospital including giving him a concussion?"

I held my breath when I heard Grandfather's question. Surely Rosenstock would deny it. But he didn't.

"The boy is a wild creature. A few times I was too angry, but he recovered, did he not? And if you're thinking I beat him Monday and killed him, you are not right and not much of a detective. I have no idea why the *Rebbe* insisted we meet with you. A waste of time."

I looked at Fink, who nodded as to say, "I got it for future action."

Grandfather was unfazed: "Then I thank you for your time, Mr. Rosenstock. Would you please ask your wife to come in?"

* * * *

Leah Rosenstock trudged into the interview room looking around wildly as if expecting some danger. As soon as she sat down opposite Grandfather, both of her hands fastened to the desk's edge as if she feared being dragged away.

Grandfather also addressed her in the same Yiddish. "A big thanks for your coming. You are safe. Our talk will not take long. Please, Mrs. Rosenstock, tell me about Yosele."

Mrs. Rosenstock did not hesitate. "He is a little boy, my baby, and I want him back. Please find him."

"We are trying, Mrs. Rosenstock, we are trying very hard, and you can help us. Again, please, tell me about Yosele. For instance, is he a happy child?"

"I can help you by telling you if Yosele is a happy child!" she responded, looking bewildered by the concept. "He likes to play, a little too much, and he makes jokes, and he doesn't like to study. I mean, he doesn't like to study the religious subjects, but he enjoys the non-religious, which causes him trouble."

"And by 'trouble,' you mean with your husband, who beats him?"

Mrs. Rosenstock's hands gripped the table more tightly, and without looking at Grandfather said with little conviction: "All children need a *pach* from time to time."

"*Paches* that send your little child to the hospital with a concussion?" Grandfather retorted with an edge of anger.

Mrs. Rosenstock looked around as if ready to flee. "They were accidents, I tell you. Yaacov didn't mean he should hit his head. Accidents."

"And was there such an accident Monday night when your husband came home and discovered Yosele had run home by himself."

"No!" she shrieked in tears, "Yosele never came home. I swear to you and would not lie to you. The Rebbe instructed us not to lie."

* * * *

Reuven's interview took about five minutes. He walked in slowly, his head down, and stopped just beyond the threshold. Upon

Grandfather's urging, Reuven took a seat and returned his gaze to his prayer book. Not for one second did he take his eyes off the prayer book nor stop rocking.

Grandfather said nothing for about 30 seconds, and then sticking to Yiddish, asked, "You are reading from Psalms?"

Reuven nodded agreement.

"Why Psalms and which one?" Grandfather inquired.

Reuven's rocking intensified. "Psalm 91, for Yosele's safe return."

"'There shall no evil befall thee,'" Grandfather quoted a line from the psalm, first in Hebrew and then in English for the benefit, perhaps, of Sgt. Fink. The Hebrew was easy to understand, even for me. Grandfather pushed on:

"I see you worry for your brother. You like your brother, I imagine?"

Reuven's voice remained flat, as if all of his emotions were contained in his rocking. "No, he is a heretic. He does not walk in the path of righteousness."

"Thank you for answering honestly, and it would help me to understand if you told me why you believe he is a heretic?"

"He does not like to study the right things, and he listens to profane music."

"Reuven, please tell me, your father sometimes hits him?"

Reuven's face showed momentary wonder as if he was filled with amazement that he had to say the obvious. "Yes, of course, because he is a heretic."

"Did your father hit Yosele Monday night for running home by himself?"

Although he did not look up, for once Reuven answered emphatically: "I'm telling you, Yosele never came home on Monday!"

* * * *

Grandfather's interrogation of Shimon and Levi was also completed quickly, as the boys sat nervously twirling their ear locks.

Grandfather leaned toward the boys and spoke to them in English. "Children, please tell me the best you can, when you would walk to school and back with Yosele, how did he behave most days?"

Shimon answered first with fury. "He's a brat. He wouldn't stay with us. He would run ahead."

"Or," Levi interjected with equal vehemence, "he would stop and just stare at things, and we would have to wait for him."

"Ah, this is helpful," Grandfather said enthusiastically. "And children, in particular, would he stop at any one place?"

The boys caught Grandfather's enthusiasm.

"Yes," both answered simultaneously.

"At the entrance to the park, always at the entrance to the park," Shimon continued. 'What are you looking at?' we would shout. 'There's nothing for you to see. It's *issur* for us to enter. You know that.'"

"Sometimes we would have to poke him to keep walking," Levi added.

"Thank you, children. You are good boys and very helpful to us in bringing your brother back home. Thank you. And now, would you be so kind as to please ask your sister to come in."

* * * *

Dinah was shaking when she sat down.

Grandfather broadly smiled at her and also in English said: "My child, you are bravely helping us find Yosele. You care for your brother, yes?"

"I do, very much, and he for me. The others don't know, but when we are alone, we talk about so many things, we laugh, and we sing."

"Ah, you sing together. What type of songs do you sing?"

We could see Dinah relaxing a bit. "Oh, mostly religious songs."

"You say mostly, but I understand your family considers Yosele an *apikores* because he listens to profane music. I promise I will not tell your family, but I wonder, do you also sing non-religious songs?"

Dinah reddened. "Sometimes, he would hum beautiful tunes when we were alone, and I would ask him to teach them to me. I would ask him where he learned them, and he would say, 'in walking around the neighborhood.'"

"Ah, I am much interested. Do you remember any tune in particular?"

Dinah did not think for long and began to sing in a gentle voice:

> *"Hey Jude, don't make it bad.*
> *Take a sad song and make it better.*

Remember to let her into your heart,
Then you can start to make it better. "

When she finished, she added: "Yosele may only be eight, but he feels so much. He said it was like a religious tune. He said Jude is the Jewish people waiting for the Messiah, and we can hasten his coming by not doing bad things and letting the good in."

"Yosele is a very clever boy, and in his way, he is also a very religious boy, no, Dinah?"

"Yes, I believe he is," she answered strongly.

"And what you sang, it is a beautiful song by the Beatles, yes?"

Dinah appeared surprised when she replied, "The Beatles, yes."

Grandfather leaned back and coupled his hands. "And so, my child, I have just one last question. Do you have a washer and dryer in your building?"

Dinah looked as if she had just heard an odd question. She shook her head no.

"Then where does your family do laundry?"

"At the Laundromat on Montrose."

"Between Lorimer and Union?" Grandfather clarified.

"Yes."

Grandfather stood and motioned Dinah that she could leave. "Thank you again. You have helped greatly in finding Yosele."

It was 5:50.

In the hallway again, with the Rosenstock family departed, the three of us had many questions as Grandfather approached, particularly about the laundry. But we never asked as Grandfather immediately took charge with rapid bursts of his own questions and instructions.

"I am sure Yaacov Rosenstock did not harm his son Monday evening," Grandfather stated right off. "I have a strong suspicion as to what happened, but now quickly let us proceed to Sgt. Fink's office, where I can share my thoughts and request information to support my premise. While I believe I know how Yosele disappeared, I do not know if he is still alive. Minutes are of the essence."

We were hardly through the door into Fink's office when Grandfather addressed Avi Raskin: "You know the laundromat Dinah mentioned on Montrose?"

"Yes, the Washomatic, why?"

"Do you know who is the owner?"

"I do, Arthur Reichman. He owns 24-hour laundromats all over Brooklyn and Queens. Why?"

"Then Mr. Reichman would not be the daily operator of any one of his particular laundromats. Do you know the operator at the Montrose location?"

"Yes, actually. His name is Moti Weiss. He's at the laundromat good parts of each day and night, six days a week. The only day he doesn't work is the Sabbath. He is known around the neighborhood as a *meshugener*, or," and Raskin looked directly at me, "what you youngsters call a 'nut case.'

"Here's what I've heard said about him, some of it scuttlebutt, and its accuracy, I can't attest to. Supposedly he was a nebishy, recluse of a kid who had a severe head injury when he was 10. Hit by a car, fell off a bike, and there are other versions. He couldn't concentrate in school on religious or secular studies and didn't get along with any family member, especially his father. Never completed high school and has gone from job to job until he stuck with managing the Washomatic a few years ago. He bounces around from one *rebbe* to another, denounces ultra orthodox Judaism as primitive and choking, and then seeks a *rebbe*'s forgiveness. He's been married three times, orthodox mail-order arrangements, each for not more than a year.

"And I seem to remember one time the Shomrim were called to mediate a dispute with neighbors. They claimed not only was he playing profane music but also playing very loud. He agreed to lower the volume, and that was that."

"And where does Mr. Weiss live?" asked Grandfather.

"That I don't remember," Raskin responded reaching for the phone on Fink's desk. "I wasn't on that dispute visit. One quick call is all I need."

As we listened to Raskin's conversation, Grandfather paced, which I rarely saw him do.

"That's right, Sruli," we heard Raskin say, "a Moti Weiss, where does he live?"

After a minute, "Yes, the one who runs the laundromat on Montrose."

Suddenly Raskin looked up amazed. As he wrote, we heard him say, "452 S. 5th. His father owns the whole building, and he has the basement apartment."

Raskin hung up the phone. The three of us looked at each other, and then at Grandfather. I couldn't contain myself.

"Zaida, that's just down the block from where Yosele lives. You think this guy has him? How did you get on to him?"

Grandfather moved toward a large street map of Williamsburg hanging on the wall behind Fink's desk. "Very quickly I will explain."

"The interviews reinforced what in the business is called a 'hunch,' something viscerally experienced by the detective that must be corroborated with testimony and facts.

"Joel, when we parted company, I slowly retraced the route between the school and the Rosenstock home and thought about Yosele's character based on the police report. If he was headstrong, if he was curious, if he wanted to demonstrate independence, what might he do to elude his brothers?"

Grandfather pointed to the map, his finger settling on Boerum Street at the entrance to Lindsay Park. "Yosele may not have known the formal principles of geometry, but he may have intuitively cut diagonally through the park to the Montrose Avenue to both evade his brothers and make it home before them.

"So I tested my hypothesis and walked diagonally through the park and came out at Montrose and Lorimer. I then walked west on Montrose toward Union, and something struck me. There were no Jewish establishments on that block. What if Yosele had become disoriented? To whom would he turn?

"I backtracked to each establishment and noticed a bearded man of about 40, thin, with a polo shirt with *Washomatic* lettering, fringes, and skullcap smoking a cigarette outside of the laundromat.

"I walked up and told him I was new to the neighborhood, and could I look inside at what machines are available. He stamped out his cigarette and walked me in. Toward the far end of Laundromat, there was a room marked PRIVATE. I walked as close as I could toward the back, and even with the din of the machines, I could hear the Beatles song *Let it Be* coming from the room.

"You know the *Let it Be* song?" I interrupted stupidly.

"Sha," Grandfather snapped at me. He then resumed.

"'May an elderly man use your bathroom?' I asked, pointing to the room. Had he let me in, my suspicions would have been assuaged. But he said firmly, 'the facilities are only for staff, boss's rules.' So you may comprehend why with this encounter and now after the interview with Dinah, my suspicions fall heavily on this man?"

Sgt. Fink rose quickly and picked up the phone. "I'll get a SWAT team out there immediately."

Grandfather put a hand on Fink's shoulder. "Please, do not Sergeant. While I am 95% certain Weiss is involved, I cannot take a chance that I am wrong. If a swat team rushes in and the man is innocent, nothing will convince the community that he is guiltless. Please, might just you with haste drive the four of us to the Laundromat. If he has Yosele, even, God forbid the boy is no longer alive, Weiss will not put up a resistance."

"Ok." Fink pressed a button on his phone.

Two minutes later we were outside of the precinct on Division Street getting into an unmarked black sedan. It was 6:05.

* * * *

When we pulled up in front of the laundromat, a man that fit Grandfather's description of Weiss was at the entrance smoking. He eyed us warily as we got out of the car, obviously noting that Fink, in uniform and with gun belt, was an officer.

"Please," Grandfather asked softly yet firmly of Fink before leaving the cruiser, "permit me to approach the man. He does not look armed or dangerous."

"Ok, but you never know," Fink agreed, his hand on the gun holster. "Avi, see if there are any customers inside and tell them it's a police action and to leave immediately. I'll keep watch out here."

Raskin dashed in without giving Weiss a look. Weiss made no attempt to stop him nor said a word. Within seconds, Raskin came out with two customers, who distanced themselves from the building.

Grandfather walked up to Weiss, keeping eye contact with him. Fink, Raskin, and I were a few feet behind. Weiss just kept smoking and did not move an inch.

"You," Weiss exclaimed matter-of-factly. "I knew there was something suspicious about you."

Grandfather disregarded Weiss' statement. "The little boy, he is still alive?"

Weiss took several drags on his cigarette and sullenly looked away like a disobedient teenager. As the tension in me was about to explode, Weiss said: "It's a good thing you came back when you did."

"Why Mr. Weiss?" Grandfather replied steadily.

"Because," and now he looked squarely at Grandfather and then at the three of us. "I would have killed him tonight. I didn't know what else I could do."

You didn't know what else you could do! I nearly erupted but kept silent.

"And he is in the back office? The little boy is unharmed?" again Grandfather asked steadily.

Weiss took another drag. "Yes, he's there, handcuffed to the heavy desk."

Upon hearing, Fink motioned to Raskin to head back into the laundromat. Raskin was about to charge in when Weiss told him to stop as he took two keys out of his pants pocket and handed them to Raskin.

"You'll need these. The large one's for the door, the smaller for the cuffs."

Raskin rushed in, and I moved away from Fink to stand closer to Grandfather. For a few minutes, no one spoke, and we heard the sounds of sirens approaching.

Then Grandfather said: "Tell me Mr. Weiss, if I have surmised correctly, you were previously acquainted with Yosele, yes?"

Weiss nodded.

"I am guessing he had been to your apartment on various occasions where he became enamored with the secular music you played, yes?"

Again agreement.

In a soothing tone, Grandfather went on: "You have been lonely, and you enjoyed his company, but he never would stay long at your apartment, yes?"

Weiss looked at Grandfather as if his secret self had been exposed. "After a few minutes, the kid would get nervous and want to leave. He said he was afraid he'd be found out and get a beating. I'd say, 'stay just a little longer,' but he'd always leave after a few songs."

"And last Monday afternoon, rushing home alone, lost, he bumped into you, did he not? How did you lure him into the back office?"

Weiss showed no remorse nor hesitancy to answer. "There was no one else in the laundromat. After he told me what he was up to, I said I have some new Beatles songs if he'd like to hear them and then he could hurry home. That's all it took. But when he got up to leave, this feeling of being left alone began strangling me, and I tried different ways to convince him to stay. But he insisted that he had to go. I had a pair of handcuffs in the desk drawer that I'd monkeyed with since I was a kid. Wasn't hard, he's so little. I grabbed him and cuffed him to the desk. He cried and begged me to let him go, that he'd be in big trouble, but I just I kept saying, 'I'll take good care of you, I will, I will.'"

Like a child seeking self-exoneration, Weiss went on. "And I did. I got him a whole bunch of tuna sandwiches which I know he loves, but he didn't eat much. I made him drink. I bought a brand new toothbrush and made him brush his teeth. Made sure he went to the bathroom regularly. And placed a cot by the desk so he could sleep. I slept in the armchair nearby.

"I thought a day or two, and he'd get to like me a lot, that he would want to stay. But he kept whimpering and begging me to let him go. And then you showed up. Who are you, anyway?"

"My name is Frank Wolf."

Weiss eyed Grandfather scornfully.

"Like the private eye Frank Wolf who solved that Boro Park murder last year and cheated a widow out of her insurance benefit?"

I could have slugged the man.

Grandfather did not debate Weiss' assessment. "Yes. But tell me, why would you have killed the boy tonight?"

"Because he wasn't going to love me, and I don't mean in a sick way, after two full days, I wouldn't have been able to explain why I didn't bring him home. When you showed up earlier, my gut said I didn't have much time left. So late at night, I was gonna suffocate him after he fell asleep, when he wouldn't know what was happening, put his little body in a bag, and dump it some place far from here. That's it."

"Yes," Grandfather sighed, "that is it. It is often that simple."

Just then Raskin came out carrying Yosele, who was pale and shivering despite the warm evening. He squinted into the early evening light.

"The boy is shaken," Raskin said, "but I think ok."

He put Yosele down and bent toward the boy. In Yiddish, Raskin said: "Everything is now good. You'll soon be with your family."

"An ambulance will be here soon to take him to Kings County for a once-over," Fink let us know.

Two police cars pulled up, and four officers rushed over. Fink informed Weiss that he was under arrest for the kidnapping of Yosele Rosenstock and read him his rights. Weiss was then handcuffed. As I watched him being led away to a car, I was taken aback by the presence of dozens of ultra orthodox, men, women, children, standing on the sidewalk onto the street. When they saw Weiss being taken away, I heard various epithets in English and Yiddish being hurled his way.

As the ambulance pulled up, the Rosenstock family arrived, shouting Yosele's name. Yosele staggered forward and climbed into his sister Dinah's arms. A roar of satisfaction came out of the crowd.

"Mr. and Mrs. Rosenstock," Sgt. Fink called loudly as the family started walking toward the ambulance with Yosele, "expect that charges of child abuse may be filed against you with the District Attorney's office. Someone from Social Services will be at your house tomorrow. Don't pretend not to be home."

Fink turned to Grandfather and me, shook our hands, and said: "Thank you both. That was incredible detective work. The least I can do is get you home. An unmarked police car will be here in a few minutes."

Grandfather made as if to wave off the gratitude. "A little boy was missing. It was imperative we help. But suddenly weariness has overcome me, so if my young colleague concurs, we will accept your offer."

Raskin came over and bear hugged both of us. "May you be blessed and go from strength to strength in the work that you do."

I mouthed a quick thanks, and Grandfather nodded sheepishly.

* * * *

In the car with a partition between the back seat and the driver, we sat silently for a few minutes. I knew from last year not to be effusive about solving the case. I'm not very good about silence at such times, so I offered:

"This was a tough one like last year, right Zaida? But at least Yosele is alive."

Grandfather placed his hand on mine. "Yes, in this case, a little boy in a grown man's body was lonely to a point of desperation. One impulsive act almost led to taking the life of another lonely, missing child. Such tragedies often entail not grand planning, not mad scheming, not greed, not revenge, just a momentary impulsive act."

Grandfather squeezed my hand and sighed. "But yes, we can be joyful for a moment. Also, I am sorry I snapped at you in Sgt. Fink's office when you asked about my knowledge of the Beatles. Every second the little boy was missing pressed on me. Of course I know the Beatles, since I am curious about all of your interests. I find that the Beatles are extremely talented. Perhaps after dinner, and with your mother home, we may listen to an album together?"

I blushed and answered, "I'd like that."

THE DORM MURDER

Monday, October 14, 1974.

I had started working at Prentice, Walters, & Reis in early July, but I still stopped for at least a moment in front of the door to my office on the 43rd floor of the new, gleaming 50-story skyscraper on Lexington near 54th. There was my name: **Joel Gordon, Associate Counsel**.

In mid-June, I had married Aliya, two weeks after graduating from law school and two more weeks before starting at PWR in their Securities Division. I had the princely annual salary of $24,100. We lived 40 blocks south in Stuyvesant Town and could easily afford the $190/monthly rent and the tuition for Aliya's graduate clinical psychology program at NYU.

"Mr. Gordon?" I heard a voice behind me.

I turned and saw a short woman with perfectly coiffed silver hair and nodded. She wore a quarter-sleeve collarless red dress with vertical stitching that came down below her knee. I took note of low heeled, shiny black shoes with a buckle that matched the color of the dress.

She moved toward me. "My name is Mrs. Ann Kimberly, and I am Mr. Reis' executive secretary."

She glanced at her delicate watch on her left wrist. "It is now 8:55, and he would like to see you in his office right away. Mayor Beame is coming at 9:30."

"Mr. Reis," I stammered. You mean Mr. Reis of …"

"Yes, of Prentice, Walters, & Reis, your boss. Please follow me to his office on the 49th floor."

She was already a step ahead of me heading to the elevators. I caught up and asked: "Would you know why he wants to see me?"

Only after pressing the up button, did she turn and face me. "Why, I couldn't possibly know that, now could I?"

Exiting on the 49th floor, I followed Mrs. Kimberly down a softly lit mahogany-paneled corridor. Portraits of the firm's founders and senior partners, as well as multiple paintings of ships in New York harbors and rustic scenes including one of hounds and horses on a fox chase, lined the walls.

We stopped before the open double-doors of an anteroom. A young woman who did not look up sat at a small corner desk typing on an IBM Selectric.

"Please wait here," Mrs. Kimberly said as she made her way to her desk. She pressed a button on the telephone and, after a moment, announced: "Mr. Gordon is with me." And then, "Yes I will."

She motioned me toward a mahogany door with **JOHN REIS, MANAGING PARTNER** etched into a brass plaque in its center. She opened it for me to enter and then closed it behind me.

Reis' office was easily four times larger than mine, with the same dark wood that paneled the corridor. There were no fluorescent lights overhead, as in my office, but rather a half dozen desk lamps that gave adequate lighting graced Reis' expansive desk and a conference table that could seat eight. One wall was all glass with a view of the East River. Another wall featured personal photos, scenes of weddings, christenings, graduations, ski trips, and one large picture of what I took to be a much younger Reis in an army uniform. Bookcases filled with law tomes covered other wall areas. A closed door to the right had to be a private bathroom.

Reis rose to greet me. He was well over six feet with a slight stoop and a broad, Nordic face. I pegged him to be in his late sixties. He loomed over me as he reached out a large hand and shook mine vigorously.

"Nice to meet you, Gordon. You're working securities, and I hear good things about you from your mentor." That would be Larry Seidman. He'd been teaching me the ropes at PWR. "Let me get to the point, since our good mayor is about to arrive."

Reis motioned me to sit down opposite him at the conference table. I was nervous, but his compliment gave me some ease.

"You have been working on the Golden Energy account out of Denver and specifically with its President, Samuel Gold, to get his company an OTC listing?"

"Yes," I acknowledged.

"Well Mr. Gold likes your work. It seems you mentioned to him that while you were in law school, you helped your grandfather—a private detective in Brooklyn, is it?—solve a few cases, including the murder of a butcher in Boro Park and the disappearance of a Hasidic child in Williamsburg."

I blushed. A few weeks ago, Sam Gold and I had had finished up a document filing. Gold said he always liked to get to know his lawyers better and invited me to dinner. Since he was an orthodox Jew who kept kosher, we met at Fine & Schapiro's on the upper West Side. As a new associate working 18-hour days, naturally I agreed. Gold insisted that we don't discuss business, and after a couple of glasses of wine, I gave him a rundown of my life, including my work with my grandfather, Frank Wolf, on the Joe Stein murder and Yosele Rosenstock disappearance.

"Yes sir," I said to Reis apprehensively. "I did tell Mr. Gold about those cases."

Reis gave me an odd smile. "Well, Gold has made an interesting request. Never came across anything like it. Do you remember around three years ago reading about the murder of a sixteen-year-old boy in the dormitory of a Jewish school—a 'yeshiva,' I believe you call it—up in Washington Heights?"

I told Reis that I had a vague memory of it.

"That boy was Ori Gold, Sam's son. The murder remains unsolved. Now here's the thing. Sam Gold wants to hire not only your granddad to look into the case, but he also wants to pay for your time according to PWR rates for you to assist him. I've got the ball rolling to set up a separate PWR account billed directly to Sam Gold and not to Gold Energy for your time including incidentals. Granddad, of course, would bill separately. So, Gordon, can you see to it?"

I was floored. Could I see to it? What was I to say besides, "I'll try my best, sir. I'll ask my grandfather right away if he will take on the investigation."

A buzzer went off on Reis' desk. I looked at my watch—it was 9:25. Reis rose and shook my hand again. "Yes, do your best, Gordon. Sam Gold is an important client, and he's only going to become more so as we expand into other states. Please keep me informed."

* * * *

The painted sign on the smoked glass door to my grandfather's office read **FRANK WOLF DETECTIVE AGENCY.** It had begun to fleck and fade after 20 years. That's how long my grandfather had been in this same office near Brooklyn's Boro Hall. I had called him immediately after meeting with Reis. Grandfather asked me to come over right away. I started a new charging section in my legal Day-timer with the heading, *Ori Gold—Dorm Murder* and headed over to the Lexington Avenue Express train. It would be a few more years before I felt comfortable charging a "no quicker" cab ride to a client.

Grandfather was at his desk going through newspaper clippings. "Zaida," I greeted him, using the Yiddish word for grandfather, "what are those?"

"Ah, Yoeli," he said. That was his pet name for me. "These are old articles from the *New York Times* on the Ori Gold murder. I began clipping them when I first read of the crime. A terrible tragedy."

Zaida put down the clipping he was holding. A slight gleam that settled over sadness appeared in his eyes.

"I see we have been brought to work together again, but in a most surprising way. I will devote my entire energies to the case. It is a terrible thing for a family to suffer over three years without understanding what occurred. You must please bring Mr. Samuel Gold to this office for an interview as soon as possible. Such a meeting is most necessary."

I was drawn into Grandfather's intensity. "So you're familiar with the case. Please give me an overview."

"Yes, of course." My grandfather removed his reading glasses and faced me where I had sat down on the office's sole visitor's chair. He spoke in an elegantly accented English never using a contraction.

"Consider my knowledge is superficial based on secondhand information, even from the best of any newspaper reporting. We must examine the crime scene, interview those present in the dormitory on the night of the murder, listen to Mr. Gold speak of his son, examine evidence, and look at the official police report. It is only then that we may allow our critical analyses engine to shape our conclusions."

I could feel Grandfather's determination as he leaned forward and continued. "As for the police report, I have spoken to our friend, Sergeant Max Fink of the 90th precinct in Williamsburg who helped us immensely with the Rosenstock case. He has arranged for it to be available at the 34th precinct in Washington Heights. If you do not mind, Yoeli, after we have a quick lunch, would you kindly pick up the report and bring it to me? I would like to peruse it tonight for our review here tomorrow morning at 8:00."

The realization that I had other client work besides this quirky Sam Gold account rushed at me, but I shook it off. Eighteen-hour days would just have to become longer, and I hoped Aliya wouldn't mind. She, too, was devoting long hours to her studies.

"Okay, Zaida, I'll pick up the report and be here at 8:00 tomorrow."

"And one further request, Yoeli. Please contact Mr. Gold and ask him if he could kindly come to my office in the next few days, tomorrow if at all possible. Consider that it is now two hours earlier in Denver for him to make arrangements."

"Tomorrow," I blanched. "Tomorrow may be…well, okay, I can ask."

"Good, good," Grandfather said. "Here is the overview you requested. During the early hours of Saturday, September 18, 1971, between one and five o'clock in the morning, Ori Gold was murdered in his Washington Heights dormitory room at the Manhattan Jewish Academy High School. It was two days before Rosh Hashonah, Ori was sixteen years old and a junior. According to the newspaper, he was struck on the head by a sharply edged, heavy object. The police found no signs of a struggle nor of a robbery. Also, they did not find the weapon.

"His body, clothed in pajamas, was discovered at eleven o'clock in the morning by his dormitory Resident Assistant, who grew concerned when Ori did not appear at Saturday morning religious services. After a few months of exhaustive police work, which led to various suspicions but no arrests, the investigation was placed into what I believe they call a 'cold case' file."

"That's it?" I objected.

Grandfather rose and reached for his brown fedora hat. "I am afraid there is no more."

He took me gently by the arm and headed us toward the door. "For the sake of the Gold family and of justice," he stated softly, "I hope we will be more successful."

Tuesday, October 15, 1974.

The next morning, I was a few minutes late, but Grandfather still greeted me with a smile.

"Before we commence, Yoeli, two things. One, may I inquire as to how is Aliya? Such a dear girl. I hope she is not working too hard."

Aliya! Working too hard! What about me, I pouted within. But I caught myself before speaking childishly. Grandfather never "poor babied" me about how hard I was working, but I knew he cared for me deeply. He had lived with my parents and me all my life in our Flatbush duplex until I moved out in July. I was 14 when my father passed away, and Grandfather assumed a parenting partnership with my mother.

"Aliya's fine," I answered. "Yes, she is working hard. She wants to present her dissertation proposal before the semester ends in December. And what's number two?"

"Ah," Grandfather leaned down and picked up a large paper bag that he offered to me. "Your mother thought you might have rushed out without a proper breakfast. I now present to you a proper breakfast."

My mother was correct. I had gulped some coffee, kissed Aliya goodbye, and run for the train. I took out a double-wrapped egg and cheese sandwich which was still warm and started eating. I was quite hungry.

"Good, then let us work as you nourish yourself," grandfather said turning serious. "First, allow me to congratulate you on convincing Mr. Gold to come see us quickly. I would have been satisfied if he had come by tomorrow, but his arrival today is very advantageous."

I smiled between bites. "As I mentioned, Zaida, when I called you yesterday, I didn't have to do much. As soon as I told Mr. Gold that you've agreed to take the case, he said he would take the first flight out in the morning. He lands at LaGuardia at 1:30. He'll take a cab directly and be here around 3:00."

"Excellent, that will give us time to review the police file this morning and travel to Washington Heights. I would like to see the exterior of the dormitory and the room itself, the scene of the crime. Again, through the good offices of Sergeant Fink, Detective John Rooney, who led the murder investigation, will meet us there at 11:00."

The orderliness and efficiency of Grandfather's mind never ceased to amaze me.

"So, Yoeli, you said that you had a chance to scrutinize the police report traveling back on the train and delivering it to me yesterday, yes?"

I felt as if I were about to take a final exam. "Yes," I answered warily."

"Then let us unfold the basics, beginning with the weather."

"The weather?" I fumbled to remember. "I think the report said it was raining the night Ori was killed, right?"

"Yes, and when did the rain end?"

"In the morning, I think." I looked to Grandfather for corroboration.

"More precisely, the report includes an hourly weather chart that indicates there were heavy rains and wind between midnight and 6:00 am."

"So, it was raining when Ori was killed," I said. Was that important? "Where are we going with this, Zaida?"

"Ah Yoeli, how often according to the report are the dorm room floors washed and when?"

I hesitated just a moment. "I believe it said once a week on Friday mornings."

Grandfather voice rose slightly. "Yes, yes, and in the report we read that there was no mud or water or shoe markings in the room, and that Ori was in his room by 8:30 that Friday evening. He ate Shabbat dinner in the school's dining hall across the street from the dormitory, thus ..."

"So," I interrupted, "it was someone already in the dorm when the outside doors locked at nine, as indicated in the report."

Grandfather looked pleased. "Yes, exactly. Next, we will review who else was in the dormitory at the time of the murder. They will be our first suspects. But before we do so, in line with what we just discussed about the weather, does not something peculiar present itself when we examine the pictures of Ori's dormitory room when forensics arrived?"

Grandfather handed me the report folder, and I looked through the pictures, including one of Ori's bloodied body on the floor. And then it hit me.

"The window is open."

"Nuh, nuh," Grandfather's switch to Yiddish vernacular prompted me to say more.

"If the window was open, and it was raining heavily and windy, you'd think at least some water would have made its way into the room. Which suggests someone opened the window after it quit raining but before the body was discovered. But why, and by whom? I don't think the police would have altered anything in the crime scene before pictures were taken."

"Two critical questions which we will keep before us as we look at who else was in the dormitory on the night of the murder."

"Well," I rushed to answer, "we know a Mrs. Wachter was there. Report says she's a widow, had been the dorm mother for 15 years, and her role is 'to nurture the boys and see to their health,' whatever that means. She has an apartment on the first floor. I don't remember a picture of her being in the file. I wonder why?"

"I would surmise that it is merely lazy analysis. The police jumped to the conclusion that such a lady could not have been involved in a murder. I want to hear her thoughts on Ori and the other boys who were there that tragic night. Since we will be meeting Mrs. Wachter shortly, let us proceed to the others. Which boy would you like to review first? As we do so, let us scrutinize the photos of each one."

"Okay, how about Sheldon Lachs, the dorm RA?" He was a senior and had a room on the first floor, cattycorner from Mrs. Wachter's apartment.

The full body photos were in black and white. Sheldon Lachs appeared to be of average build and around six foot. He was wearing a white dress shirt and dark trousers with knotted ritual fringes or *tzitzit*, dangling on both sides of his pants pockets. His eyes expressed fright, and he looked away from the camera. Also, he had short sidelocks in the manner of ultra orthodox Jews and stubble on his cheeks. A large skullcap covered his short-cropped hair.

"He looks more religious than I expected at this school, Zaida."

"Ah, I will not be disingenuous and say I do not understand your meaning, but let us remember we are an intricately woven religion and thus it is hard to pinpoint an understanding of 'religious' on a continuum. What else about Sheldon from the report?"

"Well, since he was an RA, he had his own room. All seniors were on the ground floor with freshman on fourth, sophomores on third, and juniors like Ori on second. Let's see, Sheldon's from Lakewood, New Jersey, and he was planning to go home on Sunday 'for the Jewish holidays,' I guess Rosh Hashonah." Says he 'looked pale and shaky, having found the body.' Claims he had not touched a thing in the room before police arrived. Ran to the basement where janitor named Ernest Robinson lived and asked him to call the police."

Here I paused for a moment. "But why run down to the basement to call? What if the janitor had not been there? Why not go quickly to Mrs. Wachter's apartment? She probably had a phone. Or there's probably a pay phone in the dorm. Why not use it?"

Just as Grandfather opened his mouth to respond, the answer hit me from my own training at my own Jewish day school: "Because, as orthodox Jews, he or Mrs. Wachter would not wish to violate the Sabbath by making a phone call. He would ask the non-Jewish janitor to do so for him."

"Yes, yes, Yoeli. Perhaps being a good attorney is similar to being a good detective. Each requires a scouring, examination, and explanation of the facts. Whom shall we look at next?"

"As I remember, there were no other seniors on the first floor that night, so let's look at David Spiller, a junior who was down the hall from Ori on the second floor."

Spiller's picture showed a thin, short boy wearing a satiny long-sleeve shirt with tight H.I.S. jeans that flared at the bottom over platform-elevated shoes. His hair was thickly swept into a Brylcreem pomade with a small, leather skullcap atop.

"He's from Los Angeles," I began, thinking back to the report, "and was going to spend the New Year holidays with relatives in Queens. He claimed he saw Ori alive around 11:45 p.m.—Ori was reading a book in the hallway in front of his room." I paused. "Isn't that odd, Zaida? Why would Ori be reading in the hallway instead of his room?"

Grandfather thought for a moment. "My guess is that the main light in each dormitory room is on a timer set to go off at, let us conjecture, by 11:00. The boys would not have to turn off lights, thus violating a Sabbath prohibition. I would also surmise that a small light for safety and convenience remained on in each room. So if this boy's information is accurate, at 11:45, Ori was not ready for bed and continued his reading in the hallway."

"And so David may have been the last person to see him alive," I added.

"Except for the murderer, unless David also was that person."

Grandfather then asked if he could see David's picture again. "Aha, just as I remembered. Yoeli, please look at the photo and tell me what stands out."

I looked it over. Nothing struck me. "What Zaida?"

"Observe his two hands."

I again studied the picture carefully. "His fists are clenched. That's what you want me to see?" How difficult it is to take in what is right before you!

"Yes, he is displaying intense anger and defensiveness. I will at this time not hypothesize as to why. Who is next?"

"Okay, I'm making my way to the third floor, and that means Joshua Cushman. He was a sophomore at that time." Before handing Cushman's picture to Grandfather, I glanced again at the boy's face. He reminded me of a seventeenth-century fire-and-brimstone Puritan preacher. Thick, arched eyebrows dominated a severe face. He wore a button-down dress shirt and tie along with baggy trousers that gave a Great Depression-era look.

"I would hate to have had him for a roommate," I volunteered.

"Just from the picture, you believe you know him?"

Before I could respond, Grandfather added. "You will have an opportunity to validate your judgment after we speak to him."

"Just curious, how will we get to speak to him—or any of the others—besides Mrs. Wachter?"

"We will obtain phone numbers and current addresses from the high school office and visit each as soon as possible. Detective Rooney will help us and, if necessary, Mr. Gold will exert his influence on the administration. But back to Joshua Cushman, what else does the report tell us?"

"Let's see, nothing much. From Fairfield, Connecticut. Was planning to leave early Sunday afternoon for New Year. Joshua said that he sat near Ori during dinner and then went to his room about 8:30. Did not see Ori after that. Nothing more."

Grandfather reflected for a moment. "He did not see Ori after that, but did he see any of the other residents that night? We will ask that question of everyone we interview. And now we come to…?"

I pulled out the photo of Michael Charnick, a freshman at the time of the murder with a room on the fourth floor. Grandfather saw me gawking.

"Nuh, what is it Yoeli?"

The boy, 14 when the photo was taken, gave the appearance of a sumo wrestler, already over six feet and perhaps 300 pounds. Wild eyes gave prominence to a wide, beefy face, but what amazed me was a black tee-shirt he wore over jeans with a circle of gay pride colors over a New York City background and below, **Stonewall— The First PRIDE Was a Riot.**

"He's wearing a gay pride t-shirt," I blurted out. "And it's a Jewish orthodox school he was attending. Isn't that incredible?"

"Yes," Grandfather agreed. "Also, do you remember where the boy's family resided?"

I hadn't and quickly looked. "Manhattan, on the upper West Side, just a couple of miles from the school. Then why was he in the dorm and not home that night? For that matter, why was he in the dorm at all instead of commuting."

"Yes, yes, obvious and critical questions. If I remember correctly, Michael stated that he violated school protocol and ate in his room that night. He did not see Ori at all that day. Curious and more curious."

I didn't tune in to Grandfather's musings. "So that does it?" I hurriedly asked looking at my watch and seeing it was 10:00. We were to be at the dorm and the murder site at 11:00.

"A moment, a moment, Yoeli," Grandfather shushed my haste. "Wasn't there someone else in the dormitory besides these boys?"

I kicked myself for being sloppy. "Yes, there was. The janitor in the basement." I thumbed through the file. "Ernest Robinson."

I gave Grandfather the picture of a light-skinned black man in his thirties, with a handsome movie-star face and the build of a linebacker. He wore blue overalls with Manhattan Jewish Academy stitched on the front.

I summarized for Grandfather. "He said he knew Ori, that Ori would come to his basement apartment to talk, but he had not seen him the day or evening of the murder. Robinson was under strong suspicion because his wife was murdered in 1968 in South Carolina. He was never officially charged for her death."

"I will surmise that Mr. Robinson is no longer employed at the dormitory," Grandfather said, rising. "I hope someone knows where we can find him. We must speak to Mr. Robinson."

"Because right now you also see him as the main suspect?"

"Certainly not, Yoeli. We have no main suspects at this point. We are gathering information to expose to our critical analyses faculties. Mr. Robinson stated that Ori would visit him. There is much then he can tell us, whether he is the murderer or not."

Grandfather grabbed his fedora and headed toward the door. "Since time is short, now we will not take the train to Washington Heights. Let us walk the block to Boro Hall, where we will find an abundance of cabs. And since it is my initiative, you will not charge your law firm. It will come out of my expenses."

* * * *

It had just turned 11:00. The cab dropped us off in front of a red, four-story brick building with chipped red concrete steps leading up to a large glass door with **MJAHS Residence Hall** over it. Bars covered all of the first-floor windows that ran the length of the building ending at a paved lot with four basketball courts at each corner. To the right of the building was a fenced-in grassy field with a path leading from a side entrance at the building's middle.

As we exited the cab, a wiry looking man in a London Fog raincoat ran over to us. It was a clear, warmish day, and I wondered if I had misread the weather forecast.

"Frank Wolf?" the man said loudly, extending his hand toward Grandfather.

"Yes," Grandfather answered. "And you are Detective Rooney. Allow me to introduce my grandson and associate, Joel Gordon."

Rooney gave my hand a quick shake and turned back to Grandfather. "Max Fink at the 90th in Brooklyn says you're working the Gold murder for the family and not to let my Irish pride get in the way. Although I have a lot of Irish pride, you don't need to worry about it. After three years of coming up with nothing and, I'll be honest, not getting the best cooperation from your people, I'll accept any assistance you can provide."

"We appreciate your gracious acceptance of our role. You will have our full cooperation and constant communication," Grandfather replied.

"Great, great. I believe you want to see the kid's room, where he was murdered? I've kept it sort of sealed, let it be cleaned up of course, let the family have the kid's possessions, but I'm about ready to let the school use the room again."

"After three years, I would think so," my lawyer-trained mouth added automatically.

Grandfather gave me a "how was that helpful" look, and then turned to Rooney. "Yes, might you show us to the room so that we may review the crime scene and ask you a few questions. Then we will visit with Mrs. Wachter at noon. Thank you, Detective, for giving me her number so that I could make arrangements. But if you do not mind, might we meet privately with Mrs. Wachter?"

"Don't mind at all. I've talked to the lady dozens of times."

With the students in classes, all was quiet when we walked in. We followed Detective Rooney down a first floor hallway to a spiral stairway on the left. I caught myself ascending quickly with Rooney until I looked back and then slowed down. Grandfather could not keep pace.

On the second floor, we followed Rooney down a hallway toward the back of the building. The last door on the left had no tape or any other indication of a crime scene. Rooney, in anticipation, offered: "After a few months, we agreed to remove any signs of a murder. The administration said it was spooking the kids and parents."

He unlocked the door, and we entered gingerly, as if we might disturb evidence or even the deceased. Indeed, after moving into the room and turning right, we had to stop ourselves from stepping on the faded yellow outline of Ori's slightly-curled body on the worn, thin brown carpet. Dark stains marked the area around the head that lay toward the large window, which overlooked the paved lot at the back of the dorm, with a highway and the Harlem River visible beyond.

To the right of the body, closer to the large window, were two empty bookshelves bolted to the wall and a four-drawer dresser. On the room's left side were an unmade iron-grill bed and mattress, a study desk, and a swivel chair nearer the door.

"Does this dorm just have one kid to a room?" I wondered aloud.

"Just four of the rooms," Rooney responded. "The RA's room on the first floor opposite the stairwell, and the three rooms on each floor on this side of the building. So the Gold kid didn't have a roommate when he was killed."

"And why he did not wish for a room companion? We shall inquire of his father later today," Grandfather stated as he turned toward me. "Joel, would you please retrieve the pictures of the crime scene for us to review in the context of our current visit."

I took out the pictures and gave them each another look before handing them to Grandfather. He looked back and forth from the room to the pictures.

"Detective Rooney," Grandfather began, "if I might ask you without causing effrontery, when the police arrived and began the investigation, is it possible that someone may have opened the window before forensics took photos? Clearly in all of the pictures, the window is widely open."

"No way." Rooney sounded a bit annoyed. "If any of my guys did such a thing, he'd be on foot patrol the next day."

I wondered if Grandfather would explain why he asked the question, but instead he went to something else. "Detective, did your investigation come across any pictures of Ori's room from before his murder? The lethal weapon was never found, so it was either brought in by the murderer and exited with the murderer, or it was present in the room and easily at hand. It may have been on the bookcase."

"Why on the bookcase?" I asked.

"I will share my hypothesis," Grandfather said, moving to the right side of the body outline near the bookshelves. "Absorb how the body lies on the floor. We know Ori died from a blow to the head. He must have been totally unaware or only cognizant for a split second. Otherwise, he would have put his hands up or tried to fight off his attacker in some way. But there is no evidence of his having done so, no wounds to hands or other parts of his body. Ori's assailant would have reached for a substantial object and in one motion smashed it over the poor boy's head."

Rooney remained unimpressed. "Yeah, maybe, but it all comes down to our never having found the murder weapon. If you know how to find it, more power to you."

"We will do our best. I think we have satisfied ourselves here at the physical scene of the murder. We will now descend to see Mrs. Wachter. There is one other way you might help us, Detective Rooney. Might you lend the weight of your authority in obtaining current contact information for the boys and the janitor who were in the building the night of the murder? We very much need to interview them."

"Will do," Rooney said. "I'll head across the street to the school's administration office and see what they got. They're not exactly the most cooperative bunch I've ever come across."

Grandfather bowed his head toward Rooney. "If you are quickly successful, might you bring the information to Mrs. Wachter's apartment before we leave in an hour's time? Thank you for your assistance, Detective Rooney."

* * * *

A white-haired woman who even in high heels looked diminutive answered my knock on the door. Delicate silver-framed glasses hung around her thin neck from a jeweled chain onto a perfectly fitted lavender dress that fell below her knees.

After Grandfather proffered introductions, Mrs. Wachter ushered us in and directed us to a sofa before which sat a 19th-century coffee table. The table held fine china plates of evenly-cut sandwiches on German rye bread, cups and saucers, a dark urn with coffee and a white urn with hot water near a plate with tea bags. Another plate offered gingerbread cookies and almond cake as desserts.

"It is the lunch hour," Mrs. Wachter said with the slightest hint of an accent. She pointed to a nearby sideboard upon which sat a gold-plated ewer filled with water, a large bowl, and matching cup. "I thought you may be hungry with little time to eat. The sandwiches are with tuna or egg salad. If you are interested in washing and making the blessing before eating, please do so."

Grandfather indicated that we would accept the offer and made his way to the sideboard. In the minute it took for Grandfather to complete the ablution, Mrs. Wachter sat down in an armchair opposite us and smiled at me.

When Grandfather returned and completed a quick blessing over the meal, holding the first sandwich that came to his hand, Mrs. Wachter asked him: "Where are you from?"

I knew she didn't mean Brooklyn. "From Austria," Grandfather answered affably but in German. "Und sie?"

Mrs. Wachter also answered in German. I mostly followed it, as I understood Yiddish: "I hail from Frankfurt. Based on your cultured German, I imagine you lived in Vienna and not in the countryside. Am I correct? How is it, may I ask, you have become a private detective?"

Grandfather reverted to English. "That is a long story perhaps for another time, as we do not wish to detain you. I am sure you are very busy dealing with your wards. But sorrowfully, as you know, we must take you back to the day when Ori Gold was found murdered. Surely the police have similarly questioned you, but please tell us what you remember in any order you wish—and also some reminiscences on each individual who was in the dormitory that night."

Mrs. Wachter did not flinch. She gave me a quick look as I opened my notebook to write, then she turned fully to Grandfather.

"A terrible day, a Sabbath day, right before Rosh Hashonah, a nightmare day from which we are still not free."

"How so," I asked forcefully and was immediately sorry seeing Grandfather give me a look that said "patience!"

"How so?" Mrs. Wachter's eyes darted at me and returned to Grandfather. "One of our students, a sweet, wonderful young boy, the son of a major donor to our school, is brutally murdered just a floor above my head while I slept, and the murderer who must have crept in from outside never caught. The questions, innuendos, and accusations nonsensically raised and even appearing in the press! The poor boy's room still a crime scene, yes, the three-year-long nightmare is still with us!"

"The 'innuendos,' please Mrs. Wachter," Grandfather prodded gently.

I was taken aback at how much fury appeared in Mrs. Wachter's eyes.

"Six years before, in 1965 one of our boys, hanged himself in the shower a few days before he was to graduate. From that the papers implied we are a troubled school with dark secrets. The school is not troubled; rather it was just one boy who he himself was troubled from the moment he arrived."

Grandfather leaned toward Mrs. Wachter. "And those are the accusations to which you allude?"

A blush came over her face. "I wish it was just that, but it has been worse. An unnamed former student supposedly came forward with accusations of perverted abuse by two of our faculty. What nonsense! And they allow such things to be printed in the newspapers."

I didn't like the woman and wondered how Grandfather felt. He sat with a neutral expression and said nothing.

Mrs. Wachter who may have been disappointed in not having received a sympathetic response, continued: "You wanted me to tell you about the boys who were here that night. There is nothing much to tell. There was Sheldon Lachs, who was a senior and the Resident Assistant. A lovely young man, pious, devoted to his religious studies and to the well-being of the dormitory boys. That Saturday morning, I had gone to my synagogue on Bennett Avenue where my husband of beloved memory was president before he passed away nearly 15 years ago. When I returned, the police were here. Sheldon was distraught from having found the body and the police questioning. We are still in touch, and he still carries that trauma with him."

"I will ask the same question about each person who was here," Grandfather interjected. "How did Sheldon get along with Ori?"

"Wonderfully," she quickly answered. "Sheldon told me that he would strongly recommend Ori for the RA position the next year."

When neither Grandfather nor I said anything further, Mrs. Wachter asked: "Which boy do you want to hear about next?"

"As you wish," Grandfather said.

Mrs. Wachter chose David Spiller. "I never got to know him very well, a vain boy, always concerned with his appearance. He spent an inordinate amount of time in the phone booth claiming to be speaking to various girlfriends."

"Excuse me," I said. "You said 'claiming.' Just curious why you used that term."

Grandfather gave me a quick glance of approval.

"Because the other boys would accuse him of talking into a dead phone to give the appearance of having many female acquaintances. David would become infuriated, which sometimes led to physical altercations for which Rabbi Arofsky, the dormitory administrator, would mete out punishments."

"Did David and Ori ever have such a fight?" I followed up.

"Certainly not. Ori was such a gentle boy, a peacemaker, and he would never let it come to that."

Again, we waited while Mrs. Wachter appeared lost in thought. "If I remember correctly, Joshua Cushman also was here. Somewhat of a strange boy, often picked on for his conservative political views, a member by his own admission of the John Birch Society. Right from the beginning he would rail against the boys' neglect of their religious studies and obsession with girls. He despised sports, except for ping pong, at which he was very good and had his own rackets. I believe it was in the middle of his first year when a group of boys forced him into a large duffel bag and with the help of an older brother who drove a car, threw him into the trunk and then deposited him onto the George Washington High School basketball court right before the game was to begin. There was quite a commotion with his parents over this outrage, with threats of criminal charges and a civil suit. But Joshua himself put an end to it by insisting that he wouldn't dignify his assailants with any court action. A strange boy, he was."

"And was Ori by any chance one of his assailants?" I asked.

"Oh, God in heaven, certainly not. Ori was the sweetest of boys, actually the only one who Joshua may have thought was his friend. Since Ori had a single room, Joshua visited often and would get angry when Ori wanted to do homework and suggested Joshua leave. He would then pound the desk in fury and shout, 'et tu, Ori.' I heard it often, even down here in my apartment. But Ori told me not to worry, it was just Joshua's frustration coming out. After Ori's tragedy, I don't believe Joshua had any other friendships. He became very quiet and confronted others to a much lesser degree. No one wished to be his roommate, so for junior and senior year, the school had available single dorm rooms and gave it to him at no additional cost. Except for seeking a ping pong game, he did not interact with others."

Grandfather caught the woman's eye. "You are being very helpful, Mrs. Wachter. Thank you. Please proceed."

Mrs. Wachter gave Grandfather a full smile. "Let us think, who then is left?" and with that call to memory, her smile quickly disappeared replaced by an expression of fear.

"Oh my, yes, the freshman, Michael Charnick, a brute of a boy who would lose his temper at the slightest provocation, or rather his perception of a provocation. He was so big that I thought he would surely hurt one of the boys in a confrontation."

Mrs. Wachter stopped for a moment, blanched, and looked nauseated. "Then there was the chutzpah of his openly flaunting his acceptance of deviant behavior, here at our academy where adherence to law and tradition is taught daily. Thankfully he didn't stay long. But perhaps I should feel sorry for the boy, so neglected by his parents. They were, I am told, constantly away on business and pleasure trips. Usually parents bring their child to the dormitory on the child's first day. But Michael was accompanied by a domestic, who helped move him into the single room on the fourth floor and left quickly."

Grandfather followed up. "How soon after the murder did he leave?"

"Within a few days, a day or so after Rosh Hashonah, as I remember. I had just received a call from the administration that Michael had left and wasn't returning when a few minutes later the same domestic knocked on my door and said she had come to pack up his things."

"Do you think Michael could have killed Ori?" Grandfather asked. I was surprised at the bluntness of the question. Why hadn't he asked the same question about the other boys?

Mrs. Wachter seemed flabbergasted. "Michael, one of our own boys, despite his irregularities, it could not be. And besides, Ori was the only boy I ever saw that actually stopped and had a conversation with Michael. I am sure it was someone from the outside, or," and Mrs. Wachter dropped her voice, "Ernest the janitor."

"Do you suspect the janitor?" I asked as if she were on the witness stand.

Mrs. Wachter straightened herself in her chair. "Well, if it was not someone from the outside, then it makes sense it would be Ernest. Do not misunderstand me, he was perfectly behaved during the time he was with us. But as the police discovered, he was under suspicion for a crime in the South."

"As far as you know," Grandfather inquired gently, "did Ernest and Ori have any sort of relationship?"

Mrs. Wachter's face reddened. "Relationship, what can you possibly mean by a relationship? The boys would of course speak politely to the man when they crossed paths with him, but that is all."

"And that is all that I meant," Grandfather responded while rising. "We most appreciate the time you spent with us and for the delicious and thoughtful lunch. Thank you very much."

Mrs. Wachter rose quickly. "You are most welcome," she said looking just at Grandfather. "And since you have my phone number, you are also most welcome to call me if you wish. I am surrounded daily by children, and I would welcome adult conversation."

Grandfather smiled and bowed slightly before walking toward the door. We left the apartment as throngs of boys were going in and out of the dorm. Their lunch time, I guessed. Once outside, I couldn't contain myself.

"Zaida, were you and Mrs. Wachter flirting with each other?"

"Ah, Yoeli, I will not invalidate your question but only answer that perhaps one of us was indulging in such behavior."

"Are you going to call her?"

"Allow me the same response you once gave as a teenager— 'We will see.' But for now, Detective Rooney is approaching. Let us determine if he has been successful. Since it is now 12:45, we have plenty of time to take the train back instead of a more expensive taxi."

"Okay, then, a less private question. Why did you ask Mrs. Wachter only about Michael's capacity to have killed Ori?"

"Ah, excellent, you noticed. I wanted to establish in my mind how much credence to give Mrs. Wachter's assessment of our main characters. All present that night could have killed the poor boy. Given her description of Michael, certainly she should not have been so defensive as to dismiss the possibility. When it comes to *cum grano salis*, I take her impressions of character with a doubling of salt."

"So at this point, except for Mrs. Wachter, everyone there that night is a suspect?"

Grandfather stopped suddenly, turned to me, and placed his hands on my shoulders. "And why are you excepting Mrs. Wachter?"

* * * *

We were back to Grandfather's office by 2:30.

Rooney had been unsuccessful in obtaining contact information. "The school's administration tells me that without a subpoena, they will have to obtain permission from all the parties, and it may take several days. That's the attitude I got back from the beginning of the administration. Stall and evade, as if they're protecting someone. But I do have Michael Charnick's home address and phone number, since we had to track him down for additional questioning after he left the school."

"I believe Mr. Gold may help us," Grandfather had replied.

While we waited for Sam Gold's arrival, we discussed the case. As Grandfather sat behind his desk, he insisted that we consider everyone a suspect and not allow ourselves to come to any conclusions.

"Much too premature, Yoeli, much too premature," Grandfather stated several times.

"While we wait," Grandfather requested, "please give me your one-but-not-more-than-two-sentence summary of each suspect."

I felt on the spot, but trust overtook my doubts. "Okay, here goes. Going in the same order as before, Sheldon Lachs, *nebishy*, couldn't kill anyone."

Grandfather looked displeased. "Did we not say we will not come to conclusions? Please try again without definitive evaluations."

"Okay, Sheldon Lachs, *nebishy* and piously religious."

"Thank you, and David Spiller?"

"Vain, a blowhard, someone from whom I would turn the other way if I saw him coming. Oh, yes, and angry."

"Joshua Cushman, scary-looking face, obnoxiously judgmental, but I feel sorry for him—and a bit ashamed that I might have joined in his kidnapping to the basketball game."

"Yoeli, do not impugn your integrity. I think you would not have done so. And Michael Charnick?"

"Violent, a brute, and while I try to keep an open mind, uses his deviancy as an excuse for maladaptive behavior."

Grandfather nodded. "Very insightful. And finally?"

"Ernest Robinson, the man everyone wants to be guilty, but I feel I know so very little about him or his personality."

"I agree with you, Yoeli. I am constantly struck by the superficialities that form notions of guilt or innocence."

I had learned my lesson. "And Mrs. Wachter, superficially charming but obnoxiously opinionated." I didn't want Grandfather eventually keeping company with her, so I added, "As you earlier indicated, a person whose judgment is not to be trusted."

Just then we heard a knock on the door, and Samuel Gold entered. Tall, with a boyish face that still showed some freckles even in his fifties, he was dressed casually in an orange and black plaid shirt, jeans, and a tan cowboy hat. A satchel bag hung from his shoulder.

"Joel," he said walking towards me.

"Sir." I stood up and shook hands with him.

Then he rushed over to greet Grandfather. After they had introduced themselves and shaken hands, I indicated that Mr. Gold should take the one guest chair opposite Grandfather who seated himself again behind his desk.

Gold sat and took off his cowboy hat, which he placed on his lap. As an orthodox Jew, he wore under his hat a skullcap that covered reddish hair flecked with gray.

"Your coming, Mr. Gold, particularly in such a short amount of time, is most welcome," Grandfather began. "There is much for us to learn from you about your Ori, may he rest in peace. But before we begin, might you be of immediate assistance to our investigation?"

Grandfather then explained about the delay Rooney was experiencing in obtaining the contact information.

"May I use your phone?" Gold asked.

"Of course." Grandfather pushed it toward him.

In short order, we heard Gold announce himself to an operator, ask for Rabbi Weinrab, the high school's principal, explain why he was calling, and a few minutes later say, "Thank you, and yes I hope to see you at the December Board of Trustees meeting."

The engaging smile that had filled Gold's face had fled. "Rabbi Weinrab will make a concerted effort to provide the contact information you want by 5:00 this afternoon. The office will stay open until six for it to be picked up." Then turning towards me, he added, "Joel, I certainly don't want to hold up your investigation, but could we also discuss the Golden Energy security filing while I'm out East? A couple of hours should do it."

I agreed and I heard Grandfather suggest: "If it is convenient for both of you, might you have your meeting tomorrow morning, while I establish our interviews schedule?"

Seeing concurrence from both of us, Grandfather turned to Sam Gold: "As painful as it will be for you, could you please talk about Ori? Tell us what might be most helpful in understanding his character. We will listen until you feel you have finished."

Tears welled in Gold's eyes as he spoke. "Painful, yes, exceedingly and maddeningly so. Ori was the youngest of our four sons, and five years after Lev, our third youngest, was born. His brothers had also attended the high school here in New York, inhabited the same dormitory, and each experienced four wonderful years at the school. The two oldest have now joined my business.

"It's something awful to lose a child, and to lose him to a horrendous murder, and not to know after three years why he was murdered, or what person did such a thing to him, that's what I mean by maddening. My wife is still in mourning, still wears black, does not eat, and sleeps little. She cannot stop thinking about the moment her baby was struck down, imagining endless scenarios as to how and why it happened. I believe she will leave mourning only after we find these answers. I have explored various ways to obtain the truth, and now I come to you grateful that you have taken the case and, after hearing about your previous successes from Joel, hopeful of results. And of course I will compensate you generously at the conclusion of your work, regardless of the outcome."

Grandfather put up his hands. "Mr. Gold, as I tell all of my prospective clients, to solve anything one needs the will and the effort. I can assure you both as a parent and as someone who experienced the sudden loss of a loved one, I with Joel's assistance can give you both."

Grandfather picked up a single sheet of paper. "As for remuneration, I have drawn up my basic contract. It calls for you to pay me seventeen dollars per hour, plus judiciously charged incidentals such as transportation."

Then looking at me, Grandfather added: "If you would like, your attorney is welcome to review the contract before you sign it."

A slight smile filled Gold's eyes. "I think that won't be necessary. Your terms are quite agreeable."

"Then if you will, Mr. Gold, may we hear more about Ori?"

Gold gathered himself for a moment. "Everyone loved Ori. Yes, I know, many parents say those exact words, but please understand, Ori was unique, he truly was the apple of everyone's eye, his parents, grandparents, neighbors, teachers, and I can go on, but I'll finish my list by also including his brothers. While the three of them often fought among themselves, rarely with Ori, and I don't think it's because he was the baby. Even when he was very young, just barely out of toddlerhood, Ori would be the accepted arbitrator settling disputes. When one of his brothers would get into deep trouble with us, in would trot Ori delegated to argue his brother's cause.

"His uncle, my brother joked one day that when Ori went to college, he would major in philanthropy. And my brother didn't mean just providing charitable donations but rather gifts of compassion, understanding, and fairness."

Turning both to me and then back to Grandfather, Gold—as if seeking total comprehension of his listeners—went on: "And please don't misunderstand me, I'm not trying to convince you that Ori was like an angelic being with no faults or fears or conflicts. He did, but his overall goodness and consideration stood out remarkably.

"Can you imagine, all through his lifetime as far as we know, Ori never had a physical altercation with another boy. Not once. Can you imagine?"

Here Gold paused. "What else should I tell you about Ori? He was a very good student, and it made no difference if it was science, math, English, or his religious studies. Oh yes, I know what I must share with you about Ori."

Gold stopped for a moment to wipe his eyes. "He loved sports, loved watching and playing even though he wasn't a very good athlete. What eight-year-old follows a losing minor league team and knows the stats for each player as Ori did for the Denver Bears? Same for the football Broncos, even when they were just in the AFL. You know his most prized possession? The trophy his Little League team received for winning their division when he was 12. And Ori was a bench player, just getting into blowout games, but he was always in the coaching box, always cheering his mates on, always sharing helpful observations. He kept that trophy on his nightstand near his bed, cleaning and shining it at least twice a week."

Gold stopped talking, and we sat silent for a moment. I myself had been a pretty good ballplayer in high school and made varsity as an undergraduate at Brooklyn College. There was an Ori on every team, not that good but dedicated to the game and teammates. I would have liked him a lot, and I was determined to find out why he was killed.

Then Grandfather asked: "Mr. Gold, if I may press you a bit, when you said 'faults,' 'fears,' 'conflicts,' what are examples? A fuller understanding will help us."

Gold leaned forward. "I think all three can be rolled into one. He set the bar very high for what he expected from his family, friends, people in general, even politicians, and most importantly from himself. So without admitting it, and always being a kind, loving person, he was often under stress. I think he didn't want to disappoint and didn't want to be disappointed."

Gold's moist eyes exploded into tears. "Does any of this make sense to you?"

Again there was silence. Perhaps I was too young at the time with simplistic understandings of people, perhaps because I was not yet a parent, but I had trouble digesting exactly what Gold was trying to tell us about Ori's personality. I knew Grandfather was more successful when he said softly:

"You have drawn a beautiful portrait of your child, and it will help us immensely. We will work very quickly in anticipation of an outcome. Even though it is over three years, we are sorry for your loss and hope you and your family will be soon fully comforted by Ori's memory. Perhaps a question or two before you leave us. First, why was Ori in a single occupancy dormitory room. Did he not wish for a roommate?"

A wan smile returned to Gold's eyes. "No, not at all. During his first two years, Ori had roommates. But several boys had asked if they could room with him for his third year, and he didn't want to reject any of them. So he asked if he could use his salary from summer work in the Golden Energy business office to offset the additional cost. That was our Ori."

The smile flickered out, and Gold asked: "You have another question?"

"I do," Grandfather answered quickly. "But first allow me a moment to look in the police file."

I watched Grandfather page through the folder, pulling out four photos and placing them on his desk. "The trophy you mentioned, Mr. Gold, it was returned to you with the rest of Ori's possessions?"

Gold looked perplexed and thought a moment. "I imagine so, but I'm not positive. The school packed up his things and shipped them to us after the police allowed their release. We couldn't face doing it ourselves. And there they sit to this day, still packed up in Ori's bedroom, which also has had no changes made to it."

"If it is not too much," Grandfather asked gently, "could someone in your household look through what was sent back to ascertain if the trophy was included?"

"Yes, I'll have someone do it this afternoon and let Joel know tomorrow morning when we meet."

Sam Gold sat slumped in his chair. He had come into Grandfather's office more confident, straighter, and taller, and now as he prepared to leave, he had to make an effort to lift himself. When he did so, there was a stoop in his back and a shuffle in his walk as he put on his hat and made his way to the door.

"Then Joel, I will see you tomorrow in the morning at, say, 9:00 a.m. at your firm. When we finish up, I'll head to the airport to return home. I don't want to leave my wife by herself. And Mr. Wolf, thank you again for taking our case. Please keep me informed daily."

After Gold departed, I blurted: "Ok, I knew enough not to ask while Gold was here, but why the interest in the trophy?"

Grandfather spread out the four photos on his desk and asked me to examine them. Each showed an area of Ori's room right after the murder—floor, bed, bookcase, dresser, and desk.

"What do you not see?" Grandfather asked.

I answered quickly. "A trophy! I get it! You're thinking it's the murder weapon."

"Sha, sha," Grandfather whispered putting a finger to his lips. "Yes, I am wondering where the trophy may be and want corroboration that it is not with the rest of the boy's possessions. But am I thinking it is the murder weapon? Too early, Yoeli, much too early."

I quieted down and asked: "I'm wondering how much we can rely on Mr. Gold's description of a son he lost so horribly. Don't we factor in various levels of bias as to what he told us?"

Grandfather smiled at me. "God willing, I will be alive when you become a parent. But perhaps I digress. Yes, of course there is a bias, and a very strong one as he was talking about a beloved son, a murdered child, so a bias is to be expected. But we must listen critically to Mr. Gold, as we did to Mrs. Wachter, and to the others we shall interview. We will search for where there is coalescence and where there is dissonance among the various versions that give a sense of Ori when he was alive. Then, also taking into account our own biases, we can place ourselves in the dormitory with Ori up to the very last moment when the murder weapon struck him."

My head was swirling, trying to absorb Grandfather's words. I needed to do something down to earth, so I rose and said: "I'm going to run up to Washington Heights to get the contact information from the school office. I'll drop them off with you at home so you can look at them in the morning. Then I'll see you here tomorrow at 1:00?"

Grandfather sat immersed in thought. He did not reply.

I closed the door behind me thinking that he was already in the dorm on the night of the murder making his way toward that terrible moment of death.

Wednesday, October 16, 1974.

Sam Gold was grim as we worked Wednesday morning, sharply focused on his company's business. Only once did he bring up Ori's murder. He reported that the boxes containing Ori's dorm room belongings were thoroughly searched, and the baseball trophy was not found.

"Odd," Gold said. "Ori would not have misplaced it. I'll put in a call to Mrs. Wachter to see if it was left behind somehow."

I wondered how someone as astute as Sam could not have suspected that the trophy was the murder weapon. Grief? It easily clouded reason. After we concluded our business, he rushed to catch a cab to LaGuardia for his flight back to Denver. I ran down to the kosher deli near the 53rd Street subway, picked up some sandwiches for Grandfather and me, and headed to Brooklyn.

I walked into Grandfather's office right at 1:00, and he handed me a yellow legal pad with writing on the top page as I handed him a turkey breast sandwich. I was a pastrami/corned beef/brisket type of guy, but as long as I could remember, Grandfather stayed away from beef.

"Thank you, Yoeli, for the sandwich. I did not realize I was hungry until the smell of the pickles entered with you. What you have in your hands is a schedule of interviews with those you have been calling the 'suspects'—except for Mrs. Wachter, with whom we spoke yesterday. Also, thank you for being punctual because, as you can see, the first interview with Sheldon Lachs will be here in the office at two o'clock. The other interviews, but one, are also scheduled, including with David Spiller here at four o'clock today."

I did not hide my incredulity. "You've already scheduled all these interviews!"

Grandfather returned a look as if to say, are you a naïf? "You expended great effort yesterday bringing me the contact information and working with Mr. Gold this morning, so should I have not done the same? And for the most part, it was not so difficult. Allow me to summarize."

I peered at the list quickly and saw that we were going to Connecticut the next day to talk with Joshua Cushman and Ernest Robinson. I saw nothing written for Michael Charnick.

Grandfather continued. "We are fortunate that Sheldon Lachs and David Spiller are both attending university here in New York City. Sheldon in his third year, and David in his second. I called each of the universities and obtained their dormitory phone numbers. I left a message for Sheldon, who returned my call within a half hour. I explained my role and, for the sake of privacy, asked him to come to the office. He immediately agreed. 'I think about Ori constantly,' he said solemnly, 'and if you with God's help can solve his murder, then I will repeat what I told the police many times over.'"

"And David Spiller?" I asked.

Grandfather grimaced. "Ah, that was a bit more difficult. He came to the phone right away, and when I explained what was wanted of him, he became indignant and angry at having to discuss what he had so many times told the police. I patiently waited for him to expend himself, and then I informed him that we were an official part of the investigation. I told him we could speak at the 34th Precinct Station in Washington Heights, where various newspaper reporters with cameras may be found, or he can come to my office later today."

I thought about Grandfather. I still had trouble aligning the gentle, soft-spoken man with whom I grew up with the hard-nosed detective that he could be when necessary.

"Great work, Zaida. I see we're off to Connecticut tomorrow."

"Yes, we will avail ourselves of the New Haven Line rail transportation from Grand Central. First, we will travel to Fairfield to visit with Joshua Cushman in the morning, and then on to New Haven to talk to Ernest Robinson."

"Yes, I noticed that the school had a forwarding address for Robinson after he left, or should I say asked to leave. You spoke to him? How did you get his number? And he's okay to see us?"

"Allow me to alter the sequence of your questions. You may have noted that on the contact information, Mr. Ernest Robinson is indicated as being a Junior. When I called the information operator, she informed me that there are numbers for three Ernest Robinsons in New Haven, one being an Ernest Robinson Senior on Goffe Street in the Dixwell section of the city, where a significant number of African-Americans dwell. I knew this fact from a newspaper article on New Haven I read in the *New York Times* a few years ago. I dialed the number, and I discovered Mr. Robinson is currently living with his parents. He was not at home, but his father was very gracious and contacted him at his Yale University work. He called back minutes later and asked if we could meet Ernest at the entrance to the Yale Library at 12:30 tomorrow. I readily agreed."

"I hope setting up the interview with Joshua Cushman was just as easy."

Grandfather drummed his fingers on his desk while answering me. "Joshua is an interesting subject for our investigation. His mother answered the phone when I called, and I had barely completed my introduction and asked to speak to Joshua when I heard an eruption of anger and demand for the phone. 'Are you a reporter?' a male voice screamed at me. 'It's been over three years, and I still have nothing to say to you people.'

"I quickly responded that I am not a reporter and that, as a private detective, I have been hired by the Gold family to solve Ori's murder. 'I am sure that you wish to help in this endeavor,' I quickly added, 'since I understand Ori was your friend.'

"Without hesitation, he snapped loudly, 'He was my friend. You can come if you can be here by 9:00. I can give you a few minutes, but just a few since I have much to cover tomorrow for my self-study program.'

"Again, I readily agreed, but we will need to meet by 7:00 at Grand Central Station to take the 7:15 to Fairfield, a total of 80 minutes. This schedule is acceptable to you?"

I nodded, but before I could say anything else, Grandfather continued: "In all fairness, I must disclose that while I will be resting this evening and gathering my strength for tomorrow, I have what may be a difficult assignment for you tonight."

"Okay, go on, Zaida," I said hesitatingly. What did he have in mind?

"I am very sorry to place this burden on you, but what must be done is best done without an elderly man with an accent in attendance. You see, I called the contact number for the Charnick family, and a housekeeper answered. Michael's parents were indeed away, and the housekeeper said that Michael no longer lived at that address.

"'Might you tell me how I may reach Michael?' I asked. After telling me that she could not give out that information without permission, I lied and claimed to be from the New York University European Studies Department and that Michael had applied for entry into the program indicating the Upper East side address and number

I had called. We very much wanted to interview Michael, and any delay could mean his being rejected.

"'Michael's not the bad kid most make him out to be,' the house-keeper said to me. 'He deserves a break, so I'm going to give you his address. I don't have a phone number for him.' To maximize the chances of Michael being there when you arrive, I would wait until about 8:00 this evening to go. I am sorry for your inconvenience.'"

Grandfather handed me a small piece of paper with an East 6th Street near Avenue A address written on it. I took it and looked right at Grandfather: "Don't worry about my inconvenience, but you lied to the woman! I don't know if I should be proud of you or stunned that I heard you lie for the first time that I know of."

Grandfather placed his face into his upwardly folded hands. "I choose to be proud of my action. Following my interpretation of Jewish teaching on the subject of deception, I believe a detective may lie if no one is harmed as in this case. And I hope your resultant interview of Michael will help us bring justice for Ori and peace to the Gold family."

Grandfather leaned back and closed his eyes. "And now, in the 30 minutes left before Sheldon Lachs' comes through the door, I would like to rest and gather my thoughts."

* * * *

While Grandfather retired into his thoughts, I headed over to Court Street and then a few blocks to Columbus Park. It was a warm fall day, and heeding what Grandfather had been drilling into me about premature conclusions, I needed some air to rid my head of its certainty that the trophy was the murder weapon. And I wasn't looking forward to talking to Michael Charnick in the evening. I didn't like the East Village scene, didn't feel comfortable with the type of people that lived there, and judged harshly its dissipated worldview. Part of me didn't want to find Michael when I came by, but a greater part of me said, "grow up and put in your heart and maximum effort for the Gold family's sake."

When I arrived back at Grandfather's office, it was 1:55. Sheldon Lachs was already sitting in the guest chair. He stood as I closed the door and turned to face me. He looked a bit heavier than the police picture from three years before. Stubble dotted his face, and he was wearing glasses. His eyes darted back and forth from me to Grandfather, who motioned him to be seated again.

"Sheldon, this is my grandson Joel Gordon, who is working with me on trying to determine who killed Ori Gold and why."

I greeted Sheldon and moved to stand near Grandfather so we could both be facing him.

Grandfather gestured toward me and then toward Sheldon, creating an enveloping arc. "Now that we are together, Sheldon, as difficult as we know it will be for you, could you please recount all you can remember about that terrible night."

Sheldon gripped the sides of the chair as he told of finding Ori in the morning after the murder. He spoke slowly, and what he told us matched very closely the version in the police report.

I don't know why it came into my head, but I asked: "What are you majoring in?" I noted that Grandfather slightly nodded his head in approval.

Sheldon answered eagerly, "I'm majoring in psychology. I want to understand people better—myself included."

"So you want to be a practicing psychologist?"

Sheldon smiled proudly. "Well, in a way. I'm planning to enter the seminary after graduation and become a pulpit rabbi."

Grandfather seemed satisfied to let me do the questioning, so I plowed ahead. "Thinking about everyone who was in the dorm that night, who had a motive and who do you think most likely killed Ori?"

Sheldon became agitated and looked to Grandfather as if seeking help from a benevolent presence. After a second, he said, "No one, I tell you. It must have been an outsider. That's what the school leadership thinks, and if not an outsider, then Ernest, the janitor. The police discovered he had a spotty record and was hiding from something, isn't that right?"

Perhaps I sensed vulnerability as my law school training in cross examination propelled me on. "And what would Ernest's motive have been?"

"Well, everyone knew that Ori came from a wealthy family, so perhaps robbery or anger that Ori wouldn't give him money, or God forbid something worse. I heard from the other boys that Ori sometimes visited the janitor in his basement apartment. Who knows what may have occurred!"

I scowled for a second, then hid it. "And the others, including Mrs. Wachter, might any of them had a motive for murder?"

"Mrs. Wachter!" Sheldon snapped. "How could you even bring yourself to ask? She's a nice old lady who could only hurt one of the boys by giving him too many sweet cookies. Ridiculous! And I know of no motive that Joshua, David, or Michael may have had to kill Ori."

"Okay, I retract my inclusion of Mrs. Wachter. Even if you know of no motive for those three boys, did any of them have a bad temper?"

Sheldon paused for a while before answering: "All three had bad tempers. But I can't believe one of them could strike down a fellow student. Ori was such a gentle person, kind to all three when others were not. No, it must have been an outsider."

When I discontinued my questioning and Sheldon said nothing further, Grandfather asked: "Sheldon, do you have a memory of the weather during the night of the murder?"

Sheldon hesitated: "I believe it was raining?"

"Yes, you are correct, and it was windy. I imagine your window, therefore, was closed to the elements?"

Sheldon sagged in the chair. "Yes, it was closed."

"Would you know when it had ceased raining?"

"Sometime before I woke to go to Sabbath morning prayers. It was bright and sunny by then."

"And you told the police you found the body at eleven o'clock that morning, and Ori's window was open?"

"Yes."

"And the police report indicates that Ori was murdered between one and five earlier that morning, yet there was no moisture in the room. That is odd for a windswept rain, is it not, Sheldon?"

Suddenly, Sheldon burst into intense sobbing which went on for over a minute. When he regained some composure, he spoke between sobs: "It was awful when I found him. The body lying on the floor, the pool of blood around his head. I knew he was dead, but you must believe me, I didn't kill him, and I don't know who did."

Grandfather retained his gentle voice. "Yes, Sheldon, perhaps you did not kill Ori, but you did open the window, did you not?"

It didn't take long until Sheldon nodded..

"But why?" I asked angrily.

Grandfather answered for Sheldon. "Because you were taught that, in the Jewish tradition, as soon as possible after someone dies in a room, one must open a window to at least symbolically allow the deceased's soul to depart. Am I correct?"

"Yes," Sheldon sobbed. "But I didn't kill him."

"Then, why'd you lie to the police?" I demanded.

Sheldon looked directly at me, and his voice rose. "I didn't lie to the police. They didn't ask me about the window, and I think I was in shock. I'm not so much sorry for opening the window—it was the right thing to do by Ori—but I'll always beat myself up for not being totally honest with the police." He looked at Grandfather: "Will I be in trouble?"

Grandfather stood as a signal that the interview was complete. "Our final report which the police will see will include your opening of the window and failing to inform the police of your action. I would speak to your parents and seek legal counsel. Is it possible you will be precluded from assuming a rabbinical position? I do not know. But we wish you an appropriate outcome."

* * * *

We spent the next hour reviewing what we had learned from Sheldon and strategizing how we would question David Spiller.

I was curious. "Zaida, you sort of led Sheldon to believe that you did not suspect him of the murder. Did you mean it, or was that just a ploy to make him let down his guard?"

Grandfather stroked his chin several times, and a glint appeared in his eyes. "Ah, you ask me the question because you have not seen any substantive evidence to clear Sheldon of the crime. I understand. He, like the other suspects, has no verified alibi that factually eliminates him from consideration. You are correct to question your old grandfather, but I tell you that no, it was not a ploy. My heart and my head tell me that Sheldon is not the murderer, but as I turn my attention elsewhere, I must also keep an open mind to being wrong."

"Too bland and too weak to be a killer," I judged out loud.

I didn't expect the somber look that came over Grandfather's face as he responded. "Never think that there is any human being who could be too bland or too weak to murder. Many of the people who destroyed millions of lives during the Holocaust were thought bland or weak, but certain times, certain circumstances, certain settings, certain opportunities, certain rages, create instances when those seemingly weak or bland are moved to kill. As for Sheldon, the police report, our talk with Mrs. Wachter, and Sheldon's own testimony inform us that even though he very much liked and admired Ori, he did not have much of a relationship with him. Call him what you wish, he did not possess any one or a confluence of factors for him to kill Ori, not even in a second of rage. Therefore, even as I keep an open mind, I do not believe Sheldon is the murderer."

Is there something in each of us that stands in the way of fully trusting another's intuitions even when they have been validated many times over? I had trouble accepting what was nothing more than Grandfather's hunch about Sheldon. But I respected him enough to let it go and move on to David Spiller.

It seems Grandfather also sensed it was time to focus on David. "Yoeli, I very much liked the paths you went down in questioning Sheldon. Your asking first about his intended major was a deft way to open a view into his mind. I would like you also to lead the interrogation of David."

"I'd like that," I answered quickly. "But why would it be a better approach than your taking the lead?"

"Ah, a fair question. Given my assessment of David's character as angry and arrogant, I believe he will not take questions from an old man seriously. But you, Yoeli, he will see you as someone of fairly similar age, as an opponent who is a combatant worth the battle and defeating, thus opening himself to error."

"Are you saying you think David is the killer, and he'll fight our proving it?"

"Not in the least. I have not drawn the slightest conclusion about David's guilt. Simply, I believe he has a constant anger that demands that he always be smarter, more successful, and more mastering. Thus, he perpetually is at war with others. For the next few minutes before he arrives, I will pray that I have from afar misinterpreted his personality."

* * * *

Grandfather wasn't wrong. David swept in 10 minutes late, looked at me, then at Grandfather, snickered, and demanded: "You're the private eyes that are now working the Ori Gold case? Seriously?"

Without being asked, David flopped down and sullenly acknowledged Grandfather's introductions before spitting out, "Okay, let's get it done. I need to be out of here within the hour."

He was about 5'5", and by the looks of his high heeled shoes, he was probably gaining an inch of lift. The top two buttons of his black shirt, satiny as in the police report picture, were unbuttoned, revealing both a Star of David hanging from a gold chain and that he was not wearing an undershirt. His face showed scattered acne scarring that I hadn't noticed in the police photo, and his pomaded, carefully-messy, swept-back hair promoted a James Dean type of appearance. A rebel without any obvious cause. I noted he was not wearing a skullcap. I quickly checked out his hands. Three years later, his fists were still clenched.

I moved behind Grandfather, and in a matter-of-fact voice, asked: "David, you're from the West Coast, if I remember correctly from the police report."

David seemed perplexed, as if he was expecting a more direct question about Ori's murder. "Yes, that's right," he said after a bit of hesitation. "What about it?"

I kept my tone neutral. "I guess you liked it so much out here during high school that you decided to stay on the East Coast for college?"

"That's not the reason I stayed," David snapped. "And I didn't exactly like going to MJA. I had a girlfriend who was going to attend a college in the City, so I applied to colleges in New York."

"Had?" I raised my eyebrows. "I take it you're no longer seeing that girl?"

"Nah, I moved on from her. Besides. I'm attending NYU, and next year I'm hoping to get into the Tisch Drama School. I'm taking acting lessons from a private drama coach. I want to become the first openly Jewish leading man. None of this Izzy Demsky hiding behind a Kirk Douglas name."

David paused for a moment and then glared at us. "I don't know why I'm telling you all this. What did you want to ask me about Ori's murder?"

I quickly looked at Grandfather who indicated with an upward movement of his eyes that I should continue. "In reading the police report, you stated that you saw Ori at 11:45 on the evening of his murder sitting in the hall reading a book. Do you know why was he reading in the hall instead of his room?"

David shook his head in disdain. "You'd think the brilliant police would've asked me that question, but they never did. The lights were timed to go off at 11:00 in our rooms because it was the Sabbath. I guess Ori wasn't ready to go to sleep yet."

"And why were you in the hall at that time?"

"I had gone to wash up in the hall bathroom. I remember, I snapped my towel at him to get his attention. When Ori was reading, he got really absorbed and tuned out everything around him."

I thought back to my times at sleepaway camps and how much I disliked the boys who would snap towels at others. There might have been an edge in my voice when I followed up: "And why was it so important for you to get Ori's attention?"

"I didn't say it was important. I had come over to see what he was reading, and when I saw it was *The Catcher in the Rye*, I just wanted to tell him my opinion. It's a stupid book in which nothing really happens and has that loser character, Holden Caulfield."

Here Grandfather interjected: "How, may I inquire, did Ori react to your assessment of the book?"

David kept looking at me when he answered: "Typical Ori. He said that since he hadn't finished the book yet, he would reserve judgment, but that when he was done, he would be glad to discuss it with me."

"And that was that?" I asked. "No further conversation?"

"Nope."

"And at any point that night, were you in Ori's room?"

"No, I wasn't one to hang with him. He seemed to have an open door to losers and misfits, not my kind of people. So I wouldn't go into his room."

"Losers and misfits such as Joshua Cushman or Michael Charnick?" I probed.

"Yep, they'd be the leaders of the band, especially the new Charnick kid, openly queer and, excuse the humor, fat and literally throwing his weight around."

"Do you think, then, Michael Charnick killed Ori?"

David did not hesitate. "Sure could have. Weird enough, with a wicked temper. But more likely he was killed by an outsider or the janitor."

Grandfather's strong voice took over the office. "David, the police report states that your fingerprints among others were found in Ori's room. So either that night or previously, you clearly were in his room."

The pique and arrogance that had dominated David's face until then disappeared replaced by the look of a frightened child who looked at me for assistance. I kept my gaze steady waiting for David to respond.

"Yes, I remember now, I was in his room once or twice. We were in the same trig class, and Ori was really good at it, and I came maybe twice to get some help with homework. That's it. No other times."

"David, David," Grandfather called out gently until David faced him. "Be assured that we trust your account of when you were in Ori's room. But during those times, did you happen to notice a trophy in the room?"

"You mean the baseball trophy? He kept it on the bookcase, I remember. He treasured that piece of metal."

"And did you ever touch the trophy? There are many fingerprints on it, but forensic technology is improving every day to be able to separate identities among the various prints."

David was vehement. "I never touched that stupid trophy, not once, not in the previous years or up to that night."

"Very well, David," Grandfather assured him and looked at me: "Mr. Gordon, do you have any other questions?"

"I do. David, you were on the same floor as Ori the night of the murder. Did you hear anything after you went back to your room?"

David shook his head. "No, I was way down the other end of the hall, and I sleep very deeply. Didn't hear a thing. That it? Can I go?"

Grandfather nodded.

When David left, he unclenched his fists only to open the door. He left without another word to us.

As soon as he was gone, I turned to Grandfather. "Okay, Zaida, what was that business about forensics getting better about finding fingerprints. You made that up, didn't you."

"Nuh, nuh," Grandfather bantered back. "Perhaps you should give forensic scientists more credit. I am sure they are daily advancing fingerprint detection techniques. But yes, you are correct, I did dissimulate to a degree to observe his reaction to be accused of wielding a murder weapon. It must have entered his mind. And may I inquire, Yoeli, what did you think of his reaction?"

I didn't have to think long. "I believe David was not lying when he said that he had never touched, what he called, 'the stupid trophy.' I know that he pictures himself a future great thespian, but from what I saw, I don't think he's a very good actor."

Grandfather openly smiled and swept his hands in all directions around the room. "Your detective skills are maturing very nicely, Yoeli. When I stop working, I may leave this splendid office to you, should you decide to leave PWR with its slightly higher earning powers."

I bowed my head toward Grandfather. "I am honored by your trust in me."

Grandfather's expression returned to seriousness. "As we are talking about fingerprints on the trophy, I would like to ask you to make the same point when you question Michael Charnick tonight."

I assured Grandfather I would.

* * * *

It was 7:30 and getting dark when I left Aliya and headed toward the address Grandfather gave me for Michael Charnick in the East Village. When I told her I would be walking to 6th and Avenue A from 14th Street where we lived, Aliya made me promise I wouldn't take the seedy and holdup prone Avenue A and instead go down 1st Avenue. Her request made sense to me, and besides, I wanted to take in more of the East Village as background for my visit. So I took 1st to 8th Street, which is St. Marks Place at that point, turned right, and headed west until I came to the old Electric Circus nightclub—New York's "pleasure dome"—between 2nd and 3rd Avenues.

I wanted to see what had become of that vaunted site of hedonism since its closing in 1971. It had been made famous by New York's daily newspapers, which constantly noted which celebrity actor, artist, or politician was there. Grandfather, one morning pointing to an above the fold story in the *Times* involving the club, volunteered: "Let us not imagine that what is pictured here is different from the cabaret settings in Berlin or Vienna between the Wars. A society's masking of its disenchantments through expressions of permissiveness, frivolity, and self-injury have been with us forever."

I had to see for myself, so one Sunday evening in March of 1970, just after I turned 21, I decided to go with a few friends to "check out the scene" at the club. After waiting in line for 45 minutes and making our way up the psychedelically adorned outside stairway, we entered the domed ball room. I looked up through the haze of cigarette and marijuana smoke and took in a vaulted ceiling lined with foam rubber and covered by vibrantly colored sheets. A mixed-media light show illuminated jugglers and trapeze artists. A din of music, loud talk, and laughter filled the ballroom, and straight ahead I could make out a giant bandstand with musicians, dancing girls, giant amps and speakers.

I lasted 30 minutes. After buying a beer for a dollar, I found myself separated from my friends and headed for a corner recess to observe the crowd. While the music pulsated, the mass of dancers gyrated endlessly to the same movements, their faces frozen in expressions of glee. Some were smoking cigarettes or pot, and along the walls or while sitting on sofas distributed about the room, others were dropping acid or engaging in various forms of sexual exhibitionism. Most women wore mini dresses or skirts, and a few exhibited see-through tops. The men varied in their attire from business suits to half open shirts and tight jeans, to motorcycle jackets and Converse high tops.

Contrasting emotions stirred me. On the one hand, my 21-year-old hormones raged attracted to the women urging me to abandon the standards of respect for others and myself that had been drilled into me growing up. But another part of me sensed that such abandonment would be exposing myself to the despair that Grandfather had described, concealed by the noise and smoke. When my friends found me, I said I wanted to leave. They didn't argue.

The next evening, 15 people were injured when a bomb exploded on the club's main dance floor. Grandfather, my mother, and I were in the living room listening to WINS 1010 when the news came over. My mother's face turned ashen. She was sitting on a sofa and sunk back. Grandfather came over and sat next to her. I understood. They both were upset about the injuries, but they were also reacting to my having been there just the previous evening. My mother especially, having survived the Holocaust in hiding as a child and the early death of my father, was constantly fearful for my safety.

"Yoeli," Grandfather spoke to me in a strong voice. "You will please come to services on Saturday and *bench gomel*."

He was referring to the traditional Jewish prayer where an individual expresses gratitude for being saved from a dangerous situation or journey. I didn't argue. So on the Sabbath, I recited: *Bless You Lord, ruler of the world, who rewards the undeserving with goodness and who has rewarded me with goodness.*

After the bombing, whether the Electric Circus deserved goodness or not, it stayed in business just another 16 months. It closed in August, 1971. Perhaps it was the bombing, or that the club had been just a fad that petered out, or perhaps the nightly despair had eaten away at the customers' psyches to the point where pleasures needed to be sought elsewhere.

As I looked at the boarded-up front of the club now, four years later, I wasn't surprised nothing had replaced it. An economic downturn had decimated the East Village with shuttered stores, boarded up fronts, broken windows, and rusting, ramshackle metal fire escapes dangling at various levels above the streets. Squatters who commonly referred to themselves as "artists" inhabited many of the abandoned apartments.

I turned back on St. Marks Place toward 2nd Avenue, made a right for two blocks to 6th Street, and then made a left east toward Avenue A. When I crossed 2nd Avenue, I could see the Fillmore East Theater, where the popular bands du jour had just a few years before played to sold-out crowds. Now its marquee had gashes in its white porcelain display and plastic sheeting on its top ledge. Its four-year lifespan overlapped with that of the Electric Circus.

As I approached 6th and Avenue A, I recorded more of the same blight, one tenement building after another, along with shabby stores such as Economy Loans, Plantation Drugs, Lucky Liquors, and Majestic Jewelers. Michael's residence, one building in from Avenue A, turned out to be a basement "apartment" below a shuttered storefront with a tattered sign that read **OCCUPANCY AVAILABLE** partially covering a weathered **TAQUI TACOS** and a caricatured figure of a Mexican man in a sombrero offering forth a plate of tacos, burritos, and enchiladas. Layers of sprayed graffiti filled almost every inch of the gray, begrimed corrugated steel shutter. Not one message was legible.

It was dark, and I made my way around a rickety aluminum railing down refuse laden stone stairs to a brown wooden door with a rusting lock and door knob. To my right was a small casement window protected by heavy iron bars. In case of an emergency, the window certainly couldn't be pushed out. Since the door opened to the inside of the unit, the apartment was a fire trap.

Music pulsated from within, and I could easily make out the heavy metal repetitive instrumentals of Iron Butterfly's *In a Gadda Da Vida*. I knew the song went on for around 20 minutes, and I hoped it was near its end. I rapped hard on the door and wondered if someone would hear. Seconds later, the door opened wide, and a rail-thin youth of around twenty in a tee-shirt with a *Grateful Dead* album emblazoned on it stared at me for a second. Grinning, he exclaimed: "You're not Monica!"

"No, I guess I'm not." I smiled back. "My name is Joel Gordon, and I'm here to see Michael Charnick. Is he here?"

He dramatically gesticulated for me to enter. "Come on in. I'm Dov, Mike's sometime roommate when I'm not staying at Monica's. She and me are not exactly getting along these days, and I'm expecting her to drop by for one of us to apologize to the other."

Before I moved past him, Dov turned and bellowed. "Hey Mike, some uptown looking guy here to see you."

I walked in and was greeted by stifling warmth and fetid air. The apartment was about the same size as our bedroom in Stuyvesant Town with a radiator beneath the casement window hissing hot air even though it was a warm October evening. To my right, a sink with a few dirty dishes in it, a pantry cabinet open and showing some plates, utensils, and canned and boxed goods, and then a miniature refrigerator. A grimy bathtub sat in the right corner, and behind it was a door I took to be for a bathroom, probably the size of a closet. Straight before me, along the far side of the room, was an unmade mattress and box spring on which Dov had sprawled. Black Sabbath and Led Zeppelin posters plastered the wall. To my left, a tattered red sofa with a white sheet and pillow strewn over it, and a side table on which a record player spun Iron Butterfly's challenge to understanding.

And almost filling the sofa, an immense person with sandy hair that tousled his forehead and sprawled over his neck and ears, glasses over small, wild eyes in a wide, beefy face. He wore a Lenny Bruce tee shirt over blue jeans and was holding an issue of *The Advocate*, a gay community newspaper.

He had to be Michael Charnick, and even though he did not rise from the sofa, I could tell that he had grown even bigger in the last three years.

I feared anger and perhaps violence, but he asked in a placid voice: "And you want to see me because?"

I introduced myself, explained why I had come and, preemptively, how I had obtained his address. Michael smirked and looked up at me. Luckily, the music had stopped and I could hear better.

"That was pretty smart of your grandfather to pretend he was NYU calling about admissions. Maria, my only advocate at what I used to call home, doesn't quite know or doesn't want to know how far from being able to graduate high school I've fallen. Since MJA, I've been to four New York City prep schools, and this term, I haven't bothered to attend any classes. Your grandfather and maybe you are probably a lot smarter than those cops who came around after the murder."

I was still not sure of my interview strategy, but I interrupted with: "And your parents, don't they know you're not attending classes?"

Michael sat up, and his voice rose: "My parents! No! They've had it with me, so they're happy to give me enough each month to pay for this place and keep me in food and joints. I guess I've seen to that, just like I made sure I'd get kicked out of MJA. I've got a terrible temper, but I let it loose even more when I was there for those few weeks so my parents would have to take me out. I am what they call in the Orthodox community OTD."

I must have looked confused because I had never heard the term before.

"Off the *derech*," he explained.

I knew a decent amount of Hebrew, so I asked: "derech, meaning the path?"

"Uh-huh, I am considered off the righteous path. There's a bunch of us, you know, a whole underground of us. Some are unhappy, some are angry, some—not me, although I've experimented—heavy drug or booze addicted. Some are queer, given up on or abandoned by parents."

Michael nodded toward the figure on the bed. "That's how I met Dov. Like I said, we find each other in the OTD underground."

Dov laughed and gave Michael a thumbs-up signal.

"So, are you really gay or was flaunting your propensity just an act to get you thrown out of MJA?"

"Propensity," Michael shouted, with wildness in his eyes flaring. "Meaning you think we can lean this way or that way, and if we wanted to, we could control the evil inclination to be gay? Yes, dammit, I am queer. It's who I am, not a propensity that lets me choose to be or not to be."

I held my ground and asked: "Were you attracted to Ori?"

Michael looked at me as if I were an idiot, and his voice settled down when he answered: "So what you're asking me is if I had an unmanageable crush on Ori, that on the night he was murdered I came to his room, made a pass at him, and when he said no, I became furious and killed him. Isn't that right?"

"Yes," I answered without hesitation. If I were to obtain any meaningful information, my honesty with Michael had to be established.

Michael relaxed, his body sank back, and his voice quieted. "Okay, then. In a way, you've got me pegged right. In a moment of rage, I could probably kill someone. But not because I made a pass at a guy, and he said no. Also, don't you think we can tell if someone's queer or not? I don't need the evidence of the wedding ring on your finger to know that you're not gay."

"And Ori, was he gay?"

Michael shook his head vehemently, and a momentary serenity took over his expression. "No, Ori wasn't gay, but I liked him—even in the few weeks we were in that dorm—more than anyone else I ever met. Even more than anyone I had sex with."

I relaxed a bit. This behemoth of a boy was a terribly troubled child. Tears streamed out of Michael's eyes down his cheeks. He made no attempt to wipe them away.

"What made Ori so special for you?" I asked gently.

Michael looked beyond me as if he were picturing Ori. "Since I was little, I sensed that just about everybody who looked at me was judging me. But not Ori. From his first hello, he was naturally friendly. I didn't feel like a freak, a deviant, a pity case, a salvage challenge—just myself, problems and all. He knew I was putting on the act to get out of MJA. He didn't condemn it or say stupid things like 'I'm sure if you sat down with your parents and explained how you feel, they would understand.' What BS! He would listen, and I knew he understood my desperation and pain. That was enough."

Then I asked. "Then you didn't hit him with the baseball trophy in his room that now has gone missing? Could you look at me and tell me that?"

Once again, the wildness in Michael's eyes blazed in all directions. He said nothing for a while, and even though I felt threatened, I was determined to wait him out. Finally, he answered in almost a whisper: "I did not wish to kill Ori, with or without the trophy."

"But you remember that Ori had a baseball trophy in his room?"

Again, Michael paused for a while before responding. "Yeah, maybe, I think so. I didn't hang out in his room that often."

I remembered Grandfather's instructions, so almost verbatim I asked: "Did you ever touch the trophy? There would be a bunch of fingerprints on it, but forensic technology is improving every day to be able to separate identities among the various prints."

Michael pushed slightly forward and spat out: "Yeah, I picked it up once or twice to look at it. So what?"

Better to not push the trophy importance any further with Michael. I switched focus.

"And you didn't see him at all the night of the murder?"

Michael looked uncomfortable but answered quickly. "Uh-uh, like I told the police, I ate in my room that night. What I didn't tell them is that I wanted to be alone and smoke weed."

"Then who do you think killed Ori?"

He did not stop to ponder my question. "Wasn't it an outsider? That's what I heard. And if not, probably the janitor, right?"

I was struck by how easily he bought into the school's narrative. I wasn't going to share why it could not have been an outsider, and as for the janitor, I was reserving judgment until after our visit to New Haven the next day. But I wasn't going to let it go at that. I wanted to hear Michael's reaction to the other suspects.

"What about David Spiller, might he have killed Ori?"

Michael snorted with contempt and let out an expletive filled invective followed by: "That pompous ass! All he did was sit in the phone booth talking to nobody and pretending it was one of his many girlfriends! I really wanted an opportunity to get into a fight with him and see him snivel. He might try to swat a fly, but he didn't have it in him to go after anyone else in the dorm, especially someone bigger and stronger, like Ori."

"And Sheldon Lachs?"

The flaring ceased as he replied mildly: "Sheldon Lachs, oh what a righteous *tzaddik*. He sincerely believed that he could save me. He liked to call me into his room and ask me how I am, then read me cornball quotes from religious sources and mumbo jumbo from psychological sources, like he could do something about my rage, put an end to my deviant desires, and make me not me. If Spiller might swat a fly, Sheldon couldn't kill a fly, let alone Ori. If you're in any way a smart detective, and I'm guessing you might already have spoken to Sheldon, why would he? What, Mr. Joel Watson or whatever your last name is, would be his motive?"

Michael's words stung, but I refused to be provoked. "And Joshua Cushman?"

Michael's face hardened and then went deadpan, emotionless. "You know, if I had any competition for being the biggest weirdo at MJA, it was Cushman. He was out in right field with his political views. I really think he hated anyone who didn't agree with him as opposed to my hating myself and taking it out on others. Stupid, but if I had anything in common with the others at school, it was in hating Cushman. In one of my rages, I could have killed him. He's the one who should be dead, not Ori."

I was unsettled by Michael's response, but didn't know what else to ask about Cushman. So I went on: "Okay, and the janitor, Ernest Robinson?"

Michael's voice took on more life as he leaned forward. "Not a clue. I'd seen him around the building, but we never said a word to each other. It was well known that Ori came from money, and maybe the janitor thought he had cash in his room. But a lot of the kids there came from money, so I don't know."

Michael suddenly rose from the sofa and nodded his head toward the bathroom. "If that's it, I gotta go in there."

"Almost," I answered quickly trying to keep his attention. "What about Mrs. Wachter?"

Michael started moving away and replied tartly: "That judgmental clucking old lady! Yeah right!" He moved into the bathroom and closed the door.

I didn't mind that the interview was over. I was hot, sweaty, in need of a shower and change of clothes. I said goodbye to Dov and headed to the door. But when I opened it, I almost bowled over a girl wearing the customary uniform of a mini dress, leather jacket, and western straw hat with braided leather bands.

"Hi, Monica," I said. "Are you also OTD?"

She gave me a quizzical look, and I walked away. Moments later, I berated myself for my smarmy words. I had more growing up to do.

Thursday, October 17, 1974.

I never knew my grandfather to be late, and sure enough, there he was, waiting for me under the Clock at Grand Central Station, and I had arrived 10 minutes early.

"Good morning, Yoeli." He gave me a hug, as he did each morning unless I met him at his office, his place of business. He was wearing his usual attire of a dated brown suit with dark trousers, a lighter brown V-necked sweater over a white shirt and tie. His brown fedora hat fit snugly on his head. "I have already purchased our tickets to Fairfield, then to New Haven, and return trip. I hope you have slept well. We have two critical interviews and much thinking to absorb us until evening."

I had slept well enough after showering off my interview with Michael Charnick. It wasn't just the grime that enveloped me walking around the East Village, or the sweat my body endured in that stifling hot apartment, or the cigarette and marijuana smell that infiltrated my clothes. More so, I needed to rid my mind of wanting Michael Charnick, whom I saw as an oafish, churlish, contemptuous, and threatening teenager, to be Ori's killer. I didn't like the way Michael made me feel, and I resented him for it. But stripped of these emotions, something in me said Michael didn't do it.

After talking non-stop to Aliya for an hour about the case and my visit, I realized that the instinctual is often hard to explain. Instead, I played a logic hand. "After all," I insisted strongly, "What motive did Michael have to kill Ori?"

"Did he need a motive?" Aliya answered. "Michael admitted he easily flies into rages. Does a person like that really need a motive?"

She was right, but I wouldn't waver from my belief that Michael was not the killer. I recalled that Grandfather had once lectured me about trusting my instincts, which turned out to be the key to solving a kidnapping and saving a little boy's life. So I said:

"My gut tells me Michael didn't do it, even though everything else says so far he is the most likely suspect. But Grandfather and I have two more interviews tomorrow, and I have to be at Grand Central really early. So to bed we go, and I hope that I don't sleep on it."

As soon as we were seated in the train, I wanted to tell Grandfather about my visit to Michael Charnick. But Grandfather gently put up his hand and said:

"Yoeli, if you will allow me a few moments of quiet so that I may establish my morning's mental and physical equilibrium, I would be appreciative. I'm afraid my age slows my abilities somewhat."

So we sat in silence, with Grandfather closing his eyes as the train made its way to the Harlem 125th Street Station, then into the Bronx and through the burgeoning Eastern portion of Westchester County. I was becoming impatient, but just as we were crossing into Connecticut, Grandfather sat straight up and with a new-found vigor turned to me:

"Nuh, what do you have to tell me. I want to hear as nearly verbatim as possible about your conversation with Michael."

With difficulty, I turned my mind as well as I could to tape recorder mode. I started from the moment I entered Michael's hole-of an apartment to when I departed. I left out my snarky comment to Monica.

Grandfather listened intently and at the end asked me three questions.

"I would like you to remember as precisely as it is possible for you. Did Michael say, 'I did not kill Ori' or 'I did not wish to kill Ori?'"

I didn't hesitate. "'I did not wish to kill Ori.' Why Zaida?"

"For now, it is something for me to digest. Again, I would like you to remember as precisely as it is possible for you. Did Michael say, 'I did not wish to kill Ori, with or without the trophy.' Or did he say, 'I did not wish to kill Ori, with or without a trophy.' There is an important difference in the calculation of his guilt in considering his use of *the* or *a* as the article before 'trophy.' Do you understand why?"

I thought for a moment, and I saw where Grandfather was going. "If he used *a*, then it's more of a reference to a vague trophy. But if he used *the*, there's something specific in his mind. He's well aware of the trophy, and he's trying to hide it for some reason. And I'm pretty sure he said 'the trophy.' Am I getting it, Zaida?"

Grandfather smiled. "Yes, precisely. Are you sure you will not leave your firm to join me as a partner in my noble profession?"

I laughed and continued with my memories of the interview until Grandfather again stopped me.

"Yoeli, excuse me, but I must know for certain. Michael said about Joshua Cushman, 'He's the one who should be dead, not Ori.' Those were his exact words?"

The tape replayed in my mind. "Yes, those were his exact words. Why?"

Grandfather drummed his fingers on his seat armrest. That was always a sign that he was locked onto a thought that needed rapid deliberation. But I was disappointed when he said: "If you will give me leeway for a while to assimilate this information, I would be grateful. I am not at this moment ready to present the picture that is taking shape in my mind."

I did not press Grandfather. Time passed, and I looked up and noted that we were ten minutes from the Fairfield station. Grandfather took leave for the restroom, and when he returned, he sat and put a hand on my shoulder.

"Tell me please what you think of Michael as a suspect, keeping in mind that we have much more to discover from our nearing interviews."

Nothing had changed in my mind from the previous evening. So I repeated my conclusion as to his innocence to Grandfather.

From the time I was a child, I had gotten used to waiting for Grandfather to respond after I spoke. If I tried to rush him, he would softly say, "Shh, shh, Yoeli, I am considering what you just imparted to me." Finally, after what seemed much longer but really was no more than two minutes, Grandfather said:

"Inside that angry and offensive front, there is a lonely and frightened little boy who has been mistreated all of his life. I believe in the three weeks he had been at the school, Michael had become very fond of Ori and would have been more likely to protect than harm him. But let us both suspend our conclusions for the moment as we seem to be arriving at our first stop."

Indeed we were. "Fairfield, Fairfield," a conductor called out. "Exit on your right and watch your step."

* * * *

Perhaps overly solicitous, I helped Grandfather off the train to the platform. He didn't seem to mind. The platform was deserted, but as the train pulled away, we could see activity across the tracks with the last few rush-hour travelers heading toward New York City.

Two other passengers had disembarked with us, college students wearing navy-blue blazers with the Fairfield College seal emblazoned on the front pocket. A car with a man in a black shirt and white clerical collar was waiting for them.

"Fairfield College," Grandfather remarked, "is a fine Jesuit institution with rigorous attention paid to the classics and Catholic instruction." The breadth of Grandfather's knowledge regularly amazed me, but even more so when he asked:

"Did you see the school's motto that circled the seal?"

"No." How had Grandfather, with his vision beginning to fail, made it out?

"It says, *Per Fidem Ad Plenam Veritatem*. Do you know its meaning?"

I stubbornly hadn't taken Latin in high school, resisting Grandfather's coaxing, but the French I had learned gave me some insight. "Something about faith and truth?"

"Very good, Yoeli. *Through Faith to Full Truth*. It is a very noble yet perhaps overly ambitious proclamation, is it not? Besides facts, rationality, instincts, and even faithfulness, my private detective profession examines irrationality, contradictions, and distortions which strive within a person and may get in the way of discovering a 'full truth.' Thus our challenge in solving Ori's murder. I think you understand, yes?"

I never liked being disingenuous with Grandfather, so I couldn't just reply "Yep, I think I do," when I didn't. I had motioned for a cab, so I was glad when it pulled up and I asked:

"Zaida, do you have Joshua Cushman's address?"

The cab was a beat-up Dodge Dart with white wheels and no seatbelts, and it was driven by a white haired man who looked at least 10 years older than Grandfather. A handwritten paper taped to the front glove compartment read: **HI—MY NAME IS CALEB.** When

Grandfather gave the address on Montauk Street, which turned out to be three miles north of the train station. The driver eased the car out of the parking lot into traffic

"That's the Cushman house," he said, looking at us in the rearview mirror. "Would you be family visiting?"

"No, we are not family," Grandfather replied, looking past Caleb to the road ahead. I was sure Grandfather was trying to get Caleb to turn his head back to his driving task. "We are here on business. You are familiar with the Cushmans?"

"Heck yes," Caleb answered looking at the road and turning his head back to us. "I drove their kid home from the train station many times when he was in school in New York."

"I take it you refer to Joshua? A nice boy, yes?" Grandfather probed.

Caleb's voice rose. "Well, I'm not about to take away any man's opinion, but that ain't mine. Never knew how he'd be when he got into my cab. Sometimes he wouldn't say a word, and I'd look at him in the mirror and see him stewing about something, looking mad as hell with them beetle brows narrowed together, like he wanted to kill somebody.

"And other times, he'd be yammerin' a mile a minute about communists and how American values were being rejected, and the stupid people his age who only had the opposite sex on their minds and—what was that word he used?—oh yeah, 'frivolity' and such. Then he'd catch his breath, and that look of being ready to kill someone would be back on his face."

"You haven't driven him lately?" I asked.

"That's right, and not sorry about it either. Business is good enough, even with things costing more each day than the last. Like I said, he finished his schooling in New York last year, and I heard he turned down Yale to go to the community college in town. Real strange kid."

Caleb swung hard right onto Montauk Street, and seconds later we were at the Cushman house. I paid Caleb as Grandfather asked if he could pick us up in an hour to take us back to the train station.

"Sure will, gents. At 10:00 on the nose, I'll be here."

As the cab pulled away, I asked. "Zaida, you really want to ride with him again? He really made me nervous always looking back at us and not at the road."

"Yes, I do Yoeli. He already told us a good deal about Joshua. Who knows what else we may learn from him?"

The Cushman home was a well-kept white, old colonial with a white picket fence that set off a straight line, immaculately clean stone walkway to a one-step up portico. Two well-trimmed Japanese maples in containers sat on each side of the portico, with fir, nandina, and cypress plantings equally spaced to the left and right.

I rang the doorbell, which was quickly answered by a middle-aged woman in a housedress and apron. She looked frazzled and immediately blurted out:

"You are the private detectives Joshua said to expect. I am his mother, Mrs. Cushman. My husband, Mr. Cushman, is at his office in town. He is an insurance agent."

Fidgeting with her hands, she motioned us into the foyer and pointed toward an opening on the left that appeared to be a sun room. "Joshua is waiting for you in there. Please go in. I have much to do."

As we entered, I could see Joshua sitting with his back to us as he pecked at a manual typewriter with two index fingers. He was wearing a white shirt and tie along with a mustard-colored cardigan sweater. A white crocheted skullcap covered his close-cropped, coarse hair. He struck each typewriter key with force and waited for the deadening thud on paper before hitting the next key. He must have known that we had entered, but he did not turn in his swivel chair until Grandfather said:

"Good morning, Joshua, I am Frank Wolf with my associate Joel Gordon. We have an appointment to discuss with you the Ori Gold murder case."

I glanced around the room. It was Spartan but spacious. Besides the typewriter, the desk held a black stapler, six sharpened pencils lined up one next to each other, a large ballpoint pen that I could easily read as a Sheaffer, a rolodex, and a four-tier file tray labeled PAPER, IN, OUT, and TO DO. A pair of three-drawer filing cabinets, one labeled A to M and the other N to Z, stood like sentries to each side of the window. Next to them were gray metal bookcases filled with neatly shelved books.

Along the walls hung three large, framed photos. One I identified as that of Barry Goldwater. To its right was a picture of a long-faced man in a suit with large ears, small pursed lips, and balding white hair. I did not recognize him. The third picture held my gaze for a moment. It was an enlarged photo of a man in a buttoned, pinstripe double-breasted suit holding a racket at a ping-pong table. I guessed it was from before World War II. Did they really play ping-pong in a suit and tie back then?

One other item caught my attention. Above the window we were facing hung a satin cloth with black stitching that read **EXTREMISM IN THE DEFENSE OF LIBERTY IS NO VICE**. I recognized those words from one of Barry Goldwater's speeches when he ran for president in 1964.

What I missed until I saw Joshua reaching for it on the desk to the right of the typewriter was a small leather case. Before Joshua reacted to Grandfather's greeting, he reached for the case, carefully unzipped it, and extracted a ping-pong racket. The grip was significantly worn.

"Yes," Joshua answered. He looked at Grandfather and me, then at his watch, all the while moving the racket back and forth with his right hand. "It is now 9:05. I can give you until 9:45, when I must transition to my economics course reading."

He did not ask us to sit as there were no other chairs in the room nor to move to another area of the house.

Grandfather and I hadn't discussed our interview approach, so I dove in with a question that circled our objective while satisfying my curiosity.

"Who is the man?" I asked pointing to the picture to the right of Goldwater.

As Joshua turned burning eyes on me while flicking the racket more repeatedly, Grandfather addressed my question.

"He is, I believe, Mr. Robert W. Welch, the founder of the John Birch Society. Am I possibly correct, Joshua?"

Joshua's eyes softened, and his hand motions momentarily subsided. "Yes, you are correct."

Grandfather's face broke into a relaxed smile as if he were having a conversation with a friend. "And the gentleman simulating the play of table tennis is Mr. Viktor Barna,— some time, I would surmise, between 1932 and 1935, when he won the world championships? Might I also be correct?"

Joshua leaned toward Grandfather with an expression of admiration and suspicion. "Yes, not many people would recognize him. Are you a table-tennis follower?"

"I was at one time in my life very much a follower of the sport, and if I may say, also adept at its play. As for Mr. Barna, I traveled in 1932 with my wife and young daughter to Prague to watch the matches at which he won a gold medal. It was a wonderful experience. Do you know who won the Silver medal?"

Joshua's expression showed contempt. "Of course I do. Miklos Szabados. He lost in the final to Viktor Barna in five sets."

"Yes, Joshua. Miklos Szabados in five sets. Unfortunately, I could not watch the final match because it was on the Sabbath. And you yourself, you are an accomplished player?"

"I do all right." Joshua smiled. "I drive my opponents crazy by playing constant defense. When they can't get a ball past me, it infuriates them, and they lose track of the objective of the exchange—which is to return the ball to the other side of the table, not smash my head in. The more they are enraged, the more frequent their unforced errors and my utter satisfaction."

Joshua laughed, looking from Grandfather to me for approval.

"A well calculated strategy," Grandfather replied. I could tell he was giving Joshua what he sought. "And if we may, with the time left, ask you about the night of Ori's murder?"

Joshua's wrist flicked the racket in our direction. "Ask away. As I said, I have until 9:45."

I was guessing that Grandfather was setting up a good versus bad cop dynamic. But before I started in, I had again to deal with my being flabbergasted. My grandfather was once a good table tennis player!. Did I know so little about this man that I loved who when I was born was already greying and moving slowly? But I had my task before me.

"The police statement says you had dinner that night with Ori Gold but did not see him after you went to your room, he on the second floor, and you on the third. Do you remember what you spoke about during dinner?"

Joshua gave me a look of incredulity. "What we talked about! What difference does it make what we talked about!"

Gently, Grandfather said: "If you could possibly try to answer the question, it might be of assistance to our investigation. It very well may go towards our understanding what was in Ori's mind that evening that may have provoked the murder."

Joshua remained silent for a while before angrily answering. "There was nothing in his mind that night or any night to provoke murder. We probably discussed politics or the Talmud lessons of the previous week. I was skipped into a higher level that year and was in his class. Or, as I often did, I tried to make him see how his naiveté interfered with understanding things."

For a moment, Joshua stared into space and his hand movement stopped. "And he probably said it was the Sabbath, and he didn't want to argue."

"And when he said such a thing?" Grandfather inquired. "How did it cause you to feel?"

"Made me want to get through to him even more. Because he was smart and decent, not like the other cretins in the dorm, I'd become so frustrated that I wasn't getting through."

I quickly asked, "Why were you still in the dorms that weekend? Most of your classmates had already gone home for the holiday."

"I always complete my assignments early. I remember distinctly I had a biology paper due two weeks later on Mendelian genetics, and I wanted to do research at the nearby university library on Sunday morning and then take the train home in the early afternoon. Didn't work out, since the police pestered me with the same questions over and over Sunday morning."

"If I may, Joshua," Grandfather said, "you stated that you did not see Ori after dinner that night. But did you see any of the others who were present in the dormitory? For instant, Sheldon Lachs?"

Joshua did not hesitate. "Didn't see him. He was the RA that year and lived on the first floor. I was on the third. Didn't lay eyes on him until I returned from services and saw the hubbub. That was in the morning after he found the body."

"And David Spiller?" I asked in a harder tone.

The frequency of Joshua's right wrist motions with the racket increased. "I didn't see him, and I would have made every effort to avoid seeing him. What a disgusting and demented person he was! His sewer-infested mind was taken with his good looks and fake sexual exploits."

"Oh?" I said.

He shrugged. "Everyone knew he faked speaking to girls in the phone booth. Even Ori."

"How are you certain that Ori knew?" I demanded.

"Easy. A week before the murder, I saw David confronting Ori. He grabbed Ori's shirt, and Ori shoved him away. David shouted at him, 'You think I was talking to myself? I'm telling you, the phone was working while I was on it. Something must have happened when I got off and you tried your call.'"

"And how then did this confrontation end?" Grandfather asked very softly.

Joshua's hand motion stopped. "In classic Ori fashion. 'Of course I don't believe you were talking to yourself,' Ori said. 'Phone problems can happen at any time.' That calmed David down."

"And that was the end?" Grandfather asked.

"Yes, but as he left, David glared at Ori and said, 'That's right, but if I hear you're telling others I'm a liar, I'll be coming after you.' There you go, I think you should consider David Spiller your prime suspect."

"Thank you, Joshua," Grandfather said opening his palms toward him. "The investigation is at this point very open, and we welcome your information and hypotheses. In your opinion, are there other suspects? For instance, the janitor, Ernest Robinson, was under suspicion."

"Sure," Joshua quickly responded. "I never said a word to him, but he was a low-level worker. Maybe he thought there was money in Ori's room. Could have been him."

"And what about Mrs. Wachter?" I threw in.

"Oh, please don't insult me," Joshua flicked the racket toward me. "Well meaning old lady but useless." He glanced at his watch. "Not much time left. Who else?"

"From what you said about Sheldon Lachs, I'm guessing you don't think he was the murderer?"

Joshua nodded. "No way."

"But what about Michael Charnick?"

Joshua's wrist flared back and forth as he snapped: "What about him!"

"Do you think Michael murdered Ori?" I asked, my voice steady.

Joshua turned his gaze above our heads. "He could have, yes, his perverted kind could have killed Ori. In my mind, I could see it happening. Ori constantly let him into his room. He was kind to Michael. But that's how kindness often gets repaid, with a smack to the head."

"Yes, Joshua," Grandfather replied, his voice somber. "I have also seen kindness repaid in that fashion."

Grandfather then addressed me. "Joel, do I remember correctly that as Joshua just stated, the police report indicates that Ori died from a blow to the head?"

I was certain Grandfather knew the answer and had asked for effect. I also noticed that Joshua had become quiet, his hand still, and a frightened look had come into his eyes. So I played my role and answered matter-of-factly.

"Yes, that's what the police report says."

"And isn't that what was in the papers?" Joshua blurted. He had regained his composure, the wrist flicking again as he added: "Anything else? Not much time left."

"Two last questions, please," Grandfather requested. "First, we understand that you also were often in Ori's room, and justifiably so, as you had at least one class together. Therefore, you must remember the baseball trophy Ori treasured and kept on the nightstand besides his bed. Was it there the last time you were in the room?"

Joshua answered quickly. "I don't know anything about a baseball trophy. I wouldn't have noticed. I don't follow those mindless games. Table Tennis is the only sport of substance, and Ori wasn't very good at it."

"Good, thank you. And my final question." Grandfather smiled at Joshua: "I am surprised that a person of your obvious intellectual capacity is attending the community college and not a more prestigious institution. Might I inquire why?"

Joshua had no trouble with the question, answering with a speech-worthy flourish and a grand wave of the racket: "I was accepted at Yale and asked for a deferment to take my first two years at the community college. Yale agreed. In this way, I save a good deal of money, I can combine my own curriculum with the low level demands of the community college courses, and I don't have to sit with the egotistical, pleasure-seeking barbarians who constitute the freshman and sophomore classes at the University. By my junior year, when I enter Yale, in the classes I choose to take, I hope to be free of the worst morons. Not all of them, but I hope many."

Joshua swiveled his chair back to face his desk and placed his racket carefully into its cover. Without looking back at us, he said slowly: "It's now 9:50 and time for our meeting to end. I am five minutes late on my schedule. Please let yourself out."

* * * *

Caleb was already waiting for us as we left the house. We had not encountered Mrs. Cushman.

"We will let the cab driver talk for our 10 minute drive to the Fairfield train station," Grandfather advised. "I know that there is much to discuss regarding our interview of Joshua. But we will have much opportunity to exchange thoughts as we wait for the New Haven train to arrive at 10:21 and during our 45 minute trip."

"Just one question, Zaida," I insisted as we walked to the curb where the cab was idling. "Did ping-pong players really wear suits and ties during games back in the 1930s?"

"No Yoeli, they did not," Grandfather answered waiting for me to open the cab door. "They wore comfortable short-sleeve shirts, slacks, and canvas shoes. Mr. Barna appearing in a suit, I am sure, was for photographic effect popular at that time."

Before entering the cab, Grandfather looked up at me and added: "Please do not refer to the sport as ping-pong. Its proper name is table tennis. Had you used that belittling term in Joshua's presence, his predictable eruption might have driven us from the house."

Caleb was not the chatterbox who drove us to the Cushman residence and for the most part kept his eyes on the road except to look back and hand me a business card: "Be sure to ask for me next time you're in town."

I assured him we would, and we exited the cab in front of the Fairfield train station, a large hut like structure with an interior furnished with a series of once-polished wooden benches with armrests, most speckled with gum residue and food or beverage splatters. The station was deserted except for a solitary sales window, a young man behind it smoking even though a sign above his window read: **AS OF OCTOBER 1, 1974, NO SMOKING ALLOWED IN WAITING ROOM.** He glanced up from the newspaper he was reading and languidly looked back down when he realized we were not in need of a ticket purchase.

We made our way to one of the cleaner benches, and Grandfather excused himself to use the restroom. I watched his slow and slightly stooped walk and chided myself for being oblivious to how much he had aged as I had grown into my adulthood. And that he was once a vigorous young man, a nimble tennis table player, dominated my saddened reverie until he returned.

"Nuh, Yoeli," Grandfather roused me back to our task, "You have some observances to share with me?"

"Well," I began, "I still say I would not have wanted to be his roommate."

"Come, come, Yoeli," Grandfather chided. "From a private detective trying to solve a murder case, you are capable of more refined observations."

That stung, but I quickly regrouped. "Okay, he is a very angry person, haughty, opinionated, intolerant, and I believe capable of violence. I don't know what type of upbringing he had, but something went wrong along the way."

"I agree with all of your assessments, but if I may digress just for a moment on your last comment, I do not believe that Joshua's upbringing by his parents contributed to what we summarize as his offensive character. I have on previous occasions mentioned to you that when I was a young man in the 1920s, the most gripping news of that decade to me was the Leopold and Loeb murder case in Chicago. Here we had the tragedy of two wealthy boys who committed a horrible murder of a young boy. They were refined, well-educated, and cared for by their parents. I then began to conclude that how a person is brought up contributes to the evolving personality, but at core we are all the person we were when we were born.

"I agree that Joshua as you put it is angry, haughty, opinionated, and intolerant, but I strongly suspect he has been that way since birth. But you also state that he is capable of violence. Why so, Yoeli?"

Why is it that what we often feel is so obvious is also so difficult to explain to others? I fumbled for a response: "Well, he's angry, he hates people, and I think he's capable of wishing people dead."

"Again, Yoeli, I believe you to be correct. But was he angry with Ori? Do you believe he wanted to hurt Ori?"

I scratched my head. Could I point to any reason for Joshua to want to hurt Ori? Mrs. Wachter had said Ori often asked Joshua to leave the room so he could study. But that would hardly spur someone to murder. Finally, I shook my head.

Grandfather said, "Let us hold that question for future scrutiny. But tell me, what did you think of his hand motions?"

"You mean the way he flicked the racket back and forth when he spoke?"

"Yes, exactly. What did you notice besides the constant wrist motion?"

I hesitated. Grandfather must have seen something I had missed. I tried to freeze my memory on Joshua's hands as he spoke. One frame came to mind.

"Zaida, do I recall correctly, that when he was talking about Ori, his flicking motion with the racket stopped?"

Grandfather smiled broadly. "Very good Yoeli, you are exactly correct. The motions did cease when he talked about Ori. And what else?"

"With everyone else, including us, he kept flicking, didn't he?"

"Yes, but was there anything different when he spoke of Michael Charnick?"

I answered quickly. "Yes, he was agitated, and so were his hand motions."

"Yes, yes, again, but perhaps as you are not a table tennis maven, you might have missed the following. Most of the time Joshua held the racket in a back-hand position, emulating the style and angle of Viktor Barna's defensive stance. But when he spoke of Michael Charnick, he turned the racket into a forehand position, Barna's angle for executing a decisive smash and slashing spin for a point."

"So you're saying that Joshua wanted to harm Michael! But— but—it's Ori who's dead, and Joshua was calm when discussing Ori, suggesting he would not have wanted to harm him. There remains no apparent motive, and no apparent outrage for why Joshua would want to kill Ori. So, I'm confused."

"Yoeli, let us not feel sorry for ourselves. You describe the conundrum well, and it is for such situations that we must use our critical analyses skills to unravel the riddle."

Our discussion ended at this point as the clerk called out: "New Haven, New Haven. Exit on your right and watch your step."

* * * *

"Madam, could you please drive us to the Yale University Library," Grandfather requested of the cabbie outside of the New Haven station.

"Which one Gramps?" she responded looking back at us. "There are a couple."

The cabbie was in her forties, with obviously dyed blond hair. I didn't like her. It had nothing to do with the way she looked nor the cigarette smoke on her breath. I hated when my grandfather was referred to as "Gramps," or any version of "Old Man." And especially the same day I had watched his slow movement toward the restroom at the Fairfield station. He was my grandfather who cheerily helped manage my infant awakenings, terrible twos and terrible other ages including my teenage years and never too busy or too tired for me. There had been several instances when I had noted his slowed gait or need to close his eyes in the middle of the day, but I drove that image from my mind. Zaida wasn't old, and any such mention I would take as personal denigration.

Grandfather didn't seem phased by the cabbie's lack of class. "To the Sterling Library, please."

"You got it Gramps."

I was glad the cabbie said nothing further during our short ride. At least she kept her eyes on the road.

As soon as we got out of the cab, I knew we weren't in provincial Brooklyn, nor in skyscraper Manhattan, nor in cookie-cutter suburbia. I had never been out of the New York environs, and while a multitude of students in modern garb were milling about and passing, I gazed up at the Gothic Revival library and the surrounding buildings in the university's central quadrangle with awe. I might have been in thirteenth-century Europe. I had only seen buildings like these in books, and I might have been standing before the Notre Dame cathedral in Paris or in Canterbury, England.

The front presented two arched doors of wood and stained glass. Above the doorway were sculpted representations of various ancient civilizations. As I leaned back, taking in the majestic height of the building with its thirteen oblong stained-glass windows, I estimated the library to be 14 or 15 stories high. Asking leave of Grandfather for a few minutes, I circled around the library's perimeter and approximated it to be a city block long.

It was 11:30, and we still had another hour until we were to meet Ernest Robinson. Grandfather wanted to tour the library, but this time I played the parent and insisted we eat first at a stone bench on the side of the steps leading up to the library doors. The day was sunny with temperatures in the mid 60s, perfect weather to eat our lunch outside. I opened the backpack that Grandfather had given me at Grand Central. It contained thermoses with tea and egg salad sandwiches, each with differing amounts of mayo as I liked it heavy and Grandfather liked it light. That was my mother. Of course, she had also included her sponge cake for dessert.

While we ate, Grandfather stared at the library facade and commented on the similarities of the structure to St. Stephen's in the Vienna of his youth. He said it was one of the earliest Gothic cathedrals. Grandfather seemed to remember every nook and cranny. Why had a young orthodox Jew spent so much time in a Catholic church?

Just as I was about to ask, as if anticipating my confusion, Grandfather began: "Do not think because of my own strict religious practices, I was repulsed by other religions or wanted to shut myself away. Like all great art and scientific or technical advancements that touch our souls, St. Stephen's represented the ideals, grandeur, and spirituality for which mankind yearns. And, in the case of history just 30 years ago, what the same mankind debases and pollutes in the name of what should be holy."

I sensed Grandfather had more to say, but he looked away from the building and raised his half-eaten sandwich. "And in her way, your mother touches our souls every day, does she not?"

We finished eating. I linked arms with Grandfather as we slowly walked up the steps to the library entrance. Two undergraduates held the heavy doors open for us. As with the entrance to any gothic cathedral, we walked into a massive nave with a vaulted ceiling, iron works, stone and wood carvings, and, oddly, rows of wooden card catalogues on the left that captured the presence of millions of works and the need for modern classification.

We stopped for a moment and stared straight ahead at a towering blue-and-white mural that depicted a Madonna-like figure.

"That is the Alma Mater, or 'Mother Knowledge,'" Grandfather said, "handing down learning through books to her children."

How brilliant, I mused, to have an ornate circulation desk below the mural, like an altarpiece to knowledge as students swarmed around it to check out materials.

"This way," Grandfather said, steering me toward elevators. We rode up to the various floors of the tower, where books and other library materials were housed. including special collections. Since we were running short of time before our meeting with Ernest Robinson, Grandfather said little, but he seemed determined to visit every floor.

"I had never visited this magnificent collection before, and I do not know if I will have a future opportunity," he stated with reverence.

At one point, Grandfather stopped in front of a glass display that housed the cloth Yale coat of arms—an open book against a dark blue backdrop, the Hebrew words "Urrim" on the right page facing us and "V'tummim" on the left. Beneath, within a curved black border, was a Latin translation of the Hebrew, "Lux et Veritas."

"Ah, in complement and in contrast to the Fairfield motto, 'Light and Truth,' Yoeli, is what we are given as the translation of the Hebrew words that 2000 years ago were emblazoned on the breastplates worn by the High Priest in Jerusalem as he administered his Temple duties. But the Yale translation is not fully correct. It should be 'Light and Perfection' informing us as human beings, and now particularly as investigators into a tragic death, that light in its various manifestations may allow us transitory perfection or goodness. A blotting of the light, even a momentary shadow, will move us away from what is possible to blight and destruction. I believe that is why Ori is dead. Yoeli, I hope you understand me."

At a later point in my life, I came to fully understand. As a young man back then, it may have been the beginnings of my understanding.

* * * *

It was a few minutes before 12:30 when Grandfather and I descended the stairs from the library. A man we took to be Ernest Robinson was sitting on the stone bench where we had eaten lunch. He wore blue overalls over a similarly colored tee-shirt. The name "Robinson" had been stitched in orange along the upper pocket. His work shoes were ordinary but stood out in the size of his feet, at least a 14, I guessed. In his thirties with black hair already graying at the temples, he was solidly built, just over six feet, and perhaps 240 pounds, with large hands and shoulders.

As we neared, he rose to greet us, and after ascertaining our identities, we shook hands. His grip was firm but considerate. Then he motioned Grandfather toward the bench. There was ample room for the three of us, so Ernest and I joined Grandfather sitting. I hadn't checked in with Grandfather as to who would begin the questioning. I could have saved myself that tension as Robinson, who was sitting in the middle, turned toward Grandfather and, in a low-keyed voice, asked: "You are Jewish, I believe, and of foreign extraction. Did you go through the Holocaust?"

"Yes," Grandfather responded neutrally.

"You lost loved ones?"

"Yes, my wife in 1942. My daughter—who is the mother of this fine young man—and I buried her with our own hands in a shallow grave as we hid from the Nazis. I also lost all of my relatives who believed that the Nazis were just another pogrom in the endless cycle of Anti-Semitism and did not escape Austria while there was still time. But may I know why you inquire?"

"Just wondering how a Holocaust survivor became a private detective. I suffer from intrusive curiosity, so please forgive me."

"Mr. Robinson," Grandfather assured him, "there is nothing to forgive, and you are not being intrusive. For that matter, we will be quite intrusive when we question you. I will give a concise explanation. I had been a professor of philosophy at a Vienna university before the war. After the war and as a refugee in this country, my credentials were of no use, as the Nazis destroyed all records pertaining to Jewish faculty. At first, I took a position as a security guard at the 42nd Street Library, where I sat at the exit checking for stolen books. With such an undemanding job, I possessed the opportunity to read about this country that I was coming to love, its history, literature, the wonderfully entertaining super heroes comics, political works, arts, and sports, particularly baseball which my son-in-law and grandson loved. And I was also able to nurture my affinity for detective stories, which I obtained in hiding during the War.

"I had read works by Christie, Sayers, Chandler, Hammett, and Spillane, and I was struck by how the private detective profession fit my training in critical analyses. I was 55 years old at the time, and I have been working at this noble profession for the past 20 years."

Robinson looked at me and then back to Grandfather. "So you're the philosopher detective, wise perhaps like Socrates and the other great philosophers in search of the truth."

"Not quite, Mr. Robinson. Do you remember Socrates' definition of wisdom?"

Robinson did not hesitate: "I believe it's something like 'I know that I know nothing.' Am I correct?"

"Yes, at least from what Plato tells us about Socrates."

Grandfather then looked past Robinson to me. "I find for Socrates to have said those words to be vain and pretentiously virtuous. Even the lowest slave in Athens knew a good deal. I am more comfortable with the Jewish definition of wisdom. Joel, might you tell Mr. Robinson what that may be."

I smiled. Grandfather had quoted it to me innumerable times as I was growing up.

"As noted in the Talmud, 'Who is the wise one? The person who learns from all people'," I responded.

Grandfather beamed at me and turned to face Robinson squarely. "At the beginning of an investigation, the 'philosopher detective' as you call him, should be wise in the fashion that Socrates describes—he must insist to himself that he truly knows nothing about the case. No biases and no suppositions. But then he must become wise in the Talmudic sense in pursuing knowledge by learning from all individuals involved in the case. That is why we are here, Mr. Robinson. We wish to become wiser through hearing from you about Ori Gold and the night of his murder."

"Well enough," Robinson replied. "What are your questions?"

Here I was, well-educated, working at a prestigious New York law firm and making at least three times what Robinson and my Grandfather earned each year, but I felt somewhat out of my element as a participant. So I held back and waited for Grandfather to begin the questioning.

"If you don't mind, Mr. Robinson, given your obvious depth of knowledge, would you share with us why you were working as a janitor at the Manhattan Jewish Academy dormitory at the time of the murder? And for that matter, why are you performing custodial duties at this illustrious university. We are not so naïve as not to consider that your race may be a factor, but to this extent?"

I was sure that Grandfather had remembered the information in the police report about Robinson being a suspect in a South Carolina murder in 1968. It seems Robinson also took it for granted.

"Fair enough, but perhaps a bit disingenuous as I am sure you read in a police report that I was a suspect in the murder of my wife in South Carolina six years ago."

I would have squirmed, but Grandfather sincerely replied: "You are correct, I was disingenuous, for which I apologize. Perhaps I should examine more carefully the interview tactics of some of my heroes, such as Hercule Poirot or the current fascinating television detective, Columbo."

At this point, Robinson and my Grandfather were looking directly at each other, yet I started to feel drawn into a chemistry of interaction.

"That's okay, Mr. Wolf, there's much I sense we share, including making errors in the pursuit of justice."

Robinson nodded toward the library. "But since I must return shortly to my duties, I'll be succinct. I was born here in New Haven and grew up in the predominantly Black Dixwell section of town. As you can see, I was gifted with the body and abilities of a football player, so I earned a sports scholarship to Syracuse University. I was a running back there between Jim Brown and Ernie Davis, and while I didn't nearly have the talent of those two, I was good enough to keep a spot on the team for three years and my scholarship.

"UConn accepted me into their English Literature graduate program, and I wrote my dissertation on the life and poetry of Phillis Wheatley Peters. Have you read her works?"

Robinson probably had Grandfather in mind when he asked the question, but I answered, "She was an American poet of African descent who lived during Colonial times."

English was not my forte in high school, but I remembered our American literature class when Mr. Levine handed out Wheatley Peters' poems to discuss.

"Yes, yes," Robinson said excitedly. "It's not often I come across someone who knows of her. But to continue, after receiving my doctorate in 1966, I took a teaching position at South Carolina State University in Orangeburg. It was a hotbed of the civil rights movement just a few years ago, you may remember. I became a campus protest leader. I married in 1967, and on February 8, 1968, the evening of the Orangeburg Massacre, I was leading a protest of unarmed students on campus when the police opened fire, killing three and wounding twenty-eight."

Robinson looked into the distance. "But as these innocents were dying, so was my wife. A student whom I trusted and who had recently been to the house broke in, thinking my wife was with me at the protest. When she confronted him in the kitchen, he stabbed her with a knife, grabbed some trinkets, and ran. By the time I came home and found Miriam, she had bled out.

"The student was quickly arrested after trying to pawn what he had stolen and charged with the murder. I had missed the signs, but he was a drug addict and looking to support his habit. But then the Orangeburg police had a surprise for me. They arrested *me* for complicity in my wife's murder. After holding me overnight, the chief of police informed me that as a known 'black militant' who had caused the riots which led to the students' deaths, I had a choice—I could leave Orangeburg immediately or face trial for the murder of my wife as the DA was working out a plea bargain with the student to claim I had paid him to kill Miriam."

After two years of law school through which my professors constantly preached about ethics and reverence for the law, I couldn't contain myself. "Unbelievable, this just can't happen in America!"

Robinson shook his head. "That I would be set up in front of a white jury for conviction didn't shock me. Besides its being par for the course in South Carolina, I was in the middle of greater shock having lost my wife, the deaths of the students in the massacre, and my poor judgment in letting Miriam's murderer into our home. So I didn't think twice before giving into the blackmail and fleeing from Orangeburg and from my own guilt that I may have caused the murder of my wife and had contributed to the students' deaths by spurring their protest that night.

"The local newspaper ran a story about my arrest and subsequently reported there wasn't sufficient evidence to charge me. But then I had a record of sorts, didn't I, as the NYPD later quickly found out, and I could not have gotten another teaching job. Truth be told, I wanted to hide anyway and headed to New York City. I stayed at the 92nd Street Y a few days and saw the ad for a janitor at the MJA dorm with housing in the basement. I imagine they liked the way I was built because they hired me on the spot, few questions asked. Where better to hide than a basement?"

"Indeed, where better than in a basement," Grandfather said. He must have been transported back to the Holocaust. He and my mother in the basement of a country home outside of Vienna, thanks to a kind university colleague and his wife. That's where, as Grandfather had mentioned to Robinson, my grandmother had died. My mother had been seventeen at the time.

While both Grandfather and Robinson were paused in their memories, I decided to continue the interview: "I'm guessing after Ori's murder you were let go by the school?"

"You might put it that way," Robinson answered turning towards me. "While the police had no evidence to charge me, I was still under suspicion by the administration, and the kids seemed frightened of me. The thinking went this way: it's either a stranger from the outside who broke in, the janitor, or the janitor working with someone from the outside. So I resigned and came home to New Haven. My father worked as a custodian at Yale, so I was well connected to obtain my position as a custodian at this library." A note of bitterness crept into his voice. "I spend my days surrounded by the best book collection in the world. I'm moving forward, am I not?"

Grandfather did not respond to Robinson. I wasn't sure of my footing, but I asked anyway: "*Did* you have anything to do with Ori's murder?"

Robinson snickered and shook his head. "I'm guessing that you ask everyone that question, so I won't make life difficult for you. No, I did not. I carry much hate in me, but Ori was among the last people in the world I would harm."

"And why is that, Mr. Robinson?" Grandfather inquired.

"Because he was a wonderful kid, decent at the heart of him, non-pretentious, and non-defensive. Thinking about it, maybe he was just that kind of a person who gets himself killed because he doesn't know how to protect himself."

"How's that?" I asked. What did he mean?

"Do you know how we met? It must have been September of '69, right after he arrived at MJA. I was cleaning the fourth floor hallway one morning when he came out of his room, saw me, gave me a cheery good morning, and asked: 'Did you go to Syracuse?' I was wearing an old Syracuse sweatshirt under my overalls, and he must have recognized the top of the logo. I told him I had."

A broad smile covered Robinson's face as he continued to recall their first encounter. "Remember," he said, "Ori was fourteen at the time. He asked me, 'Do you by any chance know Floyd Little, the running back? I'm from Denver, and he's my favorite player on the Broncos.'

"I laughed and said, 'Yes, We both grew up in New Haven.'

"Ori shuffled uncomfortably for a minute, the way boys do when they're not sure of something, then asked if I could get him an autographed picture of Floyd. He told me, 'I've written to Mr. Little twice, but I'm sure he is very busy.' Classic Ori. I told him I'd see what I could do.

"Two weeks later, when I saw him again, I told him Floyd had sent me the picture and to come to my basement apartment to pick it up that evening."

"The visits continued after that, did they not?" Grandfather pursued.

"Yes. I think we were both lonely. Looking back, it probably wasn't the best idea. You must believe me, nothing untoward happened."

I thought Grandfather would say something to show trust in Robinson's claim, but he did not. Instead, he asked: "And what did you discuss during his visits?"

A smile returned to Robinson's face. "Mostly sports. He wanted me to show him how to hold a football along its seams to throw it properly, how to catch it as a receiver.

"More than anything else, he wanted tips on playing baseball. He hadn't made the MJA baseball team the year before and was determined to try again in the spring. He wanted me to come out to the yard to demonstrate, but I told him it would not be good for either of us. He never asked again."

"What else did you talk about?" I asked.

"Oh, what he was studying, what books he was reading, current events. It never became personal."

A thought struck me. "Did you ever discuss *Catcher in the Rye?*"

"Not really. Maybe a week before his death, he told me there was a difference of opinion between some of the boys and their religious instructors about the propriety of reading the book. I told him I'd read it long ago and didn't remember it much. I couldn't get involved in that sort of a controversy."

"I imagine as the custodian of the high school dormitory," Grandfather said, "you were in Ori's room on various occasions to perform services. What were your impressions?"

"Of his room, you mean? Well, even when he had roommates, his area was always neat, clean, and well organized. The bed was always made."

I thought I knew where Grandfather was going with his question, so I asked: "Did anything stand out?"

Robinson smiled once more. "Well, his Little League trophy certainly did. I could tell it gave him a lot of pleasure—he loved talking about it and his team's championship."

Grandfather then spoke even more precisely than usual. "Do you recall the last time you were in Ori's room?"

"The police asked me that question, too. It was the day before the murder. I fixed the leaking sink."

"And was the trophy in the room?"

Robinson thought for a moment. "If it wasn't there, I think I would have noticed. Why do you ask?"

"We are interested," Grandfather answered openly, 'because the trophy was missing when Ori's body was discovered. We are looking into any irregularities as they may contribute to solving the case."

Robinson suddenly became animated. "I see, I see! The trophy missing is quite an irregularity. You're thinking it was the murder weapon!"

"It is a possibility, Mr. Robinson, but it would be premature to draw that conclusion. I would like you to tell us about the others in the dormitory that night."

Robinson rose and began pacing before us as he spoke. "The thing is, I'm sure no one there wanted Ori dead. I've gone over and over it in my head, and no one had a motive for his murder, no one. I doubt there was a person in the world who wanted Ori dead! And I'm telling you, no one broke into the dorm that night from the outside."

"Let's quickly go over each person there," I said, "starting with Mrs. Wachter."

"As you wish. A nice old world type of woman tolerated by the boys for the television set she had in her living room and for the sick note she would sign when one of them didn't want to go to school on a particular day. Forget her as a suspect."

I opened my mouth to continue, but Robinson moved on by himself.

"And forget Sheldon Lachs. Even though he was the RA, he was timid, more the type to get murdered than be a murderer.

"David Spiller—well, I don't know much about him, but he struck me as a pompous ass. I had one interaction with him. As I was responsible for keeping contact with New York Bell when the public phones in the dorm weren't working, I had to fill out reports on outages. I think it was the spring before Ori's murder that the third floor phone was reported out of order. Spiller was supposedly that last one to have used it when it was working, so I tracked him down to get the time he was on the phone.

"He screamed at me, 'I'm telling you it *was* working when I was on! I don't care what Ori Gold or anyone else tells you, it was working!' I wasn't interested in his lunacy, so I said 'thank you' and walked away. So maybe he had something against Ori, but to kill him, I don't think so."

"That leaves Joshua Cushman and Michael Charnick," I said.

"Since the rec room was in the basement next to my apartment, I saw the Cushman kid pretty often. He hung out there at night, trying to get kids to play ping-pong with him. But I'd usually hear the other kids making up excuses like homework to do. I can't imagine why he'd want Ori dead.

"And Michael Charnick." He paused, frowning "I can't say much. He'd only been there a few weeks before the murder. But I'll tell you this, he scared me. I am a big man, but there was something in his eyes when he looked at you. Like you were just so much meat. Did he want to hurt Ori? I don't know, but I remember seeing the two of them walking along calmly just a few days before the murder."

"What were they doing?" Grandfather asked.

"Talking. Just talking." Robinson rejoined us on the bench. "Again, I can't figure a reason for him to hurt Ori."

I said, "Thank you."

He spread his hands. "I'm sorry I haven't been able to help you more. Unfortunately, I hear the Akkadian calls of the Babylonian Collection on the third floor demanding my attention."

Grandfather stood, and I followed suit. Grandfather said: "On the contrary, Mr. Robinson, you have helped us greatly. We may not be wise, but we have become wiser by what we learned from you."

We all shook hands, and then Robinson hurried into the library to resume his duties.

* * * *

Grandfather and I caught the 2:31 train from New Haven to Grand Central Station. It was scheduled to arrive at 4:20. Although at the New Haven station, Grandfather with some effort climbed the stairs to the train tracks, when we settled in for our ride, he was relaxed and awake for the whole trip.

I waited for Grandfather to bring up the Robinson interview, but for at least half an hour, he talked about the magnificence of the library, shared his memories of the university library in Vienna, and described the vast holdings at the New York 42nd Street Public Library. I didn't think I had showed my impatience, but suddenly he stopped his commentary on libraries and turned to me.

"Nuh, Yoeli, you would like to speak of our interview?"

I didn't hesitate. "I would. I know you don't like emotional responses after an interview, but I liked Robinson, and I don't think he killed Ori."

Grandfather took in the passing countryside for a few seconds. "I do not mind at all your introduction of the emotional at this time. We are now at the end of our interview process, and all of our subjects contributed information, relationships, and states of mind from which we construct the world in which Ori lived and was killed that night. We may now release our emotional responses that we have bottled inside of ourselves."

And then Grandfather took me fully by surprise. "I also liked Mr. Robinson, and I do not believe he had anything to do with Ori's death."

Was I validated or vindicated—or both? It didn't matter. We were on the same page. Mentally, I crossed Robinson off as a suspect. But that still left all the others.

Had it been worth our time coming all the way to New Haven to interview Robinson? Sure, Grandfather enjoyed walking around the Yale library, but I could tell he was exhausted.

He turned back to me. "Yoeli, what is it we learned from Mr. Robinson?"

I thought for a moment. "I think Robinson confirmed what Ori's dad and others told us – that he was a very likeable kid, and no one had a reason to murder him. Beyond that, I'm not sure."

Grandfather put his arms around my shoulders and drew me towards him.

"But is it possible that we also learned an important lesson about the human condition when it comes to murder? Is it possible that our rigorously trained detective minds, always pursuing a motive for murder, have been dragging us in a misguided direction? What has everyone been telling us about Ori Gold?"

"That everyone liked him," I again said. "That no one wanted him dead."

"Exactly. In other words, is it possible he was killed *without* the presence of a motive? What happened that night for Ori to have been murdered, when no one wanted him to die?"

I reiterated my own confusion.

"That is why we must reconstruct the world of his murder to complete our investigation."

There's always a reason when someone is murdered, I insisted to myself. Or had it been an accident? The baseball trophy hadn't just dropped on his head. And its disappearance suggested something criminal had occurred.

By the time we pulled into Grand Central, I wasn't sure who was more tired, Grandfather or me. For the last thirty minutes, we hadn't said much. I had been lost in my own thoughts, and now I only wanted to hustle back home on foot. Hopefully Aliya would be there, and I could discuss the case with her.

Grandfather wanted to take a subway home to Flatbush, but I shook my head.

"No way, Zaida, You look exhausted Do you really want to take two trains home during the height of rush hour?"

I prepared for an argument, but Grandfather smiled.

"I shall concede to the accuracy of your assessment."

We rode the escalator up to street level where taxis were lined up. Before getting into one, Grandfather hugged me and said: "We will both get some rest tonight and reconvene at my office tomorrow morning at 9:00, yes?"

"Of course, Zaida." I kissed him goodbye and watched until his cab pulled into traffic..

* * * *

I found Aliya at home and filled her in about our visits with Joshua Cushman and Ernest Robinson.

"Wow," she exclaimed after about an hour. "Your grandfather is willing to take Ernest off his list of suspects. He's must be pretty sure he's innocent."

"That's the thing, now Zaida thinks there may not be a motive for Ori's murder. I can't get my head around it. How can that be?"

Aliya answered quickly. "Maybe it's the way our few fights happen. Neither of us sets out to hurt the other, but something, almost out of the blue, gets between us, and we say or do something hurtful. We don't mean it. It just happens."

Before I could answer, the phone rang. It was my mother.

"Joel," she said loudly, fright in her voice, "the police just telephoned for Zaida. After listening for a minute, he hung up, told me to call you and let you know that a police car was going to pick him up and take him to Washington Heights, and then he ran out. It must involve the murder case you two are working. Oh, and a separate police car will pick you up in a few minutes, too. Please be careful, and take a coat, it's getting chilly. Do your best to protect Zaida."

"I will," I assured my mother.

As I hung up, I could hear a siren nearing. Was that my ride? I grabbed a jacket and garbled an explanation for Aliya.

"Go," she said, motioning me toward the door. "Go."

The police cruiser screeched to a halt just as my feet hit the sidewalk at 1st Avenue around 14th Street. An officer jumped out from the driver's side and shouted to me,

"Are you Gordon?"

When I indicated I was, he opened the passenger door. "Okay, get in. Another car with your grandfather is on the Brooklyn Bridge, a few minutes behind us. He's on the radio and wants to talk with you."

I was still fumbling for my seatbelt when the police car shot away from the curb, siren again blaring, made a U-turn that threw me against the door, shot diagonally left on 14th Street—just missing cars that had no interest in yielding—and raced toward the FDR Drive. All the while, the officer was pressing buttons on the police radio. Static crackled, then he said:

"Rizzo, can you hear me? I've got the Gordon guy with me. Almost on the FDR. Your passenger ready to talk to mine?"

"Yep, Martinez, he's ready. Go ahead, sir. They can hear you."

In between crackles, Grandfather's voice came through. "Joel, we are rushing toward the Manhattan Jewish Academy dormitory.

Detective Rooney called me and arranged for us to be picked up. It appears the Michael Charnick has been on the roof of the dormitory for the past hour threatening to jump. Detective Rooney believes that we may be of assistance in bringing Michael down."

"But how can we help?" Had my interviewing him led to this suicide attempt? "What can we do?"

Grandfather must have understood my distress and guilt. He called me by his pet Hebrew name, something he almost never did in public. "Yoeli, it is not just that a young boy, terribly frightened, wishes to harm himself, but his being on the roof certainly is tied to our solving the Ori Gold murder. Simply, it falls to us to try to help, yes?"

I took hold of myself. "Of course, we need to help." But I also remembered my promise to my mother. "And you'll be careful, whatever we do?"

"Yoeli, I will do my best."

By then, as Officer Martinez swished his cruiser around one car after another at breakneck speed, and as we were crossing over to the Harlem River Drive, I turned my head and saw another cruiser with its lights and siren on keeping pace with us. Officer Rizzo with Grandfather had caught up.

We slowed down just before we reached the dormitory. The police had cordoned off the block. Uniformed officers waved us through. When we stopped just short of the dormitory building, I jumped out, ran to Grandfather's cruiser, and opened the door for him. He allowed me to take his hand to help him out of his seat.

It was a beautiful twilit evening, with the skies above darkening and the sunset fading to the west, toward the Hudson River. Other police cars and fire trucks were parked along the street, with personnel in front of the dormitory, in the grassy area to the right, and no doubt in the paved yard at the back. Hundreds of people stood around talking and staring up at the roof, among them MJA students. Many were pointing toward the street side roof of the MJA dormitory where, even in the fading light, I could see a large, hulking figure standing with one foot on the parapet. That could only be Michael. He was pumping his right hand aloft, and in it he held a long, metallic object. I squinted. What was it?

Suddenly two floodlights came on and crisscrossed the building. They came to rest on the figure. When the light hit him directly, I saw it was Michael Charnick, dressed in a tee-shirt and sweat pants. And he was holding a trophy—I recognized the silver figure of a baseball player swinging a bat at the top of a black base. It had to be Ori's missing trophy.

Detective Rooney in his London Fog raincoat jogged over to us.

"Gentlemen, thanks for coming so quickly. Mr. Wolf, as I told you, the kid suddenly appeared on the roof around six o'clock. He's been waving that trophy around and howling, 'I killed him, I killed Ori Gold, and now I'm going to kill myself!'"

"It's Michael Charnick," I said. "He was in the dorm on the night of the murder."

"I remember. We sent up a negotiator, but the kid starting screaming and cursing and put one foot over the parapet. He said he would jump if the negotiator didn't get off the roof. That's when I thought of getting you two involved."

"We will go up to the roof and talk to the poor child," Grandfather said firmly and without hesitation. "One boy is dead, and we cannot allow another to die. The good news is that he has not jumped so far. He is confused, frightened, and, I am thinking, desperately wishing to be rescued. But all can change in a minute in his mind—an additional dark thought, the need to punish others through his death, anger that he is not being rescued,. We must go up immediately."

I don't believe it was just my mother's plea to look out for my grandfather's safety that drove a fierce determination in me to protect Grandfather. His going up on the roof with a lunatic murderer seemed out of the question.

"Zaida, you can't go on the roof," I ordered, but my voice also contained a pleading note. "It's much too dangerous. I'll go. He knows me, and I'll do my best to talk him down."

Grandfather took hold of my shoulders. Looking up at the figure bellowing, Grandfather said: "Yoeli, there is no time for the two of us to negotiate, and I must as part of my responsibilities also go to the roof. I will propose a non-negotiable compromise. We will both ascend, and you will come closest to the boy and do the majority of the speaking. Good?"

I braced myself and nodded.

"Then let us proceed."

Turning to Rooney, Grandfather indicated that we were ready to enter the building. My hands shook, and I pressed them together to hide it. I had never been in a situation like this before, and the empty cliché of *failure is not an option* leapt to mind.

"Let these guys into the building," Rooney called to a phalanx of police and fire personnel. He led the way, and we followed as quickly as possible with Grandfather somehow keeping pace. Once inside, we headed down the first floor hallway to the stairwell on the left. I held the door open for Grandfather and said: "Zaida, you go first, at your own speed, and I'll follow."

"Yes, Yoeli, I will do my best to walk up as quickly as possible. But when you approach the boy and speak to him, trust both to your instincts and to the resolve in your own self. Insist that this boy will not die. And do not lie to him at any time, as a stratagem or even if you believe he will not want to hear the truth. Do this and I know you will be successful, yes Yoeli?"

I half-laughed when I responded: "I'll put the no lying rule into effect right away. I hope so Zaida. I don't have your confidence, but I do trust in your confidence in me. I will do everything possible to talk Michael down."

Grandfather stopped at each landing, breathing hard, but delaying only momentarily. When we pushed the door open to the rooftop, I immediately felt a chill breeze. Good thing I had worn a jacket.

A large television antennae, bent by the wind, sat in the middle of the roof. To either side, a pair of whirring fans in large vent covers spewed exhaust. Over the noise, I heard Michael's hoarse screaming voice: 'I killed him, I killed Ori Gold, and now I'm going to kill myself!'

I got my bearings and turned toward him, with Grandfather following.

I stopped around five feet from Michael. His back was turned to us, but I could see he was wearing the same gay pride tee shirt he had worn three years before, when the police report picture was taken. It looked grotesquely small, exposing his bare midriff over those loose-fitting sweat pants.

How should I approach him? I didn't want to spook him and send him over the edge.

Grandfather said I should go with my instincts, so I let my interaction with Michael in his apartment swim back to me. Then I said, in a matter-of-fact voice loud enough for Michael and Grandfather both to hear: "Hi Michael. First time we met it was in your stifling hot apartment. This time we're on a chilly roof where the world below can still bother you."

Was I right to engage Michael with questionable humor? Would he get my sardonic take off on the *Drifter's* hit song?

Michael did not turn immediately nor flinch in any way. Had he heard me? I turned to Grandfather, who indicated with his hands for me to be patient. After around 15 seconds, Michael turned slowly, one sockless, sneakered foot on the parapet. He lowered the trophy. In the dim light, I wasn't sure if he was glaring at me or calculating what to do.

I absorbed his response as just a jab, glad that he had not jumped immediately and that he was willing to talk, at least for a moment. "So it's Mr. Joel Watson or whatever your last name is." Then his eyes focused on Grandfather behind me, and he added: "And that must be your genius grandfather who tricked Maria into giving you my address. Boy, does he look ancient, And he climbed all the way up here to try to save me, only there's no one to save. I killed Ori, and that's that, and now I will pronounce judgment on myself—guilty of murder and set for self-execution in just a few minutes. Then you can feel good that you've solved the case and collect your fee."

I moved a foot closer, and Michael still did not flinch. "But we don't deserve to collect our fee because we didn't really solve it, did we? You just up and confessed all by yourself. And knowing my grandfather, he won't take a penny because we didn't solve the case. We still don't know why you killed Ori. You want to tell me?"

For someone who for over an hour had exhibited manic behavior, Michael now looked at me as if I were the maniac. "You'll never be as crazy as me, but you're weird, and I like you," he said slowly in almost a whisper. "Come a little closer, and I'll tell you what happened that night."

I moved to within two feet of Michael, and Grandfather followed. He still hadn't said a word in the standoff. Was he all right?

"Okay, Michael," I said gently. "Please tell me what happened that night."

Michael looked me directly in the eye. "Not much to tell. I was stoned and decided I needed some company. Came to Ori's room a little after midnight, and he was getting ready to go to sleep. I was wide awake and feeling high, didn't want to sleep, and after a few minutes, Ori said he was tired and wanted to get ready for bed. I have a bad temper, especially when I'm stoned, so when he became insistent that I leave, I lost it, grabbed the stupid trophy, and smashed him on the head from behind. I didn't mean to kill him. It was an accident, but I did it and I deserve to die."

Michael exploded in tears, wails of grief and self-loathing pulsing down to the crowd on the street. His chest was heaving, but he still clutched the trophy, and his left foot remained planted on the parapet. With his free hand, he beckoned to me.

"Come closer and tell me you get what I'm saying, that I have to punish myself because no one else can really ever do it."

I moved forward, and before I could get a word out, Michael's free hand shot out and grabbed my jacket. He yanked me forward, his face an inch from my own. His breath was hot on my cheek.

His strength was terrifying. But his foot remained planted on the parapet, and we did not go flying over.

And in Michael's clutch, I wasn't sure if what I felt was the power of constrained violence or one person's demand for connection with another. I knew there was no way to free myself. I gasped, "Michael, what are you doing?"

I sensed a slight release of his grip, but not enough for me to escape. "What am I doing? Simple. As big as I am, as tough as I am, as angry as I am, I feel scared to die alone. I'm a coward who needs to hold on to someone when I jump off. Sorry that you were convenient."

Then Grandfather's voice, crisp and cool as the evening's air, pierced the rooftop. "No Michael, you will not jump, and you will not take the life of my grandchild, my one and only grandchild. You understand me! And you will not take your own life. In our history, too many children have died needlessly, Ori died needlessly, and you and Joel will not suffer the same fate!"

Grandfather moved forward and put his arms around Michael and me. With the three of us in this embrace, one thrust by Michael towards the roof's edge would cause all of us to fall to our deaths. My mother's plea reverberated through my head.

"You are a precious child, Michael, as is Joel," Grandfather continued, emotion and concern dominating his tone. "And you have been neglected, misunderstood, shamed, and abused. But as righteously as you feel your anger, I am convinced beyond your gruff exterior, you are striving within yourself for goodness. Whatever occurred previously, you must allow that goodness to prevail. And I believe you are already doing so. It is not fear that has prevented you from jumping. Despite what occurred with Ori, you are not an evil person, and you are not a murderer."

"But I killed Ori," Michael whimpered.

"You say you killed Ori," Grandfather responded, lifting his right hand to stroke Michael's face, "but that does not necessarily make you a murderer. Allow us to descend together, and tomorrow morning after some rest and reflection, we will sift through what occurred and establish the level of your guilt to determine appropriate punishment."

Seconds that seemed forever ticked by in silence. Then I felt my jacket come loose from Michael's hold. I grasped his left arm, steadying him, and Grandfather took his right. Michael was bawling. Grandfather took the trophy from Michael, and together we led Michael away from the roof's edge toward the stairwell.

We slowly made our way down to the street. Grandfather held onto Michael's arm the whole way. When we hit the street, clapping and cheers erupted from the bystanders which obliterated a few heartless taunts. Detective Rooney and two uniformed officers rushed to us with their hands on their holstered revolvers. After determining that we weren't hurt, Rooney indicated to an officer to handcuff Michael.

"A moment, please," Grandfather requested. "Michael, the officer will need to handcuff you and take you for medical attention and detention overnight. Is that correct Detective Rooney?"

When Rooney said yes, Grandfather continued. "But Joel and I will come see you in the morning. There is much to sort through, even though you have confessed to Ori's murder. Please be cooperative with the police. Right now, they only wish to help you."

Michael gave a nod and was led away to a nearby squad car. Rooney shook hands with us.

"After a psych and physical checkout at Columbia-Presbyterian, we'll hold him at the 34th precinct. You can visit him in the morning. Thanks for talking the boy down. Much appreciated. A squad car can take you guys home when you're ready."

"One thing further," Grandfather said to Rooney. "I would like please for you to call Joshua Cushman tonight. Summon him to be at the station by 10:30 tomorrow morning. If he refuses, say that Connecticut state troopers will be at his door with lights flashing to take him away. He will come. And please order him to bring his table tennis racket. He will not object."

Rooney gave Grandfather a bewildered look, but Grandfather offered no explanation.

"Okay," Rooney finally said. "I've got a lot of trust in you, but didn't the kid admit he killed Ori Gold? Isn't the case solved?"

"And why bring in Joshua Cushman?" I asked.

Grandfather smiled. "Detective Rooney, Michael did on the roof confess to hitting Ori with the trophy on his head from behind in a moment of rage. But please look at the coroner's report in your police file. Ori was struck in the front of his head. Look at the picture of Ori lying on the floor when he was found. It is not the position of a murder victim who falls after being hit on the back of the head, but very much like a victim who was smitten by a blow to the front of the head."

"So you don't believe Michael killed Ori?" I asked. It seemed incomprehensible.

"Joel, I did not say I did not believe that Michael hit Ori and killed him. I very much believe the boy. But for the case to be fully resolved, we must understand *why* Michael is lying about how he killed Ori, and I believe Joshua Cushman has a role in that mystery."

Shaking his head, Rooney turned to leave. "You got it, Mr. Wolf. I'll call the Cushman home as soon as I get back to the station."

A gaggle of reporters had surrounded us and began machine-gunning questions.

"Who are you?"

"What did he say up there?"

"Did he really kill Ori Gold?"

"How did you talk him down?"

To which Grandfather wearily responded: "I am a tired old man who will now proceed home to rest. You will excuse us please."

The reporters let us through, but a few who weren't satisfied with Grandfather's answer swarmed after us. They were stopped by two officers who shoved them back toward the others.

"You heard the man," one of them barked. "Leave them alone."

As we neared the squad car, Grandfather stopped me and clasped me to him. He was crying helplessly, and since I had never seen my

Grandfather cry like that before, I found tears welling in my own eyes. I fought them back.

"Zaida, what is it? Why are you crying?"

After regaining his composure but still holding on to me, he said: "Yoeli, I was so frightened when Michael grabbed you. I wasn't able to save others I loved, and now again I was terrified that I could not save you."

"Yes, but I'm here, and everything is okay."

"Yes, now, everything is, as you say, okay. And I am proud of you, how you dealt with Michael. Is it possible you have grown up into a fine and courageous young man who can with confidence trust to your instincts? Yes, I am sure of it. Again, if you wish to leave your lucrative position at your law firm and join me at a somewhat reduced salary, you are most welcome. But regardless, tomorrow we will together complete our case."

Friday, October 18, 1974.

The next morning, Grandfather took a cab from Flatbush and picked me up at my apartment. Together we rode to the 34th Precinct. We arrived right at 10:30. We introduced ourselves, and the desk sergeant said he was expecting us.

"Head straight back and you'll come to Rooney's office and a couple of interview rooms. You can use Interview Room 1. Those folks from Connecticut are already there, sitting in a hallway bench. The kid from the roof is in a holding cell in the basement."

"Is he okay?" I asked.

"He's under a suicide watch, but yeah. His parents are on their way back from Geneva. Should be here tonight."

The sergeant looked down at log book. "According to the log, the kid didn't sleep at all last night. He's going to be woozy."

"Thank you," said Grandfather. "I would like first to speak with the Cushman family. Is it possible for you tell Detective Rooney we are here and in 15 minutes to please bring up Michael Charnick from his holding cell? I believe the detective is aware to first ask the boy permission to talk to us. He is only seventeen, but deserves that legal courtesy."

"Sure. I'll call the detective right now."

We headed down the hall. On the wall to our left was a plaque marked *34ᵗʰ In Memoriam*. How many officers had lost their lives over the years!

We rounded a corner and the Cushman family came into sight. Holding firmly onto his table tennis racket's case, Joshua Cushman sat next to a woman I recognized as his mother. He wore the same mustard-colored cardigan over a white shirt and tie. A bespectacled, balding man in a suit and tie sat on Mrs. Cushman's other side.

The woman jumped up as soon as she spotted us. She straightened her powder blue suit, then strode forward to meet us.

"You are the two private detectives who were at our house yesterday. Is it your doing that we are called at night to appear with our son at a police station? What is it you want with Joshua? Is it about the Gold boy's murder?"

"It is," said Grandfather.

The bespectacled man rose but more slowly. "I am Harold Cushman, Joshua's father. I saw you on the news last night. They said that another boy had confessed and threatened to jump off the dormitory roof. Then two unknown men—I guess the two of you—talked him down."

"You are correct," said Grandfather.

"So why are you harassing our Joshua?" Mrs. Cushman demanded. "He hasn't done anything!"

Mr. Cushman looked down and muttered: "I also would like to know why we were asked to come."

Joshua remained seated, gripping the covered racket. "Mom, Dad," he said sharply, "I can handle it." He stood and looked at Grandfather and me. "What is it you two want from me? As my mother said, that oaf Michael Charnick admitted to the murder. So what else is there?"

"Let us discuss it in private." Grandfather walked over to Interview Room 1 and opened the door, indicating that Joshua should enter. He sauntered in. His parents were about to follow, but Grandfather held up a hand. "Just Joshua, please. He is eighteen and an adult. If you wish that we should wait until an attorney is present, that is Joshua's prerogative. But Joshua, if there is nothing else, then perhaps you will not mind just a few more questions for final resolution of the case. I believe there is more to what happened that night, but perhaps not?"

Joshua, clutching the leather racket case, plopped down in a chair at the interview table. "I don't need a useless attorney. I can handle your questions on my own."

Detective Rooney had come out of his office. He nodded to the Cushmans, then whispered something to Grandfather and departed. I followed Grandfather inside, shutting the door behind me.

The interview room contained a rectangular metal table with two metal folding chairs, one on either side. A mirror framed the long side of the room.

Grandfather took a seat opposite Joshua. Pointing to me and then to the mirror, he said: "My associate, Mr. Gordon, will repair to the observation room."

I left quickly, closed the door behind me, and headed into the adjoining room. The setup was similar to the police station in Williamsburg, where we conducted interviews last year in the Yosele Rosenstock case.

I watched the scene, but neither Grandfather nor Joshua were speaking.

Joshua had both elbows on the table, and he looked half bored, half angry. He fingered his racket's handle. Finally, he muttered:

"So, are we going to just sit here all day? The Sabbath starts around 7:00. I guess I have several more hours before I need to be back home."

Before Grandfather spoke, he directed his gaze toward Joshua's eyes, but Joshua looked past him.

"I believe everything will be resolved by the time the Sabbath arrives, yes Joshua?"

"Why are you asking me? You dragged me here."

"Ay, ay, ay, Joshua," Grandfather retorted in a paternal, admonishing tone. "Once again, were you in Ori's room when he was killed?"

Joshua screamed, holding himself from rising by holding the table. "I told you, I did not kill Ori!"

"But Joshua, Joshua, you are a person with a sharp acumen. Was it my question? Did I in any way accuse you of killing Ori, or did I simply ask if you were in the room at the time?"

"I'll say it again," Joshua said, teeth gritted. "I didn't want Ori killed, and I didn't kill him."

Just then I heard a knock on the interview room door. A moment later, it opened. Michael Charnick walked in, with Detective Rooney behind him.

Michael wore an orange prison uniform, his long hair even wilder than its windswept appearance on the roof. There was a light fuzz on his cheeks, and his eyes had dark, puffy bags under them. Rooney took a position at his side.

"Charnick!" Joshua gasped.

"Cushman!" Michael recoiled. "I didn't—"

"Shut up!" Joshua yelled. He leaped to his feet and faced Michael. "Just shut up!"

"Why are you here?" Michael persisted, his voice stronger. He looked from Grandfather to Rooney then back to Joshua. "Why are you here, Cushman? What are you telling them? I killed Ori. I gave them a full confession."

Joshua backed away. "I don't know why I'm here. And I'm telling you, just shut up!"

I could see the weariness in Michael's eyes being replaced by anger. His back stiffened, and he glared at Joshua.

"Don't tell *me* to shut up. I told you—"

"You idiot!" Joshua raised his racket case in slam mode and moved toward Michael.

Michael raised his right fist to strike. But Rooney leaped between the two, and that's when Grandfather roared, "Stop!" as loudly as I had ever heard in my life.

He rose. Everyone was staring at him.

"Please, hold your positions. What we have before us is a reenactment of Ori's killing. Michael, Joshua, you each wanted to strike the other, did you not? And Ori came between you as a peacemaker, did he not? And Michael, you struck him, as the pathologist report indicates, at the front of his head and not the back, as you claimed. His last sight in life was his beloved trophy coming down upon him, was it not?"

Michael suddenly slumped. "Yes, yes, that's what happened. I killed him, and I deserve to die for it."

"Shut up, shut up, you idiot," Joshua intoned, with little conviction behind it.

Grandfather's tone was businesslike but at the same time soothing. "Michael, please tell us what happened that night."

Michael looked at him. "Like I told your associate, I stoned myself that night. It was about one a.m., and I couldn't sleep and didn't want to be alone, so I decided to see if Ori was still up. He often read late into the night. I heard voices in his room, so I went in. Cushman was there, and they were talking about *Catcher in the Rye*. Cushman was insisting that Ori should stop reading it because it was a deviant book.

"I told him to butt out, and within a minute or two it was all me and Cushman arguing and calling each other names, and him attacking me for who I am. Ori asked us a few times to leave saying he was tired, but we ignored him, and our argument got hotter and hotter until Cushman moved toward me with that stupid little ping-pong racket. I knew he was going to hit me with it. I was standing next to Ori's bookcase, so I grabbed the trophy to hit Cushman first. But out of nowhere, Ori jumps between us, and I crashed the trophy on his head. The last thing I remember was him looking into my eyes, and then he fell to the floor with blood spilling out. It was as simple as that. I didn't want to kill anyone the moment before, not even Cushman really, and I didn't want to kill anyone a moment after. But in between, I killed Ori. It was as simple as that."

"And why did you not immediately call for assistance. It is possible that Ori was still alive and you let him expire," Grandfather asked somberly.

Tears were streaming down Michael's face. "I've thought about that a million times. Cushman said Ori was dead, and that I hadn't wanted to kill him, and that it would just mean trouble for both of us for the rest of our lives. We swore each other to silence, came up with what we'd tell the police, and went back to our rooms. I hid the trophy with my possessions. I've been carrying it around from place to place for the last three years. It was like I was carrying my guilt around. Then after the Joel guy visited me a few nights ago, it all came up to the surface, and I couldn't stop reliving the moment I killed Ori, and I wanted to be punished for it."

Michael looked directly toward Joshua. "But Cushman, I kept my word. I never told anyone about you being in the room or how it happened. I'm the one who killed him, and I'm the one who should be punished."

Joshua looked down at his two hands folded over the racket. "I categorically deny being in the room when Ori was murdered. It's the perverted maniac's word against mine. I want to see my parents, and I want them to obtain legal counsel. That's all I have to say."

Rooney opened the door and summoned an officer to take Michael back to the holding cell before he approached Joshua. "That may be, buddy, but for now I'm arresting you for complicity in the murder of Ori Gold. Get up and come with me."

As they were leaving the room, Rooney began reading Joshua his rights.

* * * *

After our presence at the 34th was no longer needed, Detective Rooney again provided a police car to drive us home. I decided to go back to Flatbush with Grandfather. I called Aliya on Rooney's phone and told her what had occurred. She agreed to meet us there.

As we were leaving the precinct, I heard a woman's wail from behind us, and Joshua's mother charging toward Grandfather. I thought she was going to attack him, but she stopped just short.

"What have you done to my boy," she shrieked. "Joshua is a good boy. He will achieve great things. Why are you trying to ruin his life?"

Grandfather looked neither afraid nor angry and answered in a voice filled with pity. "I am sorry. I understand. He is your son."

Then Mr. Cushman caught up with his wife, put his arm around her shoulders, and led her away.

* * * *

We rode in the police car without siren or flashing lights. Traffic was heavy on the FDR. I stared out toward the East River while Grandfather settled back and looked out the window toward the city. A constrained weariness had descended on Grandfather. I could see it in his face and the slumping of his body.

I have never been good at remaining quiet when I am unsettled, so I asked as neutrally as possible: "Zaida, what do you think will happen to the boys?"

Grandfather sighed. "Ay, to start, I am sure bail will be set, and even if it is high for Michael, his family has means and will have him released pending trial. But will there be a trial? Will he be tried as an adult? Let us remember he was fourteen years old at the time. And Joshua, he was but 15. If he maintains his claim that he was not in the room at the time of Ori's killing, then it is his word against Michael's, and defense attorneys can easily make Michael out to be unstable and an unreliable witness."

"Yes, I think you're right, Zaida."

Grandfather continued. "Truly, they were but children, two very troubled children who engaged in lethal play. They were not plotting to hurt anyone, but in an instant, an innocent met his death. Do you recall what Michael said at the station? 'I didn't want to kill anyone the moment before, not even Cushman really, and I didn't want to kill anyone a moment after. But in between, I killed Ori.' That is the way most murders occur, and often not of just one innocent, but of millions."

* * * *

That weekend, the *Times,* the *Daily News*, and the *Post* all ran stories about the Ori Gold case. While the *Times* and the *Post* provided inside-pages updates, the *Daily News* blared the headline on its front page: **ARRESTS IN THE DORM MURDER.** It showed a picture of Michael Charnick being led away in handcuffs, with barely identifiable images of Grandfather and me in the background. But the *Daily News* and the *Post* both identified Grandfather as the Brooklyn private detective Frank Wolf. I was listed as an "unidentified man." The articles in one sentence indicated that 18-year-old Joshua Cushman of Fairfield, Connecticut was also arrested for obstruction of justice.

For a week, the phone didn't stop ringing both at the Flatbush apartment and at Grandfather's office. Newspapers, television stations, national magazines all wanted interviews, and some offered to pay handsomely. Grandfather refused every one. Relatives and friends of cold case victims all over the country, both Jewish and non-Jewish, entreated Grandfather to investigate. He would listen politely, sometimes spending an hour on the phone, but in the end explaining that he wasn't in a position to take on a new case at the moment. My mother was relieved as again she was concerned about Grandfather's weariness and overall health. After a few weeks, the calls stopped.

I, too, had my moment of fame. Although the newspapers never published my name as the person standing next to Grandfather, friends and colleagues easily identified me, and my own calls and back slaps at work were numerous. Should I, listening to these accolades, have been as exhilarated as I was after getting a game-winning hit in high school and being carried off the field on the shoulders of my teammates? I simply wasn't, and I understood it was the still-emerging Grandfather part in me.

* * * *

In early November, Samuel Gold came to New York and asked if he could see us both at Grandfather's office. When he walked in, I thought I detected a small bounce in his step. Or was I imagining it because the case was solved? His eyes immediately lit on Ori's baseball trophy, now standing on Grandfather's desk.

After warm greetings, Gold sat down and reached toward the trophy. His cheeks were wet with tears. "May I?" he asked gently.

I reached over Grandfather's shoulder and handed him the trophy. He held it close to his chest for a few minutes, his fingers caressing the metal.

He then vociferously thanked us for our work, took a checkbook from his briefcase, tore out a check, and said to me: "PWR, as arranged, is billing me for your time, Joel." Then he looked at Grandfather. "But Mr. Wolf, after you invoice me for your time and expenses, I will write you a check, but in addition I'd like to give you an additional ten thousand dollars in reflection of my family's gratitude."

Grandfather shook his head and gave a quick wave of a hand. "It is most gracious of you, Mr. Gold, but I cannot accept. We made a business arrangement for the work we did, and I do not deserve and cannot take more. I do, however, have a fully itemized invoice for much less for which you may write a check before we part. But a suggestion. Perhaps you would donate the money in our names to a charity of which Ori would have approved."

Gold broke into a smile. "As it happens, we are starting a foundation in Ori's memory called The Ori Gold Baseball Youth Fund. It will award grants to youth leagues in need of baseball equipment and training in any part of the country, in the cities, in rural areas, anywhere there is a need. We will then dedicate your donation to the fund in Ori's memory."

Gold held the trophy slightly aloft. "And this trophy will be a symbol for the foundation appearing on all of its materials."

Before leaving, Gold once again thanked us and added: "My wife is doing somewhat better since she learned what happened to her little boy. I have seen her smile, and perhaps over time...over time..."

* * * *

The Sunday after Gold's visit, Aliya and I came over to Flatbush for brunch with my mother and Grandfather. After an hour of eating and conversation, to which Grandfather seemed to give less than his usual attention, he rose and said:

"You will all please excuse me. I have an engagement in Manhattan for which I must prepare myself."

After Grandfather went into his bedroom, I looked at Aliya, she at me, and both of us at my mother.

"Mom," I asked the child in me coming out. "Where's Zaida going? What engagement in Manhattan?"

My mother, who has some of Grandfather in her, gave us a Cheshire cat smile: "Is it possible I would not have all of the facts to reply to your inquiry?"

When Grandfather came out dressed in his High Holy Days suit and carrying his best overcoat, Aliya nudged me and whispered: "Do you smell that? I think he's got cologne on."

Then it hit me, and I blurted: "Zaida, don't tell me! Are you by any chance going up to Washington Heights to see Mrs. Wachter?"

Grandfather grinned and put on his overcoat and doffed his hat to us: "Then, as you requested, I shall not tell you. A good afternoon to all."

ABOUT THE AUTHOR

Saul Golubcow writes from Potomac, Maryland. His commentary on Jewish American politics and culture has appeared in multiple publications. His fiction centers on the complexity of and challenges facing Jewish Holocaust survivors in the United States. The Cost of Living and Other Mysteries is his first book-length publication featuring private detective Frank Wolf.

ACKNOWLEDGMENTS

Before I put him on paper in *The Cost of Living and Other Mysteries,* my detective hero, Frank Wolf, had been with me for decades. In graduate school, I had started to scope out stories about Jewish Holocaust survivors in the United States. I had wanted to offer my perspective on these extraordinary people who came with their shattered lives to this wonderful country and, somehow, emphasized living and the future despite the death and destruction they had experienced.

For one of my projected stories, I thought about the life and personality of my father-in-law, Kalman Teglasi. He had lost his first family during the Holocaust, and he arrived in the United States in later middle-age following the Hungarian Revolution. He was well versed in religious practice, history, arts, the sciences, and the technologies of his time. I was also struck by his various observations of the human condition. Although he never attempted private detective work, he often spoke of "critical analyses" as an imperative for reining in impulsive and rash decision-making, the core skill of a good detective. I back then wondered, might I create a Holocaust survivor character who becomes a private detective in Brooklyn?

But everyday life happened for me, which included raising two wonderful children. I put my notes away in a desk drawer, which I carried around from dwelling to dwelling. Upon my work retirement a few years ago, I took out the notes and started writing. I created various stories about Holocaust survivors, including an aging private detective named Frank Wolf, which I published in short story form. But once I was with Frank in his world, I wanted to keep writing about him and his relation to his family and the Jewish community in which he solves mysteries.

As central to his persona, Frank Wolf represents that spirit of Holocaust survivors which has insisted that, while they suffered horrible victimization, they would not succumb to victimhood. Even before I met my father-in-law, this response to suffering was bred in my bones. I also saw it in my own family. My parents, Harry and Sonia Golubcow, also lost whole families in the Holocaust. Grateful for the opportunity to make a living as poultry farmers in Southern New Jersey even though they knew nothing of farming, nor later of being hotel managers in Atlantic City, they demonstrated a resilience in the midst of enduring pain, building a new life in which my sister and I were protected and a path into our future developed. My father often insisted, "I can't give up."

As it turned out, my sister Molly Golubcow is an author in her own right and has written a touching memoir of growing up as the child of Holocaust survivors who would not give up. The family joke is that she is my "publicist." Her enthusiasm in promoting my writing, both fiction and non-fiction, is most welcome, as I am not a comfortable Facebook or Twitter user.

The behaviors of my father-in-law and parents may have been tied to the tragedy of the Holocaust, but the breeding of my bones was more encompassing. I am the proud benefactor of over 3,000 years of Jewish history, tradition, religion, and culture that shaped me and found expression in Frank Wolf, in his senses and sensibilities, and thus his ability to solve mysteries in the New York City Jewish communities of the early 1970s featured in this book.

Frank would tell you that in the millennia-long Jewish (and really of many other cultures) journey, there has been a beginning but no end. It's how we with kindness understand others, how we observe boundaries, how we control our egos and impulses that are critically important to living with dignity and satisfaction at any step of the journey. When there are breakdowns and crimes (isolated or mass), a good detective (historian) must use analytic skills, while at the same time being aware of the irrational, to solve the "case." I am thankful to my myriad teachers who have given me these insights to share with my readers through Frank Wolf.

Closer to home, my inspiration and thanks must go to my wife Hedy Teglasi, who has kept me honest in all aspects of my life, including my writing. The slightest hyperbole or discordant expression does not get by her eye, and while rewrites can be defensive and tiring, I always recognize they must be done.

My children, Jordan and Jeremy, have in their way also been my teachers. During toddlerhood, they would amaze me with their "from the mouth of babes" wisdom. Mealtime was always a time for conversation. I realized after they left home how much I learned from them, even when I had gone into "I'm the adult and know better" mode."

Finally, what's a writer without a publisher who believes in him and an editor who will meticulously polish his prose. I am fortunate to have found both in John Betancourt of Wildside Press. John, a winner of the Black Orchid Award for excellence in the mystery genre, read my stories and saw in them "a fresh take on the classic detective formula." To help me enrich my stories, he had to first sharpen his own understanding of the mind, emotions, history, and world of Frank Wolf. He did so with patience and trusted me along the way. John spent hours of editing and discussion time, all to the betterment of my writing. I look forward to buckets more of the "red ink" in the future.

Saul Golubcow
Potomac, MD
June 30, 2022

CPSIA information can be obtained
at www.ICGtesting.com
Printed in the USA
BVHW082251160123
656420BV00004B/68

9 781479 473014